THE NEW IMPROVED SUN

THE NEW IMPROVED SUN

An Anthology of Utopian S-F

Edited by
THOMAS M. DISCH

Harper & Row, Publishers

New York • Evanston • San Francisco • London

For my niece Sarah
and my nephew Eric

in the hope

CONTENTS

Contents

Introduction

BUCK ROGERS IN THE NEW JERUSALEM

In one sense, all s-f is utopian. In the sense that u-topia is not only the good place but no-place-at-all. To describe in patient, plausible detail a world that doesn't exist—what else is that but to write science-fiction?

The fact is, however, that with the looming exception of Wells there has been very little overlap between s-f and utopian fiction. Anti-utopias there have been by the droves: *Brave New World, 1984, The Space Merchants, Player Piano,* and all their vast progeny. But the genuine ameliorative article is rarely encountered. Except, sometimes, inadvertently. For it may be that good old hard-core Sci Fi of Triple-A vintage (Amazing-Astounding-Analog) represents an implicit program for reforming society along technocratic lines: the world *as* a better mousetrap. Surely the most delectable diorama of such a utopia has been the monolithically bland, sublimely monotonous *mise en scène* of *2001,* a movie unanimously loathed by the surviving Gernsbackian contingent of the s-f fraternity, who saw more clearly than those who had never shared their dream that Clarke and Kubrick had decisively betrayed the utopia between the billion lines of all their stories.

In that respect, *2001* epitomizes the relations between s-f and utopian speculation. No sooner does a bright hope glimmer on the page than it is shown to be delusive, specious, or downright sinister. Even in a solid, progressive, Triple-A story, the nice inventions have decided kinks in them, so the good scientists have something to cope with (if aliens are lacking).

There are several reasons why there has been so little utopian s-f, and the best of these is that utopias are notoriously dull. How can there be conflicts when everyone is nice? And without a conflict, what story is possible?

Basically, only one. The story of the Visitor from Here-and-Now who goes to Utopia, misunderstands and misjudges its citizens, and finally comes round to seeing that it is, verily, Utopia. At which point narrative ceases and the Virtues take over. This scheme can accommodate any number of worthy books (e.g., the *ur-Utopia* of Thomas More, Bellamy's *Looking Backward,* even the longest of them all, Austin Wright's *Islandia*), and it is the basis for at least three of the selections here—those by Brian Aldiss, B. F. Skinner, and James Keilty. In the story of the Visitor, what is required is that the utopist's bare ideas be so good, so ingenious, so just, that all by themselves they can arouse and sustain the reader's interest.

This, however, should not be an insuperable requirement for s-f writers. Isn't it the commonest complaint against us that we're all too willing to offer mere ideas in place of fully fleshed-out fiction? And why not, after all? A good idea doesn't *need* to be dressed up as a narrative. Accordingly, some of the stories that follow—John Sladek's, Joanna Russ's, my own—aren't stories so much as manifestoes, recipes, and calls to arms, more or less barefaced as the case may be.

A much more serious impediment to the creation of utopias than their inherent dullness is that they're silly—in real life as much as in literature. The same dolts who expect Babylon to go sliding into the Pacific tomorrow morning are also expecting their messiah, what's-his-name, to lead them to the Promised Land by tomorrow night. Utopia is the reciprocal of Armageddon, and neither locality can survive long in the cruel world of reality. After the ninth or tenth trip to the mountains to escape a certain doom, anyone may legitimately conclude that the world isn't coming to an end. And as for the bright new day a-dawning, that hope is surrendered along with one's dreams of becoming a movie star, a great ballerina, or a saint. Even the truest believers seem to run out of good intentions before they've paved the road all the way to hell. Shakers end up selling homemade jam, Flower Children wilt and die, Mormons become advisers to Nixon, and life goes on, a mixed bag at best.

And isn't it just this, the grand equivocalness of everything, that's always been the subject of good fiction, s-f included? Utopias require a deliberate singleness of vision, a decision to accentuate the positive, that can be death to a limber intelligence. If s-f writers characteristically have portrayed anti-utopias, it isn't due to their inherent pessimism or contrariness, but simply because there is a natural tendency for logical minds to pick nits and look for loopholes. I remember that Gordon Dickson, surely the least black-hearted of men, once described the process by which, knowing the background of a story, he finds the ideal protagonist to place against it: he considers who will be most seriously harmed or threatened by the world of his invention. This, while a quite workable principle for storytellers, would never do for a sincere utopist, whose only interest in loopholes is in plugging them. The better the utopia one devises, the freer it should be from all that we post-lapsarians regard as drama, and what cannot be achieved by ingenuity is accomplished by fiat. In Campanella's *City of the Sun,* for instance, there are only beautiful women, since "ugliness is unknown among them. Because the women exercise, they acquire good complexions, become strong of limb, tall and agile; and beauty among them consists of tallness, liveliness, and strength." Well, certainly we all benefit from exercise, and a good complexion doesn't need make-up. But still. I think of all the strong, tall, agile women (and men) I've known who were, nonetheless, rather uglier than not. Even Campanella wasn't wholly persuaded by his own prescription, it seems, for he added: "Therefore, if any woman were to paint her face in order to make herself beautiful, or use high-heeled shoes so as to look tall, or wear lengthened garments to cover her thick legs, she would be subjected to capital punishment."

Which takes us to the final consideration that can be urged against utopias as a class: they are repugnant. Once one has eliminated all that is dull, silly, and unworkable, there usually remains a great unredeemable mass of black bile. Often, as with Campanella, it is that touchiest of all utopian problems, Sex, that brings out the city planner's worst, but it can be anything. Plato had it in for the arts, as did Francis Bacon, who forbade the inhabitants of his New Atlantis—"under pain of ignominy and fines, that they do not show any natural work or thing adorned or swelling, but only pure as it is, and without all affectation of strangeness." Shades of Mies van der Rohe! But, in all fairness to Plato and Bacon, utopias bring out the totalitarian in all of us, for the simple and sufficient reason that whatever a utopia's ostensible mode of government, it is always ruled by an absolute tyrant, the author.

Nevertheless.

Nevertheless we need utopias, and we need them, like other necessaries, fresh each season. Our hopes must be a function of our possibilities, and these keep changing at an ever-increasing rate, as both our environment alters (no full-scale utopia of our time, for instance, can ignore ecological problems) and our own image in the age's mirror changes—and changes again. We need utopias because . . . But the reasons are, I hope, so obvious that I will make the editorial leap of faith and stop already.

But only to catch my breath.

For what good are anthologies of utopian fiction if they don't allow their editors the liberty (which we hold to be self-evident) of writing separate introductions to each story? Yes, I know—a good wine needs no bush, and in this particular instance editorial comment is especially superfluous, since I have nothing more to say about John Sladek than that he is beyond compare science-fiction's supreme satirist, that he's my oldest and best friend, and that all his collected works deserve to be cast in bronze and graved in marble, thereafter to be prominently displayed all over the amber plains of his native Iowa. Beginning with . . .

HEAVENS BELOW

Fifteen Utopias

by John Sladek

Getting There Is $\left(\frac{n-1}{n}\right)$ th the Fun

Professor Lodeworm made one last adjustment. "If my Utopia-ray works according to plan," he said, "it should make life for everyone a continual round of delightful anticipation, ever closer and closer to satisfaction. Now I'll switch it on."

Professor Lodeworm made one last adjustment. "If my Utopia-

5

ray works according to plan," he said, "it should make life for everyone a continual round of delightful anticipation, ever closer and closer to satisfaction. Now I'll switch it on."

The Bright Side

On Dr. Freeman's desk at the Astronomy Institute we found a list headed "UTOPIAS." The first items were:

1. Arrange the planets in order of size, of color, of mass, and in alphabetical order.
2. The world population, laid end to end, ought to reach about eleven or twelve times to the moon. Test this.
3. Make friends with a black hole.
4. Adjust the earth's rotation so that my watch always keeps perfect time.
5. Land a man on the sun.
6. Carve Mercury, Venus, Earth, and Mars with the faces of Washington, Jefferson, Lincoln, and Theodore Roosevelt.
7. Paint the moon's bright side black.

The remainder of this list was obscured by blood from Dr. Freeman's throat. He lay with his head on the desk, having apparently killed himself with a piece of broken glass. We think the glass came from the objective lens of the Institute telescope, which he'd smashed earlier in the day.

A talk with his physician cast more light on the matter. He had diagnosed in Dr. Freeman a deterioration of the optic nerve.

"I can understand an astronomer's being unhappy at going blind," he explained. "Wish I hadn't told him to look on the . . ."

Mr. and Ms. America

"I know they always say it's hard to be a judge in these contests," George said. "But you know, it really is hard. Hell, we've got at least fifteen possibles here, and they all look good to me."

Lotte yawned. "Not to me. Vanity surgery isn't much, nowadays. Look, each of these characters has sunk half a million in his own body, and what have they really got? Look at this one, now."

Mr. Florida was parading above them. George saw little enough wrong with him. With Mr. Florida's three-foot coxcomb, rib fins, and real eyes set into his female breasts, he was at least the Number Three contender.

Ms. South Dakota looked even better. She had restricted herself to a hundred pounds of implanted fat, extra fingers and toes, and a small, shapely pair of antlers.

Next came Ms. Iowa, an atavism of the 1950s: ninety-inch bust, ten-inch waist, thirty feet of trailing blond hair, and feet equipped with tall spike heels. A decided washout, along with Mr. Alaska and his fifty-pound penis that looked like a case of elephantiasis, nothing more.

By lunchtime, they'd narrowed it down to five men and four women. George and Lotte agreed the contest was tawdry, grotesque, and decadent. Over lunch, they tried to puzzle out what was wrong.

"The trouble is," George said, "most of the young surgeons have no ideas. Laszlo Goodwin's okay, but the rest—amateur copyists."

"Not like our day," Lotte said. "Your outfit still looks good, you know?"

"Thanks. Yes, old Morton knew his stuff. A simple concept like this never looks out-of-date: seal fur all over, eyes on stalks, and a toroidal torso. My tailor says it's a real pleasure and a challenge, making clothes for a man with a big hole through his middle. But you still look great, too."

"Thanks," said Lotte. She cut a bite of steak and delicately stuffed it up her armpit.

Empty Promise

"Just sign here," said the Devil, "and name your wish."

Jonathan Palmer signed. "I wish for Utopia," he said. "A perfect world without blemish or unpleasantness."

"But—" said the Devil, looking surprised as he vanished forever.

"Things seem better already," said Jonathan Palmer as he vanished forever.

"Better and better," said his wife, turning from the keyhole to embrace her lover, Raoul. As she vanished forever, Raoul recalled that he was the sole beneficiary of her sizable insurance policy. He immediately vanished, followed by the cunning insurance salesman, his grasping boss, and the rest of imperfect humanity.

I alone am left. Ha-ha—

The Paradise Problem

Blenheim won his island by correctly guessing the number of coffee beans in a boxcar. He named his utopian republic Boxcar, its capital, Bean.

The island population consisted of two tribes, the Ye (who always told the truth) and the Ne (who always lied). A man from one tribe or the other was always posted at a fork in the main road, where one branch led to the city, the other into cannibal country.

By the river, Blenheim found a party of missionaries and cannibals, waiting to row across. The rowboat could carry only two men. If the cannibals on either shore outnumbered the missionaries, they would eat them.

Farther down the river was a pair of men with the curious names of A and B. A could evidently row upstream half as fast as B could swim downstream, while A and B together could row upstream twice as fast as B alone.

The two men explained that they were always engaging in contests, such as chopping wood, pumping water, racing a bicycle against a car, and so on. B was as many years older than A as A's age had been when B was as old as A was when B gave him half his apples plus half an apple.

In the city of Bean, the baker, draper, tailor, and smith were named (not respectively) Baker, Draper, Tailor, and Smith. Baker was the tailor's uncle, and Draper was the smith's son. Tailor had no living relatives. If Draper was the tailor, then the smith was named after the occupation of the man named after the occupation of Draper. Otherwise, the city was very beautiful.

Blenheim spent many happy years in Boxcar, drawing various colored socks out of a drawer in order to get a matching pair. Exactly how many happy years did he spend?

What Changed Doyster's Mind

Doyster stepped out of his time machine and strolled up the shady avenue of the Academy grove to Plato's house. The philosopher was just now supervising workmen who were placing a lintel over the door. On the lintel was inscribed: "Let no one enter here who is unacquainted with geometry."

"It won't work, boss," called one of the men. "The posts are too far apart. It won't reach across."

"Nonsense," said Plato. "Let go your end."

As one end of the lintel crashed to the ground, Doyster was already walking back down the shady avenue.

Handout

The League of Nations rules put it like this: Everyone in the world was entitled to go along to his nearest Dispensary and collect, free, a large box of God.

The first problem was a big riot in South America, owing to a rumor that supplies were running out. The League made a reassuring broadcast: No shortage was imminent. Indeed, the supply was expected to last indefinitely.

The riots in the Indian subcontinent were harder to combat. Local officials began to gripe: "Oh, sure, there's enough to go around, but it's not in the right places. Rich Americans have enough to burn, while poor Indians are shelling out a hundred rupees a box on the black market. Is that justice? Why can't we straighten out the distribution?"

The League looked into it, and sent a memo: God was already present everywhere in great quantities. Containers, alas, were not. Applicants should be urged to bring their own boxes, baskets, pails, envelopes, etc.

Next came the staff shortages in Africa. People might walk fifty miles to the nearest Dispensary, only to find it closed. Perhaps the overworked official had collapsed with fever, perhaps he had gone AWOL, or deserted, or been murdered by black-marketeers. No one knew. Angry crowds began burning Dispensaries, not only in Africa but across the world. Officials now began to desert in greater numbers, or call for military protection.

At the end of a year, the League reviewed its campaign: The costs (of troops, compensation for riot-torn cities, etc.) ran to billions. The results were disappointing. Fewer than a tenth of those in need had actually been reached.

Reluctantly, the League voted to dispense no more boxes of God.

Assessment

Our machine slaves have now taken over all tedious or disagreeable occupations. They paint, write and perform music, make scientific discoveries, and handle pretty well everything from fashion to philosophy. This leaves us plenty of time and freedom to do whatever we like—extract square roots, say, or calculate payrolls.

Art News

Sisyphus jammed a block of wood under the stone to keep it from rolling back, took a swig from his canteen, and squatted down to explain his work to the tour group.

"Of course, it's a very healthy life—outdoor work, and so on. Then, too, I've always liked working with natural materials like stone. Not that the stone itself is important. No, what's important here is not gross physical change. I think I can safely say that ever since Oldenburg dug a hole in Central Park, filled it in, and called it a buried sculpture—ever since then, physical-change stuff has been dying a slow death. Nowadays, the artist is not concerned with torturing Nature to 'make' something. He's concerned with 'doing' something *within* Nature. . . ."

After stopping for ice-cold orangeade, the group moved on to Tantalus.

Pax Gurney

As a young man, Gurney said, "If I were world emperor, the first thing I'd do would be to introduce a compulsory world language." For the next twenty years, he actually worked on such a language, Unilingo, on the off chance he might become emperor. Unilingo was designed to guarantee world peace forever. In this language, no one could lie or express hatred or discontent. No one could hold an opinion contrary to fact, or hold any opinion at all about non-facts. No two speakers of Unilingo could ever really disagree. Gurney described it in his memoirs as "a calculus of good sense and good taste."

Of course he *did* become world emperor, and the world prospered for many years under his "rule of grammar." People stopped talking about matters that did not concern them, and spoke wisely of those that did. The world was at peace. Gurney abdicated, and the institutions of government withered as people learned self-control.

A century after Gurney's death, an American compiling a new dictionary of Unilingo made a curious discovery. While in America the word *orth* had kept its original meaning ("to fray the edge of an old blanket, from left to right"), in Eurasiafrica it had taken on a new one ("to fray the edge of an old blanket, left-handedly"). He wrote a letter about it to a Eurasiafrican colleague. The trouble was traced to photocopies of Gurney's original manuscript, on file in the two continents. One copy showed the word *riin* ("from left to right"), the other showed *riin* without a dot over the second *i* ("left-handedly"). An interesting dispute arose between the Universities of Tübingen and Nebraska.

What had been on the original manuscript (long since lost)? Was a dot added, correcting a mistake? Or erased? Was the addition or erasure itself a mistake? Physical chemists were called in, and photography experts. The debate became more heated, and opinions were split along continental lines. An American professor was booed at Tübingen; Nebraska fired a foreign archaeologist.

Over the next century, the two continents grew apart. The dotless Eurasiafricans developed a philosophy aimed at defining the final meaning of life. The dotted Americans preferred a harsh form of skepticism, summed up in their motto: "That which does not exist is nonexistent." Two centuries later, these philosophies had become articles of faith for two bitterly opposed religions.

Knowing this background to the present war, we can more easily understand . . .

A Fable

The snails, discontented with their free and easy life, held a noisy meeting to petition Jupiter for a king.

"We're not complaining," they insisted. "We know we already have portable homes and other luxuries. But we'd like a strong leader. After all, you gave the frogs a stork to follow. And even the men have their presidents. How about us?"

Jupiter threw an old log down into their pool and said, "There is a king for you!"

The old log has proved a wise and compassionate leader. Under his guidance, the snails have prospered, until now they are seen in all the best restaurants.

Utopia: A Financial Report

Utopia is laid out in four planned nations: Fascesia, Commund, Capitalia, and Anarche.

Fascesia is a half-tamed land. The cities are sophisticated, filled with monumental architecture, opera houses, and elegant night clubs. The countryside, on the other hand, is a wilderness teeming (in theory) with savages and wild game. Alas, Fascesians tend to hunt both to extinction, and the cost of replenishing these is considerable. Therefore we recommend closing Fascesia.

Commund cities are bleak and industrial, while its rural areas undergo intensive agriculture. Communders are excellent organizers and produce surpluses yearly. Unfortunately, these surpluses seem to lower the morale of Communders, who rather enjoy mild discomforts and privations—proof that they are continuing their "struggle." Accordingly, we remove their surpluses from time to time, as well as causing them to have minor shortages. The costs of removal and destruction of their surpluses have become excessive. Moreover, the materials destroyed are our loss, in the last analysis. We recommend closing Commund.

Capitalia is a uniformly settled nation with a monotony of maple-lined streets and white frame houses. Capitalians have no incentive to work (though of course they refer to their play activities as "work"; e.g., signing their names to pieces of paper). They also require huge outlays of energy, materials, machines, foods, and medicines. We recommend closing Capitalia.

Anarche seemed at first a viable nation, with few requirements. Now it is entirely deserted. Anarchers are evidently unstable, and frequently migrate to the other three nations.

Summary: We feel the experiment has served its purpose. We now know more than enough about the social institutions of *Homo sapiens*. We feel, therefore, that Utopia should be closed and its inhabitants destroyed. The ground can then be used for a study of the social behavior of another interesting species, the armadillos.

Utopiary

Utopia has turned out to be like a well-planned garden: Each change of season brings its fresh cycle of pleasing color, heavenly scent, and backbreaking work.

Luck

General Holme threw the dice. "Tough luck, General Vladiful," he said, chuckling. "I've just captured your fourth army. Do you want to surrender?"

The other sighed. "No, no. After all, we are playing for real armies. Let us play on awhile. I may yet turn the turtles on you, eh?"

"Tables. We say turn the tables. Ha-ha, I must say, this beats the old system of waging w—"

The door burst open and a soldier strode in, pointing a submachine gun at them. "You'll have to surrender. This sector has just been captured by the forces of General Heinz."

"Heinz? Heinz?" Holme scratched his head. "Never heard of him. He's not in the game."

"He plays a bigger game," said the soldier. "Come with me, please."

Vladiful nodded. "So, there is a bigger war than we know of, even. I wonder who Heinz opposes?"

From the darkness outside came a burst of automatic fire. The soldier flopped to the floor, bleeding from a dozen wounds. In a moment, a man in a Germanic uniform was prodded into the room at bayonet point.

"I am Heinz," he said. "Are you my captors?"

"Not us." Holme offered him some brandy. "Ask the man with the gun."

The man with the gun cleared his throat. "This sector—

namely, Earth—has just been captured by Planet Marshal Gordon. You are all under house arrest."

As if echoing him, an amplified voice rolled over the dark parade ground outside. "You are all under house arrest. This sector has just been captured by the 119th Galactic Army under Commander Noll."

"Noll?" said Holme. "Lucky bastard. I wonder what *he* threw."

A Picnic

Bill Nolan was thinking out loud. "In a way, I guess this *is* Utopia. I mean, people in the past would have been horrified at the idea of having a picnic in a junkyard. They weren't like us."

Jimmy stopped kicking at an old tire. "Why, Dad?"

Nolan rescued the baby, who was crawling around elbow-deep in sump oil. "That's enough, hon. Mommy'll bring your bottle in just a minute." He waved to his wife, who was climbing over a crumpled Buick.

"You see, Jimmy, our stomachs are different. Everybody has a lot of little helpers in his stomach, to help him digest his dinner. But the way it used to be, the helpers couldn't handle much of anything. So people had to eat things like—oh, cows, pigs, and so on."

Jimmy looked up at him. "Cows! No kidding?"

"I used to eat pieces of cow myself. (Hey, did you strip that insulation like your mother said? Good boy.) No, what happened was, some scientists changed the little helpers. See, we were running out of cows and stuff, so we needed helpers that would help us eat new things. Now just about everything is edible."

"You're not supposed to say 'et.' "

"Yes, but 'edible' means 'eatable.' I used to wonder why myself."

"Mumf chmumf—"

"Don't let your mother see you talking with your mouth full, son."

Janet Nolan came back to the picnic site just then. "See what? Oh, God, Bill, you let the baby get herself *filthy*. Couldn't you have spooned up the sump oil instead of letting her crawl right in it? And, Jimmy! What are you doing?"

A large piece of the old tire was gone, and the boy was now swallowing a strip of muddy tread.

"I was hungry," he mumbled.

"Hungry? That's no excuse for bolting your food. You'll have a tummy ache."

"Stomach," the boy corrected.

"I don't see why boys who bolt their food should have any dessert, do you? And we're having polyethylene seat covers."

"Aw, Ma, can't I have some?"

"Hmm. We'll see."

Bill looked at the baby's bottle in her hand. "I see you got it."

She smiled. "Yes. Real high-octane lead-free stuff. Only a little rusty water in the bottom. We were lucky to find it, she's so fussy."

Janet delivered the bottle into the frantically waving arms of the baby, who rammed it in her own mouth and started sucking. Long before the others had finished twirling up masses of plastic wire insulation on their forks, the bottle was empty. The baby lay back, flushed and drowsy. Nolan gave her a cardboard cookie, but, after slobbering at it for a moment without really biting it, she gave an aromatic burp and went to sleep.

"Utopia," he murmured.

"What, darling?"

"Nothing." He brandished the carving knife and fork. "Now for the main course. White sidewall, darling? Or dark?"

If Necessity is the mother of Invention, then its other parent, surely, is Unnecessity. The synonyms of Unnecessity are all, alas, pejoratives: uselessness, needlessness, fruitlessness, futility, vanity, and labor lost.

It isn't fair, Roget. The sweetest fruits of civilization have their source in play much more than in prayer, and this is even truer of the civilizations of the imagination.

A case in point. The Teachers and Writers Collaborative has published a delightful booklet called *Imaginary Worlds,* which outlines an experimental curriculum developed at P.S. 70 in Manhattan, where students in two social studies classes designed their own utopias. Among the diverse forms this project took, perhaps the most diverting was a parody of a sixth grade geography book written by six sixth-graders. I cannot pass by their imagined Land of Withershins without quoting at least two of the essays about it. The first is Randy Besman's "Religion in Withershins": "The religion in Withershins is Betrusminy. This is a prejudice." And Jason Brill's more extensive account of "Mining in Withershins": "The major mining fields are for (and especially) rivers which are red with 3½ legs sticking out of its awnie which makes it look something like a dindle. Another major thing that we mine for in Withershins is a wemmel-warsal. This is a gold colored thing that looks somewhat like a Terge with antennae. Of the newer mines there are antenumps. They are very valuable because if you don't have antenumps you can't live in Withershins. Antenumps are holes with walls around them, they are usually furnished with dooks and fendys. You sleep in dooks with assorted fendys around the house for sitting."

(This booklet, with the complete run-down on Withershins and on the development of a utopianizing curriculum is available for $1.00 from the Teachers and Writers Collaborative, 244 Vanderbilt Avenue, Brooklyn, New York 11205.)

My point, beyond getting in that plug for *Imaginary Worlds,* is that first, last, and foremost, utopias are a form of play—if for no other reason than that by making the world a game we can begin to imagine other rules by which to win the game.

However—and this is where the difficulties begin—a true utopia, if it is not to be dismissed summarily as "a fond thing vainly invented" (as the Book of Common Prayer defines Purgatory), must have its roots in the realities of human nature. One must adapt the solution to the problem. And if the problem seems insoluble . . .

REPAIRING THE OFFICE

by Charles Naylor

1

It was beginning to be winter but Hally had chosen her favorite cotton print—evenly spaced clusters of sweet william on a white ground, crisp and efficient. She hadn't had the occasion yet to learn that it was inappropriate. And she was surprised, not cowed, to see Joyce Babcock sitting behind the personnel desk at Bonton's: a face remembered, a hand and flutter of football banner jabbed high in a fall sky. *The* Bonton (she made a mental correction). Joyce had graduated with her sister four years ago from River Heights High, top in the class.

"What activities were you in?" Joyce asked pleasantly. Her lips were thin and defined by a coloring that showed the barest trace of blue.

Hally smiled. "I wasn't in cheerleading." An inverted compliment. "But I was Secretary of the Red Cross for my homeroom in junior year." As Hally knew both then and now, no one else had wanted the position. Like a deflated volleyball, it had fallen to her.

"And . . ." Joyce, embarrassed, looked down at her memo pad.

"And I was—" Sweat oozed from her palms into the primarily white cotton. "I was in National Honor Society." It was a lie, of course. Even her normal awkwardness couldn't excuse the poor timing.

"Oh," said Joyce with a broad smile, "so was I!" They both laughed. "Is Mrs. Beebe still the adviser?" Mrs. Beebe, the Latin and Greek teacher, had taught for over forty years at River Heights and had always been in charge of the National Honor Society chapter—since so many of her own students were regulars on the honor roll. She was short, unfathomable, shopped in the A. & P., and not two words had ever passed between her and Hally (who'd barely squeaked through two terms of Spanish with a circled sixty-five).

"Uh-huh. We dedicated the yearbook to her. She's retiring, you know."

"Oh, you were on the yearbook, too?" Joyce's interest held.

"Yes." She tensed. (Hally had donated two snapshots for one of the collages.)

"I didn't see the yearbook this year."

Just as well, Hally thought, picturing the half-page devoted to the Honor Society in their robes, Mrs. Beebe in her green and comfortable Roman sandals that she wore only for special occasions. "It was real nice."

Joyce leaned forward on her elbows. "I remember she used to say, 'Greek trains the mind.' Did you do Xenophon?"

Hesitating, "No . . . I had her for Latin."

"Oh! She used to tell us how good the Cicero class was and—

what was it?" Joyce stared affectingly up and beyond Hally's
eyes. "I bet you a cookie—that's what she always said—I bet
you a cookie."

". . . Bet you a cookie?"

"Didn't she say that?"

"Oh . . ." Hally fixed the cotton belt straight. "Yes."

How the times had changed, Joyce mused to herself. These
new girls were cute and fresh, even eager to change the world,
leave their mark, but they hadn't the spark—they didn't seem
to have the good times or the memories that *she* had. Her eyes
went blank for a moment, recalling the smell of the cafeteria
wing an hour before lunch. Her figure had begun to fill out
pleasantly, and whatever character was destined to show in her
face was there. She eyed the cotton sleeve and the delicate vac-
cination scar. "How would you like to be in our accounts re-
ceivable department?"

Hally's mouth trembled. "I sort of wanted to be a salesgirl.
I thought . . . with Christmas?" She looked toward the clattering,
brightly lighted area beyond the glass wall of the cubicle: six
or eight old brown desks huddled under a light snow of waybills.
A telephone somewhere on the floor had been ringing for fully
three minutes. The chipped Docustat. A single microfilm viewer.
Middle-aged women hobbled to and from the files in spike heels.

"You know, it's a very interesting job. You will be doing lots
of different things: answering telephones, looking up people's
accounts, speaking directly with the clerks on our sales floors."

Hally ventured a timid smile.

"And the girls are real nice." She paused. "Before you know
it, you'll be promoted—"

"To what?" Hally asked a little too quickly, then shying. "I
mean," she said, blushing, "what would my job be then, if I . . ."
(but she couldn't suppose) "if I work real hard?"

"Mmm." Joyce shifted her weight again forward to forearms
and elbows, thrumming. "Well, sometimes people come up here
to discuss their accounts or to pay bills in person with cash, and

—I don't know—possibly if things work out, you'll be our liaison working with them."

Despite herself, there was something tempting in this talk of being singled out, promoted, though her real wish was to feel pretty and (but she couldn't say *what*) in the dress department or like a courtesan behind a battery of crystal perfume bottles. Nevertheless, she liked Joyce for her grown-up . . . what amounted to poise, the way she said what there was to be said pointedly and then smiled. "Do you mean I have the job?" Almost meekly.

"Be here Monday morning at nine. I'll introduce you to Mrs. Metcalf—she'll be your supervisor—and the other girls."

Christmas promised never to come. The faces were all familiar, although she had not known any of her co-workers previously. River Heights, one of the largest towns on the Muskokee River, was not so grand that one couldn't (if one were a politician, for example) meet all the regular residents with a little effort over a two-year period. But the random sampling of people at The Bonton *was* unfortunate and, as Hally's mother frequently reminded, *she* had never been the outgoing kind.

Hally was in charge of "H" to "K." Most of the day she filed sales slips, first sitting at a pull-out steel shelf and alphabetizing them within the letters (there were always more "H"s) and then filing the white copies and credit memos in front of individual ledger cards that bore the charge customers' names and addresses. She had her own credit authorization telephone, and it rang constantly, making her very nervous, since there was no safe place to put down her *un*finished work, and as often as not the flimsy white slips fluttered down to the floor or in between the great green file units, so that the files had to be moved by one of the maintenance men (they wore khaki uniforms and had to be summoned from the basement) while Hally, all red-faced, was obliged to go down gracelessly on hands and knees to reach into the dusty crevice.

" 'H' to 'K.' "

"Hally?"

"What?" It was her mother.

"Hally, who do you know in Chicago who's writing you letters?"

She reached for a pencil and memo pad. Mrs. Metcalf was strict about personal telephone calls. "Mother," she whispered, "Mother, I'm not supposed to be getting calls on this phone."

"I know. I know. I just thought you might like to know that you have a letter. There isn't any return address. You don't have any friends in Chicago, do you? Should I open it and see who it is?"

"No," Hally whined, and then tensed, remembering the probable surveillance.

"There's something in the corner, just a word. I can't read it."

"Mother . . ."

"No, baby, I called because I thought maybe you'd like to know. You're expecting something from somebody, maybe."

As each day passed, the size of the pile grew. That year, Christmas fell on a Thursday, and when Hally came in Monday morning of Christmas week her umbrella (it had been raining since dinnertime Sunday) caught in the elevator door on three. It would never work again.

She walked autistically over to the great pile of rubber-banded sales slips and found her own bundle. It was not as big as the one she had had the previous Tuesday. On that occasion there'd been so much to file that she'd come in early the following morning (without pay) just to keep from drowning. The Bonton each year before the holidays drew business from (she noticed, riffling through the mass) as far away as Harrisburg, Pennsylvania.

She thought about the umbrella: With luck, the rain would change to snow and the snow just keep falling and falling. She fantasied a perpetual Christmas, clove-scented and warm before the fire, remote. She might never need buy a new one—but then the spring would come. She was seventeen and so far as she knew she didn't have leukemia.

Joe, fiftyish and short, hurried in and took his seat. He had
"L" to "O."

"Oh," he said. "Oh, Hally, how are you today? Well, it's almost
Christmas now, isn't it? Just a few more days and Santa Claus
will be coming down your chimney. You have a chimney, don't
you?"

"No." She shook her head. He knew she didn't have a chimney.

"Well, you'd better have a chimney, h'how's Santa Claus gonna
come down your chimney if you don't have a chimney? H'ha-
ha-ha. Say, say did you get wet this morning? D'you think the
weatherman's gonna give us snow for Christmas?"

Hally reddened. Hughes. Hujsa. Catherine V. Hughes. Catherine F. Hughes. Inskip. Hunter. Hurley, she thought.

"Oh, oh, Hally, Hally, wait till you see what I have for you,
wait till you see what I made for you."

She looked over, feeling an absence of blood, the tension at
the base of her neck. Joe's life: small, overripe, futile. Each day
he chattered in that soft manic monotone. She knew what it was
he'd brought. She wanted to scream.

He peeled away two rain-speckled sheets of heavy cardboard
from his sketch pad and there it was—big round face, eyes like
a greeting-card puppy, hyper-pretty, silly little curls, the head
supported by a starched and tiny all-purpose body. A pinup
c. '44 (but fully dressed). And underneath, in a large effeminate
scrawl—*"Hally."*

"Oh!" Tears flooded her eyes, making Meg Statler, at the
other end of the room, loom bulbously in and out of her vision.
"Oh, Joe . . ."

He beamed.

She clutched the charge slips (still loosely bound) in one hand
and held the other up to her mouth. Ran, stumbling, for the
ladies room; only stopped when she'd reached the window and
forced it up a little higher.

The river menaced at a distance, while in places it hid itself
in a thickness of trees. Cars below streamed past in a hissing rain.

Hally pounded the sill with her arms, grunting, wanting to vomit, at the same time fighting it, resisting the impulse to scream and rage (which would only bring in the total work force to crowd around and gape at her). Down and down again, she slammed her arms, mute and rhythmic.

The charge slips fell to the floor, bundle intact. They lay in a little pool between her and the washbasin.

She stopped.

Looking out over the city again, she saw whole large un-daunted groups of holiday shoppers: single men, wearing ties, bundled to the knees in proper grey winter coats; young modishly dressed women in twos and threes; a dowager on her yearly shopping mission; stout housemaids with woolly hats. A blue roadster zipped past, tooting the horn. She knew no one of her own age, background, and sex who owned a car—but it still seemed one and indefatigable, however unreal.

She stooped, picked up the bundle, and calmly undid the binding. In no more than a minute, they were all flushed down the toilet.

2

Mary Ruth Cristecu leaned forward to untie the bow of her sneaker—her single sneaker (the mate was in a closet at home). She slipped out of the comfortable canvas shoe and put on the other grey leather pump for the long subway ride to Brooklyn. Still forward, she took up the conversation again that had died a natural death minutes ago. *"Now* I'm glad I di'int give huh my umbrella. Y'see, Carolann, it *is* raining."

"Oh, shuga, y'right," turning in her swivel seat to look out the dirty, rain-specked window behind her. Carolann Gano was forty-two.

Mary Ruth (a tall and attractive sixty-two) was kind but odd.

Carolann was perfectly ordinary. Short, unmemorable in her three-inch heels, she spent half her weekly salary on a hair stylist in Flushing—shampoos, settings, comb-outs—but her skin had been pitifully pocked as a child and so one forgave her the indulgence. Really, she had only one other weakness, a fifteen-year-old daughter Cathy.

Minutes passed.

"But I think she *woulda* returned it . . ."

"What?" Carolann looked up from the daily ledger. "Mary Ruth, I'm tryin' to close out an' I can't do it if you keep talkin' to me."

"Sahree . . ."

A door slammed at the other end of the small room.

"Good night, Mista Ticker," Mary Ruth said quietly as he brushed past the opening to her cubicle. As president of the company, Herman Ticker had a little room all to himself.

"Good night, Mary Ruth—Carolann, Marco."

The walrusy office manager looked up. "Uh, Mr. Ticker, would you mind . . ."

"Marco, I have to pick up the car myself tonight—Freddie couldn't leave the warehouse—make it quick?"

"As quick as I can, boss. I think we just lost another mail-order clerk."

"You think."

"She went out to cash her check a few minutes before three and never came back. Mary Ruth passed her downstairs in the lobby and offered to lend her an umbrella."

"I tried to tell huh," the spinster added, "the radio said this mawnin' it was gerna rain."

Ticker (sun-tanned, flashy tie) leaned on one hip. "And she didn't come back . . . wise-ass broad. You think she quit."

Marco held up a set of keys like a boy scout applying for his first merit badge. "In her desk drawer, boss."

"Oh, shit. Marco, put an ad in the *Post*. No, the *News*. To-night—"

"F'Christmas' sakes, you guys," Carolann said, fingers punching away at the calculator, "my cousin's sista is coming fa dinna,

I gotta balance, I mean. . . ." She lifted both palms. "Y'know? I tell you the truth, we're betta off without huh—"

"But, Carolann . . ."

"Listen. In t'ree weeks I go on my vacation, and I don't give a" (very quietly) "you know what . . . *what* happens hea, becawse I'm gonna be out on *the island* with my sista."

Mary Ruth spoke gravely: "Marco, you let me ask around my neighbahood—"

"No," Ticker cautioned, raising a hand. "I want Marco to put an ad in the paper, but this time," addressing the old man, "you don't take the first fish that bites."

"Yairr," Mary Ruth chimed in, "that last one was a real *crab!*"

"Right," Ticker continued, "and this time try to get a man."

"A veteran," Marco added.

"Well, I don't care if it's a vet or not, but you should try to get a family man, someone who can't be moving from job to job. How long did it take you to train . . . Dolores, Marco?"

Marco paused a second and then exploded: "What do you mean? It takes years!"

"Marco, Marco, it doesn't take years. Two days. *You* take care of it, okay?"

Hally checked her hair in the stainless-steel elevator paneling, but someone had bored a hole into the metal, making her face appear distorted in an odd, rather realistic way, as though her jaw were dislocated. The door jolted open.

"PIXIE PICKLES," the gold letters read on the bumpy glass. She pressed the buzzer, then tried the handle, but it was locked. From inside the sound of approaching footsteps—and out of the grey light a form gathered. The door opened.

An owlish woman with teased hair stood staring at her: "Yes?"

"I have an appointment to see Mr. Spinelli at three?"

Over her shoulder: "Marco!"

"Yeah, okay," came the response from somewhere deep within. "Put him in the other room."

"It's a *girl*." To Hally: "Would you come with me." She led her to a dismal, cluttered room off to one side, then walked away.

Hally sat, but after several minutes had passed, got to her feet again and went to the window. The Jersey skyline could barely be seen through the thick air. Somewhere below, a crane was wielding its power with great groans and sighs. Pixie Pickles, she thought. Little West 12th Street. The names were nice, the area, too, dated and having a smell all its own. She watched in the distance men loading garbage onto barges near the Gansevoort Street Pier.

He'd interviewed eleven others, all men, all bad. Three couldn't speak English, and when Hally had called he thought, Well, it *is* a woman's job: paperwork, answering telephones, and the mail; she had a wholesome sound, a shyness that made her seem more malleable than the others.

"Well, Miss Hally, it looks like you've got yourself a job. Be here at nine Monday and I'll start to break you in."

"Oh." (It was all she could say.) "Oh, thank you."

The previous girl, or one like her, had left a pair of cracked imitation leather boots in the file drawer. Reams of shorthand notation. She set them up on the desk, wondering all the while which of the women (the one on the left or the taller one, in the cubicle) was Carol Ruth, whether it was all right to call her Carol instead. She spread the things out, then set about reorganizing them into neat piles, not having been given anything else to do. They were all the same. She looked up—three more hours (the clock read 2:30). Marco had begun to explain how to write up an order and then been called away to take the phone. That was at eleven. With the lunch hour and other interruptions, he had forgotten her.

She sat facing the water cooler and the clock; behind her, a broken duplicating machine—people came regularly from the warehouse to use it, having her squeeze uncomfortably forward into the desk until they had judged for themselves the degree to which it was, in fact, broken. To her left was . . . Carolyn (she'd heard the other woman say it). To the right, separated from her by a narrow aisle, was Marco's desk. The second mail had come and the few new orders been opened, stripped of any checks, stapled, and left on the green blotter. Beyond Marco was another cubicle, in the corner just outside Herman Ticker's office. Myra, his secretary, stayed there.

A week passed. Through sheer invention, Hally learned how to write a mail order and have it filled by the men in the warehouse without immediate repercussions. While she'd never before known the differences between kosher dills and bread-and-butter pickles, red relish and chow-chow, she soon had at least an abstract idea of all their forty-two varieties and the infinite shapes and properties of their possible containers. She knew which customers got the fancy labels, which supplied their own, and which received the square green one (lettered in Old English) that bore the Pixie Pickles coat of arms and attested to the fact that the firm had been in business since 1903.

It would be difficult to say when precisely she understood that the job was awful, that she mustn't stay. Was it Carolann's upbraiding her for bringing back the coffee with milk instead of Melloream? Passing the suspect cardboard cup from Mary Ruth to Mel Golden (v.-p.), back again to Carolann. Had Hally decided to quit the first day? (But then it seemed . . . funny to give two weeks' notice, and she had no other job to go to.) She would, she decided finally, work a month, give the work and the people a fair chance.

A month passed. She would prepare a little speech to give on her last day explaining why neither she nor anyone else *ought* to stay: Everything was old and ugly; the desks, the chairs, the

people—even the telephone books were four years old. And the
place was dangerous. (A mugger had once, before Hally's time,
walked in at three o'clock payday wielding a pistol, demanding
that everybody throw his cash into a heap in the middle of the
floor.) The space was too small for the number of people it
housed, consequently noisy, and on Thursdays Darla Blechman
came, officially to dun late-paying customers (less officially, as
Mel Golden's mistress); and she, old as the others, spent hours
on the phone having loud personal conversations with a homo-
sexual nephew. Add to that Cathy Gano's calls, each day at
11:30 sharp, to her mother: all long, all repeated word for word
to Mary Ruth the minute the receiver was down. "That prin-
cipal's gonna hea from me. If my dawta tells him she cou'nt
help getting back from huh lunch late, that's it; what she says
goes. I tole huh to tell him that I said he should shove it up his
you know what. Cathy's so cute . . . y'know what sta'ted this? Last
week one day, she got so involved wit cleaning huh closet that
she f'got to go back to school. Listen, Mary Ruth, if my dawta
tells him she's sorree, she's sorree, I mean, it's *unreal*." Or last
night's TV situation comedy blow by blow, or ". . . I shua wish
I had a Godfatha." Hally would mention the *Godfather* business,
too—something about men and their heroes.

But finally she decided not to, as to do so would be too painful. And her school speeches had been consistently substandard.
The company was failing. The others spoke about it in whispers.
Opening the morning mail was a ritual significantly denied her.
Mary Ruth, Marco, and Mr. Ticker would crowd around Carolann as she totted up the checks. They'd failed because times had
changed. Larger firms that could afford more attractive packaging
and more expensive sales campaigns were slowly killing them.
Of course the *Godfather* was their hero. The Mafia boss represented power (something this tiny, foundering group both desperately needed and fantasied), power for the little man.

She would write a letter to Herman Ticker, leave it on his

desk, say only that she had been unhappy with the job. Or lie:
tell him a family tragedy had called her back to River Heights.
They understood family.

But that wouldn't do either. Even if she mailed the letter outside. Marco had shown her the eleven letters *he* had written to
those applicants who had been turned away. His courtesy had
amazed and pained her. And he'd shown her the bill for the
three-liner in the *News* that she'd read herself and answered.
She couldn't.

"Carolann," Hally said one day, setting the cardboard box full
of coffee cups down on the edge of the receptionist's desk. "I was
thinking the other day how we don't any of us really know
each other, how there's never time to talk here in the office. You
know?"

Carolann looked up from her chipped file drawer of unpaid
accounts, jowls just beginning to show in the loosening flesh of
her jaw. She hated the Midwestern accent. "Yeah, Hally, but
we gotta lotta work to do—"

"No, be serious."

"You'll get to know us afta a while."

"I was thinking I'd like to have you all come over to my
place some night. Some Friday or Saturday night for a little party.
It'd be nice, y'know? Just maybe spaghetti—something simple."

The big day came. Hally'd laid in a supply of Chianti and
paper cups, and Pixie Pickles had donated an assortment of their
best. There were candles. Hally washed the windows and swept
the floor (she had only a single room), and bought four loaves
of Italian bread at Zito's on the way to work in the morning.

"Hally," Marco said, leaning sideways from his desk chair
(it was just after two), "you could go home early to get things
started if you want."

"Gee, I do have a couple of last-minute touches—thanks."

"You mean you have the spaghetti sauce already?"

She nodded with a broad smile. "Fer sher, I made it last night —great big pot."

"It'll have to be, with the gang of us coming."

They both laughed.

"Alma's really excited," he continued. (Alma was Marco's wife. She'd invited her, too.) "She's bakin' you one of her surprises."

"Oh, Marco, she shouldn't have." Hesitating, "Is it a dessert?"

"Yeah. You'll see. She made me promise not to tell you."

"I'm glad it's a dessert, because I *didn't* make anything."

They were thirteen. Marco and Alma. Herman Ticker and *his* wife (pretty, forty-fivish, bleached). Myra Winston had threatened to bring her black militant boyfriend but, providentially, they had "broken up" the night before. Miss Cristecu also came without an escort; she wore what Hally thought was a very chic red-orange stripe. Hally had insisted that Carolann bring not only her daughter Cathy but also her mysterious, rarely alluded to Ray. Mel Golden, she averred, would not be allowed in the door without *his* wife. (He'd wanted to "just stop in for a drink.") Fortunately, Hally remembered to include Darla, as she would certainly have heard about the dinner later and felt slighted. The one person whom she did significantly leave out was Gus.

Actually, Gus didn't work for Pixie Pickles at all but rather, representing the Federal Food and Drug Administration, manned a tiny laboratory-office at the warehouse where he tested sample batches of the product for contamination and infestation before giving his seal of approval. It was not a romantic interest, and perhaps for that reason Hally had not included him on the guest list, for the others had taken note of the friendship already and begun to talk.

They came together (she knew they would). Probably they'd

discussed the problems of walking in smaller groups through the tough neighborhood and decided against it. Or it might have been just another expression of their solidarity as a group, their tacit war on Hally. The buzzer sounded and she ran down the two flights of stairs to open the front door herself.

"Hi!" brightly swinging the door wide open, one palm flat against her apron. "Do you smell the spaghetti?" Indeed, the odor of garlic *had* reached the other residents of her floor.

Miss Cristecu sniffed the air. "Smells like gawbage to me," she said naïvely.

"They must keep it behind the stairwell," Carolann whispered to Cathy. (Several had already started up the stairs behind Hally.)

There weren't enough chairs, of course, so Alma Spinelli (sixtyish and plump) suggested that, with Hally's permission, she and Marco teach the others to do the tarantella until dinner was served. "Do you have a record player?" she asked.

"No, Mrs. Spinelli, I'm sorry. Not even a radio, but how about if we all clap?"

"That's quite a door you've got there," Darla Blechman remarked, standing alone. "I've never seen such a lock."

"It keeps me from worrying while I'm away at work," Hally called across the "dance floor." "The trouble is, I have to use a key to get out, too, and sometimes . . . I lose it!" She laughed and wiped her wet hands back and forth over the apron.

Darla touched the steel mesh. "Must have been expensive."

"I don't know, Darla, it was here when I came."

"And you don't have a fire escape."

"No, I don't. I think if a fire inspector ever came by he'd shoot me."

"Y'could give him a little something," Carolann interjected, tugging at her husband's sleeve and laughing. "Ray's a fiaman!"

Her husband turned and smiled, shy in the company of the others.

Alma Spinelli had dragged fifteen-year-old Cathy out into the middle of the floor to help with the dancing. Cathy stood there, angular, plump around the middle, sullen, a little frightened, her dark hair limp and coarse. Like a cheap china figurine about to shatter.

"Help yourselves to wine," Hally called over the clapping. "I'll start dishing out the spaghetti." It was nice. Mary Ruth and Herman and Mimi Ticker had brought big fiaschi of wine. People could get drunk if they wanted to. And Myra, who stood (arms folded) laughing in her throaty way, had come with a bouquet of violets. Hally was touched. "Okay!" She handed the first plate to Mary Ruth with a plastic fork. "There's cheese on the window sill."

Then Mimi Ticker: "Oh, Hally," sighing, "it looks so good"; and each of the others.

"Thank you. It's my mother's recipe. Eat up while it's hot, Mimi, okay." Last of all, she heaped a large plate for herself.

"*Meat* sauce, and it's so good," Carolann raved. "You're a real goombah, Hally."

"Yairr," Mary Ruth interrupted, "I ain't Italian but this is the best spaghetti I *eva* tasted. You really did a beautyful job. . . . Oh, and thank you, Hally, f'remembrin' that I can't eat meat."

"Oh," Hally gulped, "you're welcome." (Had Mary Ruth ever alluded to an intolerance of meat?) "Yes, I added it at the last minute—"

"I hope not just on account of me," the elderly spinster said quickly.

"Yes and no." Leaning against the refrigerator door, she glanced over in the direction of Alma (winded from the dance), who hadn't begun to eat yet. "Please don't let your meal get cold, Mrs. Spinelli," Hally said, laughing, and wound the long strands of pasta through and around the tines of her blue fork.

The grey-haired lady began to eat.

"It's not that I shou'nt eat meat; it just makes me . . . I donno. I can't digest it, y'know?"

Hally smiled reassuringly at Mary Ruth and cleared her throat. "Now that I see you've all started to eat, I wonder whether anybody notices anything unusual in the sauce," she asked in a confiding way.

Marco took a taste of the ruddy preparation separately. "Pizza-pie spice?"

Hally shook her head.

"I awrys put in a little *Accent* and some shuga," Carolann confessed.

"I can't taste nothing unusual, Hally," Mary Ruth said despairingly.

"That's all right," she reassured. "You wouldn't. It has something to do with the meat, actually." She paused. "I'm just nervous, really."

"Oh . . ." Mary Ruth sighed. "Hea, Carolann, just gimme a taste—"

"No!" Hally ran forward and stopped her. "You can't." She hesitated. "It's a game and it would spoil things if you tasted it, too."

"Oh . . . listen to huh—it's a game. I *love* potty games!" said Mary Ruth. ". . . And I'm the only one."

Cathy screwed up the last several strands on her paper plate. "I don't taste nothin'."

Hally grinned. "Well, Cathy, you're every bit as bright as your mother says you are. There shouldn't *be* any peculiarity to the taste of this spaghetti sauce—"

Eagerly Mary Ruth raised her hand. "Didja pickle the meat? I was thinkin maybe—because we all work at Pixie Pickles?"

"That's a good guess, Mary Ruth. But . . . no." (Confusion.) "But you're warm, I . . . Myra?"

"Hally, I noticed—I didn't want to *say* anything but—the little bits of meat were all cold. They weren't hot like the sauce."

"*Very* good. They weren't cooked, in fact. I prepared the meat days ago, bottled it, and then added it after I'd put up Mary

Ruth's plate." She paused. "Has anybody here—oh, of course you have—heard of botulism?"

"You're surprised?" She smiled. "Darla, you should know better than to try to leave; anyway, there's nothing to be done for any of us. Oh. For the benefit of Cathy—you look a little puzzled—possibly you were cleaning your closet the day they explained botulism: it's a poison. I assume your mother and father know about it, because until 1925 it was a terrible problem here. And the reason, Mimi, why you couldn't taste anything unusual is because the poison is tasteless and odorless. We will all—but Mary Ruth—die. Not immediately, but you may as well stay here, since the reason for our getting together tonight *was,* after all, to get to know each other." She looked at each of them. "Mel, I don't believe you introduced me to your wife?"

"Sarah . . ."

"Well, Sarah, I'm glad to meet you. I wonder: have you by any chance met your husband's mistress, Darla?"

Herman Ticker set down the wine bottle he had been holding.

"You won't be experiencing any symptoms—I should say *we*—for another four hours. Or possibly as long as six days. Carolann, it is of no use to try to vomit. Just a taste of contaminated meat is usually fatal." She paused. "You'll feel more comfortable knowing what symptoms to expect. No need worrying about vomiting and diarrhea—constipation is more likely—in any case, the toilet is outside in the hall and the door is locked. After midnight you may begin to experience dizziness and double vision. Botulism attacks the nervous system. Your coordination will be altogether, as *you* say, Carolann, 'unreal.' Later, possibly tomorrow or the next day, we'll all have increasing difficulty breathing and speaking. We die of asphyxiation."

"But . . ." Carolann sobbed.

"You're wondering why I chose to single out Mary Ruth? I decided after some consideration that she was the only one of us *worth* saving. She isn't married. She isn't mean. Unlike you, Myra, she works hard. Unlike both you, Carolann, and Marco, she isn't a backbiter. In fact, Marco, this might be a fine opportunity to tell Herman Ticker to his face some of the things you say to us about him every day. Go on. You can even call him Herman. Mary Ruth, I'm sorry to put *you* through all of this but you will not be able to leave until we are all dead—I've swallowed the key. Oh, and I forgot: if you—or anyone else, for that matter—become hungry, we still have Alma Spinelli's prune pie."

Mimi Ticker shook her head and a tear rolled down one cheek.

"That, incidentally, was a very nice idea you had before, Alma, teaching everybody to do the tarantella. You realize that it was once believed the dance was the only cure for the tarantula's bite. Now we know that the spider's bite wasn't poisonous at all, just painful; however, once the dance was prescribed regularly for the nervous condition known as tarantism. The afflicted person danced and leapt and shrieked. Well. I doubt we'll resort to that." She cleared her throat. "I feel I should tell you why I am doing this. Would you like to know?"

No response.

"I am your savior in a way. I'm saving you from the slow, painful death of Pixie Pickles, the rupture of your unhappy life together as a family. Cathy, you will never have to tell your parents that you're pregnant—you thought we couldn't see it, didn't you—and, Marco, you can stop worrying about your blood pressure: there's enough garlic in my spaghetti sauce to keep you kicking until the very last. Darla, you would have been the first to go anyway. The money's run out—am I correct, Mary Ruth?"

Myra began to wail.

"That's all right. Make as much noise as you want. The floors and walls are thick. Cry. Rave. Mary Ruth, I think you'd better sit this one out in the closet."

Just as Babylon, that great city, must fail before the New Jerusalem comes down out of heaven, prepared as a bride adorned for her husband, so an honest despair is an essential precondition for any utopia worth the imagining. If that seems a dire pronouncement, I can add the authority of H. G. Wells, who describes the moment before the world's awakening with great conviction in *In the Days of the Comet:*

"I stood upon the edge of the great ocean, and I was filled with an inarticulate spirit of prayer, and I desired greatly—peace from myself. . . . Tomorrow I should be William Leadford once more, ill-nourished, ill-dressed, ill-equipped and clumsy, a thief and shamed, a wound upon the face of life. . . . It entered into my thoughts that I might end the matter now. . . . To wade out into the sea, into this warm lapping that mingled the natures of water and light, to stand there breast-high, to thrust my revolver into my mouth—? Why not?"

One's despair may be as private and intense as that described in Wells's novel or in the foregoing story, or it may be coextensive with the globe. There's this to be said for sublimation: anxieties become more supportable when transferred to India or Ulster, to the Population Explosion or the Cold War, to wherever or whatever seems as unsolvable as one's own problems.

These are not, after all, unreal problems. Not one's own and not the world's. Nor are they unsolvable, though they may seem so until someone comes along to solve them. Like Henry Kissinger. Or Brian Aldiss.

WHAT YOU GET FOR YOUR DOLLAR

by Brian W. Aldiss

It has been my pleasure to travel on the Probability Machine only twice in my life. What follows is a report on my visit to Probability A395, which I undertook during the winter of 1973; that is to say, during the period when the world was first suffering from the effects of the Great Energy Crisis, after the oil-producing countries of the Middle East had refused to increase the rate at which they withdrew the dwindling supplies of fossil oil from their national territories.

The Probability Machine at the University of Oxford is surprisingly little known. True, it is under the control of that secretive body, the Hebdomadal Council, and is kept, not in the Physical Laboratories, as one might expect, but in the old Logic and Probability Theory building, which stands outside the university and the city, on the Kennington side of Bagley Wood.

The Probability Machine was invented by two Englishmen of genius, Charles Babbage and Charles Mansfield, the latter making practical application of the former's theories. The machine was built by members of the Oxford University Scientific Experimenting and Investigating Society in 1861. It was powered by a revolutionary propellant, first suggested by Mansfield in 1849, consisting of a benzene-oxygen mixture. Because this mixture caused the death of an undergraduate in the early stages of development, the Probability Machine was sheltered from publicity, and has remained out of the public eye ever since.

My journey took place on 16th December, 1973. I was making the three hundred and ninety-fifth journey in the machine. As I signed the faded old leather-bound log book, I noted that Journey Number Five had been taken by a don on the University Maths Faculty, C. L. Dodgson.

I was in the machine no more than six minutes. As soon as the gigantic strobe plates ceased whirling, I climbed down, nodded to the attendants, and made my way into the streets of this world of alternate-probability.

At first, everything appeared much the same as in the probability-world I had left. But so it generally does. One comes across a small difference—say, a new street or an unexpected name over a bank—and there is a curious feeling of tension, for at that point you do not know if the difference is insignificant, affecting only a family history, one genealogical chain, or whether it forms a clue to a whole radically altered world-history.

Radically altered worlds are naturally much rarer than the minor variations but, on my previous probability-trip, I found myself in a Britain changed beyond belief; I fled to the United States and found that country equally incomprehensible. In neither country was a tongue spoken that I could comprehend. Matters were almost as bad in Europe, until I found myself in Florence. There I learned what had happened, almost a millennium earlier. The Romans had made contact with the Chinese in the Red Sea; trade links had been established; the Roman legions had been directed towards the riches of the East. As a result, Gaul and Britannia had never been invaded. Instead, the British Isles had been carved up by various Germanic and Scandinavian marauders until, by the twentieth century, they were divided into six small kingdoms and a republic, with twenty-four main languages between them. North America had been colonized by Laplanders.

But in Probability A395 it was clear that nothing so drastic had happened. I walked into a department store and took an unhurried look around. Little seemed to have changed. All the same, one is never too certain, for you are challenged by items of which normally you take no notice. Was household furniture always so cheap? Were those lamps better designed than the ones you might expect to see "at home"?

Again, I thought that the people in the store, both staff and customers, looked slightly more cheerful and perhaps more smartly dressed than they had been "at home"; but it was a subjective impression; I could not be sure.

Only in the pet department did I get a shock. They had glass tanks of tropical fish. The last tank contained something different: "Trilobites, £20 each." Trilobites!

I recognized them even as I read the label. There were about ten of them in the tank, none more than three inches long. Their carapaces varied from sandy red to a dull crimson. Some flittered through the water, some rested on the bottom of the tank. And I knew that trilobites had been extinct for millions of years.

"Of course they're genuine," the manager said when I approached him. "They're imported from the State of Sinai. This is only the second consignment we've had. There's a terrific demand for them all over the world."

I went to the public library and looked up the State of Sinai in an encyclopedia. There it was, attended by a photograph of "the brilliant geodesic structure of the University of Eilat." From the brief article, I learned that the nation, which gained its independence in 1963, was comprised mainly of Arabs and Israelis living in unity. Here indeed was something which had never happened in my previous Probability.

Flipping idly through the same volume of the encyclopedia, I came across an article on space-travel. It was brief, and concluded by saying that the United States had sent a rocket into orbit in 1970. The Russians and Japanese had followed suit a year later. The U.S. and Japan were planning to send a manned rocket to the Moon before the end of the seventies. . . .

Here was a major difference in Probabilities. I thought immediately, I've materialized in a more primitive Probability! So much for egotism!

That comforting reflection was dented a little when I emerged into the streets again. At the end of the article on Sinai, I read that it was one of only three countries where passports had been abolished; on impulse, I decided to go there myself. As I made my way to a travel agency, I observed that darkness had fallen, but the streets were all brightly lit. Only yesterday, in my own Probability, a blackout had descended as a result of the energy crisis and the action of the Arab countries in cutting off oil to the West.

Well, I made it to the new State of Sinai. There I found an answer to all the differences between Probability A395 and mine; it is embodied in the following report.

(I say *all the differences*. I mean the differences which are verifiable matters of fact. For—alas—I cannot help feeling that there was also a very slight but meaningful difference in the outlook and morality of the world in which I found myself.)

Just how inevitable was the space race in our Probability, and in all the other Probabilities in which it took place? Can we think back to a time when the Americans and Russians might not have turned towards the Moon and planets, but instead engaged their vast resources and know-how in a project designed directly to improve mankind's lot, such as the development of the Amazon basin or of Siberia?

Events look inevitable only after they have happened. The space race appeared highly unlikely to almost everyone before the first sputniks went up. What of that .000001 per cent for whom space-travel was a lifelong creed: Robert Goddard, Konstantin Tsiolkovsky, Hermann Oberth, and of course good old American Wernher von Braun? It may have been just an accident of history that events went their way; in Probability A395, events went another way.

One year before the first sputnik was launched, in October, 1956, the world-nightmare in our Probability had reached new heights. There was abortive revolution in Hungary against the oppression of Russian Communism; and British and French forces, acting in collusion, bombed Egyptian airfields and started to invade Egypt, as old imperialist illusions of power—personified in the Prime Minister, Sir Anthony Eden—enjoyed a last fatal fling.

Just possibly, that folly could have been made a world turning-point. As the British and French ignominiously withdrew from Egypt, another .000001 per cent might have risen up and been heard. In Probability A395, it did rise up and it was heard. From then on, a slight divergence in possibilities can be noted. The UN Forces did more than just take over in the Canal Zone.

In addition to occupying the Canal Zone, the UN set up a new department, MERO, the Middle East Reclamation Organization. MERO officials announced that first practical steps would be taken to solve the hitherto intractable problem of the Middle East, the oil-producing centre of the world. Instead of selling arms promiscuously to the rival Middle East nations, the Western Powers and their friends (and of course the Communist Bloc if it cared to join), through MERO, would reclaim the melancholy wastes of the Sinai Desert, and the adjoining Negev Desert, apportioning the area reclaimed between Egypt, Jordan, and Israel.

Israel immediately agreed to join in the MERO project; her farmers were already raising bumper crops of wheat and barley in parts of the Negev. Russia, anxious to increase her influence in the region, exerted pressure on President Nasser, so that Egypt also co-operated in the project. Anthony Eden headed for Jamaica.

The first MERO task forces arrived on the fringes of the Sinai in February of 1957. It was a miscellaneous cohort of Swedes, Brazilians, Jugoslavs, Icelanders, Indians, Americans, Dutch, and two Norwegians. The World Press had an enjoyable time at their expense, especially when one of the Norwegians was shot by an itinerant Arab who hadn't heard that his world was going to be improved, and would not have liked it if he had.

"Promises to become an international ground-nuts affair," commented the *Times* wryly, in a leader.

"BRING EDEN BACK!" bellowed the *Daily Express*.

But the work got started, and the cynics and idiots were—well, they were not silenced, but they began suddenly to praise the vision of a scheme which, they claimed, should have been commenced years earlier.

MERO was a costly enterprise. As the equipment piled up and the experts gathered, and the nuclear-powered desalination plants grew along the Mediterranean coast, astronomical sums were bandied about. The first twelve months alone were said to have cost £28.5 million (coincidentally, the cost of the American Survey 4 Moonprobe, written off as a failure in our Probability).

Nor was the enterprise carried through without mistakes. Just before Christmas, 1957, the great El Arish scandal blew up, as a result of which several eminent gentlemen lost their eminence. El Arish, capital of the reclamation area, grew from a dozy Mediterranean port of some 11,000 people to a bustling city of almost a quarter million within a couple of years; it was only to be expected that rackets would be operating—as the leader of the Turko-Armenian gang pleaded when convicted for fiddling two million pounds' worth of earth-shifting equipment and exporting it to Cyprus on a MERO ship.

There was, too, the unfortunate case of the four hundred thousand eucalyptus trees, a gift from Canada, which were wrongly planted and not ringed with oil to preserve moisture, so that they perished.

These were minor setbacks, after all. Grasses began to grow over dunes, the sisal plantations to spread. Thousands of sturdy acacias and eucalyptus saplings gave increasing shade to new highways. Desalination plants, powered by British nuclear reactors, began to spew forth almost drinkable water; a denazified German in Egyptian employ perfected a cheap solar-powered pump which would freshen as well as raise water. The Lussan dam began to generate hydro-electric power; pipelines cut the barren land into an uberous geometry. Meronized villages began to grow up here and there, each making its own impression on the desert; each had its varieties of specially-developed maize, cane sugar, rice, cotton, and selected vegetables to grow in its new fields. The East-West system of canal, road, and rail between Suez and Eilat on the Gulf of Aqaba began to extend inwards from both directions; near Nakhl El Tur, Dutch engineers struck oil. They were looking for dates and found oil.

To the few local inhabitants of Nakhl El Tur, oil was an incidental—at least at first, and until the full extent of the oil strata was realized.

The Nakhl El Tur oasis stands on the edge of true desert (or did until 1958, for it is now a strenuous market-city, as I discovered for myself), beside an extensive dried-up salt lake. In the bad old days, Nakhl grew little but dates, and even the date palms bore poor crops, owing to under-irrigation and lack of drainage. A three-man Dutch engineering team set themselves the limited objective of improving this disposition, after a UN doctor had reported on the high incidence of malnutritive diseases in the area. Utilizing the new solar-powered pumps, the engineering team watered large areas of land south of Nakhl, thus leaching residual salts out of the topsoil; at the same time, they lowered the water-table by drainage. The result was a spectacular trebling of the date crop within three years. The discovery of oil was mere "spin-off."

For the industrial managers of the West, this oil find marked a turning-point in their attitude to MERO. However reluctantly, they were now convinced of the viability of the project. Oil was to their superstitious minds what gold had been to their ancestors; they began to investigate (and invest in) the reviving area. Stock markets everywhere indulged in a euphoria unknown for decades. After an appropriate time lag, this optimism led to many urban regeneration schemes all round the world.

As the rigs spread further into the difficult terrain about Nakhl, technologists on the spot found themselves in need of more adequate transport. So the first Tumvec ("tumbling vehicle") was developed, a crawler machine with tracks, which could engage its legs in crane-activity when necessary, striking its typical "sit-up-and-beg" attitude. This machine was the predecessor of the tumvecs we today take for granted when they appear at the scene of an earthquake or similar disaster. No doubt they will be working on the lunar surface before so long, and just as efficiently.

But the first Nakhl tumvecs were clumsy and expensive. One-man machines were more suited to local conditions. So the Baliped came into service, a tall-walker that in the cities of A395 today often takes the place of automobiles. Balipeds can be used by the aged and the invalid, responding as they do to minute balancing movements by the operator. This machine has already changed the lives of hundreds of thousands of people for the better.

The three Dutchmen of Nakhl were soon enlisted on a new project connected with the subterranean waters they had discovered. This was no less than the construction of the world's first underground dam, a seminal step towards the development of El Tur Science City, that peculiar blend of showmanship and high endeavour which still attracts so much popular attention today.

For anyone who has worked or lived in the fantastic underground environment of El Tur, this by-product of MERO is the most interesting of all, and promises to lead furthest. The claims that its thirty-hour day is developing an "anti-circadian man" may be poppycock, but El Tur's renowned "freedom from day-night tyranny" has certainly led to the development of calescent behaviourism—which may, when more widely studied, alter our whole theory of the function of Man. Like hypnosis before it, calescent behaviourism is initially hard to credit; yet, in fifty years' time, we shall probably accept it as a commonplace that man powers his own vehicles by a simple act of will. Oil will then be properly employed and not wasted, as it still is, as an inefficient means of propulsion.

Other so-called "spin-off" bonuses appeared here and there in MERO territory. Turquoise and manganese deposits were found, as

well as subterranean lakes containing water from the Paleocene
epoch, sixty million years old and 1,750 feet down. Living in that
water were remarkable survivals, various species of the trilobite
genus, including Callavia and Agnostus, which I had seen in the
Oxford department store. Long believed extinct, these forerunners
of our crustacea emerged from a mile below Sinai to delight and
puzzle the scientific world. More recent findings in the same area
include the cave of a fifth-century anchorite in which was pre-
served a remarkable Codex of the late-third or early-fourth century, throwing new light on the relationship between Moses and
Aaron, and the tribes of the Sinai in Biblical times.

By 1959, it had become fashionable to visit the Sinai Project.
Travel agencies moved in. Student parties arrived from all over
the world to form work-parties in their vacations. Many young
men and women stayed on to enjoy the life of dedication and ad-
venture, or to contribute to the populist movements developing in
the area. Early agricultural schools expanded into colleges. The
University of El Arish gained its charter in 1960, the University of
Eilat in 1961. By then, the desert was blooming, yellow becoming
brown and green, and of the 23,800 square miles involved in the
project, almost one third lay under active reclamation.

From then on, progress was fast. Throughout the sixties, there
were even more amazing developments. After no more than nine-
teen months' wrangling, and the appearance of American and
Russian fleets off the coast, Sinai declared itself an independent
sovereign state, to be run jointly by Israelis and Arabs who re-
joiced in declaring their common Semitic heritage. Sinai's populist
politics serve to give it an identity distinct from either of its immediate neighbours—between whom it is emerging as something
more positive than a buffer state.

Independent Sinai has declared itself to be "a warmer, friend-
lier Antarctica," open to science, its boundaries closed to no man.
Its pleasure resorts have pioneered new perspectives in tourism.
Its daring scheme for the damming of the southern end of the Red
Sea and the reclamation of Saudi Arabia is now in stormy debate in

the UN (whose investments in the area make it now a powerful para-national force). Perhaps Sinai's most impudent achievement was the announcement only last year of the Abolition of Passports Act. Sinai, Chile, and Iceland are now the only countries one may enter without that restrictive twentieth-century invention, the passport. Egypt, Iran, and other countries may soon follow suit.

As for MERO, it was officially discontinued in 1969, to be reconstituted under a new charter as TWARO (Third World Aid and Reclamation Organization). This new body has much wider powers than the old, thanks chiefly to massive investments from giant corporations in the USA, USSR, and UE. Under its stormy and capable Chairman, Lord Ritchie-Calder, the TWARO charter enables it to draw 1.1 per cent of the GNP from eleven contributory nations to ameliorate the complex socio-historico-economic problems resulting, at least in part, from the depredatory expansionist policies of European powers in colonial times.

This is not the place in which to discuss the tentative solutions to the population explosion (perhaps the biggest problem mankind has ever surmounted); my concern is with the reclamation of the Sinai-Negev complex. But it is worth remarking in passing that from those humble beginnings in February, 1957, has flowed the present astonishing reawakening of hope in the West, and the banishment of the old Cold War cynicism. This had contributed to a concurrent decrease in mental illness and diminished crime rates, and the global blossoming of the arts—led by Negro, Brazilian, Egyptian, and Danish personalities. That simple creative act, the forming of MERO, has had consequences which have released a new epoch of human creativity.

For the State of Sinai itself, there is still a long way to go. The initial project could hardly be termed complete. But the new Sinaiese development of inertial-flow control opens up dazzling prospects for world-transport, space-travel, and mechanical operations in general; while the success attending the project has encouraged other developing countries to invest money and capabil-

ity in similar reclamation ventures (often supported by TWARO)
rather than in high-prestige, low-yield projects such as national
airlines, nuclear power stations, opera houses, and independent
deterrents.

The cost of all this has been substantial. Experts put the price
of MERO at $24 billion (coincidentally, the cost of the space race
to the United States of America between 1961 and 1969 in our
Probability).

In this brief report, I have simplified much. For instance, I have
written as if I still regarded the Probability from which I started
as "our" Probability, and the main one. But "our" Probability is
just one of myriads; and I have settled permanently in A395—it
is now "my" Probability.

It's just like the old one but different.

Then again, I've simply treated figures as if they were equiva-
lent between all probabilities. But who's to say if $A395 1
= $X7000 1? There's no Rate of Exchange between changes of
heart. The point about cash is how much peace of mind you get
with it. Where I am now—as things have worked out, I'm married
to a Sinaiese girl and have a minor post on the faculty of the University of Eilat—you get just that bit more peace of mind for
your dollar.

In closing, I would like to offer my 1970's definition of Utopia.

Utopia's the place where the hopes you feel for the world at the
age of seventeen don't seem ludicrous, dangerous, or plain old-
fashioned when you reach the age of forty. . . .

I've always wanted to be James Mason. The last movie I saw him in was *The Last of Sheila,* and I wanted to be James Mason more than ever. Elegant. Funny. Wise. Modest in triumph and graceful in defeat. Utterly ripe. The Dryden of movie stars.

Prashad is a utopia for James Mason—a utopia's utopia. It does all the things a utopia should do, it does them thoroughly, it does them well, but most of all it does them with consummate grace. When the possibility of doing this anthology first began to glimmer and before I knew anything else of its contents, I knew that it would have to contain "The People of Prashad." (It first appeared in *Quark,* the excellent and ill-fated paperback quarterly edited by Samuel Delany and Marilyn Hacker.) Prashad is, hands down, the most *agreeable* utopia I know of, and if some modern *Mayflower* were to set sail in search of it I'd seriously consider signing on. That, surely, is the final test of a utopia.

THE PEOPLE OF PRASHAD

by James Keilty

To so much as approximate, let alone pin-point, their location would be doing a gross disservice to a people to whose forbearance —say more—to whose hospitality I shall remain forever indebted. It is sufficient to say that the nearest landing strip, as we count

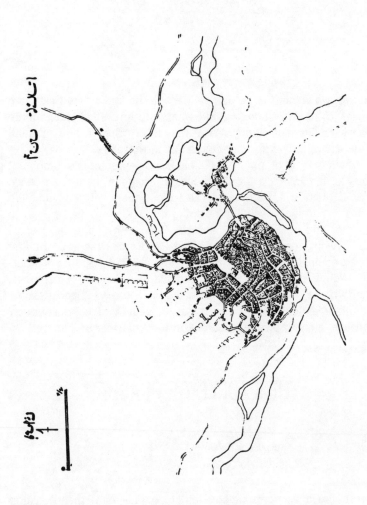

PLATE 1

nowadays, lies a good three days' riding from the valley of the high fields, *ta tamtilselyav,* and much of that time is spent in a narrow declivity between awesome cliffs whose tops more often than not cut off any view of sky or sun.

My introduction to the remarkable place and people, Prashad and the Prashadsim, was through Lalmital Tolkom, a friend of my father (all this was many years ago), a member of Prashad by birth, who left there in his adolescence to become a successful, though I fear not a very happy, businessman in our world. He knew, of course, of my interest in out-of-the-way languages and peoples and, in due course, it was he who arranged that not only was I to go to this remote corner of the world, but that I was to be able to live there for a period exceeding a year in the relative comfort of his clan-house (an approximate translation of the institution known to them as the *khudkharad,* which is not nearly as difficult to say as it is to explain). It also needs to be said that it would have been impossible to remain there for such an extended period of time without such an arrangement, for there is very little provision for the casual visitor in Palad Agormas, the tiny Prashad metropolis.

In the play *Sholsidimsum Goisidimin* (Foreign Visitor), a copy of which I was fortunate enough to bring out with me, reference is made to the fact that Prashad is *not* in either Russia, China, Afghanistan, or India. It is, as they say, independent (*balsushamsum*), no matter what theories any of these neighboring lands might have about where *their* boundaries might fall in relation to the people of Prashad. But this independence is maintained only through a highly developed ability to remain quiet, unknown, uncontending, and low. To the degree they can they remain invisible, and it is not my intention to repay their kindness with a gratuitous betrayal.

One might well ask: in that case, why write about them at all? In extenuation I can only say that a description of their culture and society has a value and importance that will be made clear in the telling; it provides a salient challenge to what in contrast seems an insane world; I mean the one the rest of us live in.

At any rate, I was brought in from a place I could get to in the normal course of traveling, and my "disappearance" for a period of over a year went unnoticed since it had been prepared for at this end among family and friends, and no enquiries as to my whereabouts were ever made. It was fortunate—indeed it was a condition of my entry—that I was as unknown as the people I was intending to visit.

On landing I was met by a representative of the family with whom I was to live, a handsome young man by the name of Birital Tolkom who, fortunately for both of us, knew some English. He had horses, and the first day we spent riding across the flat, stony alpine desert whose only vegetation was a kind of dry scrub. By nightfall we reached an oasis where there was a cluster of houses, a few fields sown with wheat and barley, and the only trees I had seen since leaving my place of arrival. Before noon of the following day we had reached the mountains, and we began that long tortuous climb within what seemed the very bowels of these fierce, jagged, and thoroughly inhospitable peaks. The range seemed to be, at most places, over 20,000 feet above sea level. Our own altitude was considerably below that, although by the time we had reached the summit of the pass we were well over 10,000 feet. It was at the summit that we spent our second night, this time completely in the open.

The next morning a fantastic sight greeted the eye. We were looking down into a valley, but the valley itself was not visible, as it was blanketed by a cloud that lay below us, covering all but a range of distant peaks on the opposite horizon. As we descended, now on a fairly good road, we entered this cloud that year-round hangs over the valley of the high fields, breaking up somewhat around noon and forming again in the evening. It is this perpetual mist and the rain it produces that account for the high agricultural productivity of the valley and, at least in part, for its isolation, the fact of its being utterly unknown to the outside world,

except to a few inhabitants of the surrounding desert and a very
few intrepid travelers who have found their way here by pure
chance.

In point of fact, the descent into the cloud does, for a second,
take one's breath away, as if one might drown in this mass of
vapor. In a short while, however, one comes down out of the
cloud into a land of spectacular greenness, a sight enhanced considerably by its contrast with the long stretch of completely arid
territory crossed on the preceding days of travel.

On all sides now there were fields of grain in terraces where
wheat, barley, corn, rice, hay, and other feed crops were growing.
There were orchards of pear, plum, apple, apricot, peach, cherry,
something that looked like but probably wasn't mango, and other
fruit trees. Just below the summit of the pass there were many fir
trees, but these gave way to mulberry, pepper, chestnut, elm, and
deodars as the road continued its gradual descent into the valley.
In some areas sheep were grazing in lush pastures; elsewhere there
were cattle and a variety of domestic fowl, chickens and ducks for
the most part. Occasionally we passed through a neat village lining both sides of the road with low, whitewashed cottages, solidly
built out of stone and beaten earth, with flat roof terraces fenced
with brushwood.

At about noon, just as the overcast was breaking in places so
that one could see patches of sky and a glimpse of sun, we reached
the wild, tumultuous river that runs through the center of the
tamtilselyav. The river has a twisting course, for the smaller, secondary valleys that run down to it, used for intensive agriculture,
are separated by high ridges of rock around which the river is
forced to bend. To prevent excessive erosion by this extremely
rapid flow, willow trees have been planted thickly along its sides;
but even these, here and there, are washed into the stream by the
violent, tearing thrust of the water.

After we had followed the river for a few hours, the sound of
which was almost deafening at times, suddenly the city of Palad
Agormas swung into view, perched on the ridge which it covers

and which divides it roughly in two. The city occupies this steep, rocky site, around which the river makes one of its many bends, in order to leave the valleys on either side as much as possible free for agriculture. At first sight it appears to be all one complicated, terraced structure, its color a general dull brown or yellow. There appears to be little or no vegetation within the city, which only covers, however, a little more than a half-mile square. In other words, Palad Agormas is extremely compact. Indeed, this small area—along with a tiny, straggling suburb on the opposite bank of the river, which is connected to the city by a sturdy stone bridge —contains a population of around 50,000 people.

What struck me immediately was an odd lack of differentiation. As I have said, at first glance it appears to be all one structure. There are no towers, no steeples, no spires or minarets, no mosques or cathedrals, no fortresses or castles, no palaces, not even a soaring smokestack. All of the buildings are of about three stories or less, all built of much the same materials: wood, stone, and packed earth, with yellow unglazed tile on the roofs. Indeed the whole of it struck me as if it were some lichenous growth on the rock-formed ridge. If the city itself has no punctuation, the surrounding nature, culminating in snow-covered peaks at the horizon, has that to spare, and in that respect, the city seems to defer to the magnificence of its surroundings; it doesn't contend. Palad Agormas, like all cities, reflects the values and ideals of the people who built it and live in it. I was not completely aware of how much so this was the case when it first came into view, but in many respects the whole story was there in that first sight. What I was being told was, among other things, that the people of Prashad have no institutionalized government or religion—but that they do have a deep respect for nature, for the world of which they form a relatively insignificant part.

Entering the city, we plunged into a maze of very narrow streets, some of which followed the contour, while others, composed mainly of steps, connected one "terrace" of the city to another. In comparison to the width of the streets, the houses were tall; these are the *khudkharad'l,* the so-called "clan-houses," each of which contains about fifty people. They are rambling structures, much added to over the years, composed of a series of open courtyards, usually surrounded by wooden balconies or galleries which give access to the many rooms. The ground floor, with its great door upon the street and often a secondary door on an altogether different street, contains the workshops, storage rooms, the kitchen, the stable, the laundry, the bath and the privies, in fact all the utilities required for the maintenance of the *khudakhad,* which is the name for the residents of the structure as a group. The upper floors (there are usually two) contain the individual rooms of the members of the *khudakhad,* including the nursery or nurseries.

The streets for the most part are paved with stone, quite clean, and, because there are no shops open to the street on the ground floor, rather quiet. In other streets I saw rows of smaller structures, also of two or three stories, with open terraces let into the front of the building on the ground floor, where there were small tables with stools around them, and people could be seen eating and drinking and conversing. These were the *drukharad'l,* of which more will be said later.

While crossing the town on our way to what would be my "home," we came across one large open space, one of two market places in Palad Agormas (the other is across the river), the *unsa* where all commercial transactions occur. At one end of this was a large but rather low structure of one story. This was the *khomidakharad* (a name which in only the roughest approximation may be translated by "bank"), again one of two, the *divi* and the *boir* (to rhyme with "no-ear"), the "new" and the "old."

When finally we arrived at the *khudkharad* where I was to live during my stay, we entered by a rear door that led directly into the stable. Here I had my first lesson in how life was conducted in a family of this sort. To begin with there are no servants; therefore our first order of business was to unpack and unsaddle the horses, rub them down, and see to their feeding. After a long trip and

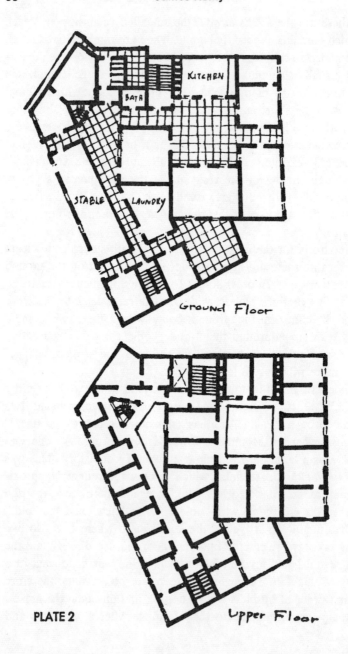

Ground Floor

Upper Floor

PLATE 2

three days' riding, this seemed somewhat an anti-climax; but I realized that it was simply a necessity, the performance of which was taken for granted. The first "law" of this society, and particularly of the *khudakhad,* is that if you see something that needs doing, you do it. You never leave a mess for someone else to cope with.

Birital, my guide, then proceeded to show me to my room, which was on the floor above the ground floor. It was large, rather dark, as all the light came from a window on the courtyard, and warm. This warmth, which I learned to appreciate in the generally cool, damp climate of Prashad, came from the flues in one wall which were connected with the kitchen ovens on the floor below. On our way to my room, Birital showed me, on the ground floor, the privies and the bathroom. This last consisted of a room occupied by a large vat of hot water where, Japanese style, one soaked after one had soaped and rinsed. The facility was used simultaneously by both men and women, our inspection revealed.

It was curious, I thought as we walked down the passages and through the courtyards and up the stairs and along the galleries around the courtyard, how little curiosity or interest of any kind my sudden appearance seemed to evince. Birital had said that he would make a more general introduction when we went down to the kitchen, after I had deposited my gear in my room, to have something to eat. But the people we met on our way scarcely raised an eye as we passed each other. I didn't detect any hostility in this, and later I came to realize that, living in such close quarters as all the Prashadsim do in the *khudkharad'l,* and indeed in their extremely densely populated little city, they leave as wide a margin as possible as far as personal contact is concerned; they don't impinge, demand, or importune on each other. In other words, they leave each other alone unless there is something that has to be said or something that needs to be done involving someone else.

The kitchen, where all meals are prepared and eaten (I was about to say "served," except that the whole process is very much every man on his own), is a huge room lined on one side with tile-covered charcoal stoves, and on the side opposite the stoves with a range of brick ovens. Another wall is taken up by shelves and bins where kitchen utensils and staple foods such as rice and flour, tea, and the usual seasonings are stored. In the center of the room is a great wooden table with benches and stools around it. The general procedure was that everybody did his own marketing and cooking, except for the very young and the extremely old. In practice, this meant that there was at any time a great variety of foods available, and it was quite acceptable to pick and choose, cafeteria style, among what had been prepared, since no one who cooked cooked only for himself, and there was always something left over. In this way I was provided with a quite adequate meal. The food was reminiscent of Chinese cooking, and though the people are distinctly not Chinese, they use chopsticks to eat with. After we had eaten, we went out to a well in the courtyard and rinsed out our bowls and cups and other utensils, and deposited them again on the shelves in the kitchen.

During the meal I was introduced to a few of the people with whom I was to live during the next year, but since there is no set time for eating—they have a horror of schedules—by no means all of the clan was present. In due course I did get to know them all, some well, some very casually; but this was only the result of my having been there over a long period of time. Naturally everyone living in the *khudkharad* knows everyone else—since he or she was born there. And this is the salient factor about this peculiar institution: no member of Prashad ever leaves his *khudkharad,* as a place of domicile, except that he leave the country entirely. A woman may have children, but these children are born and brought up in her *khudkharad,* with her brothers and sisters and aunts and uncles, not those of the father (assuming, as is almost invariably the case, that the father belongs to another *khudakhad* or clan group). The only woman who would come to live with her "husband" in his *khudkharad* would be a peasant woman belonging to the so-called *sholnai sidim'l* (literally the "other people") who work the land. In other words, for all intents and purposes, the institution of marriage does not exist among the Prashadsim, but rather, more importantly, the family does; the family is the all-important and most basic element in their society, and it serves almost every purpose that the institutions of government in other countries have delegated to them.

In this respect, the *khudkharad*—I mean the building—serves as a school, an emergency hospital (even though there is a hospital of sorts in Palad Agormas), a fire department, a police department, an insane asylum if need be (though this is very rare), and as any other kind of institution that on occasion might be needed to serve the society. By virtue of its lack of rigid structure, it is extremely flexible; by virtue of the deep, mutual understanding of its inhabitants, it is a remarkably warm and nourishing environment for its children as well as its adults, despite, oddly enough, the relative stand-offishness that one senses immediately, especially among the older people.

The question came up after lunch, and in a certain sense as a result of it, as to how I was to make my contribution as a temporary member of the *khudakhad*. I had, naturally, brought along funds which would allow me to repay any expense made necessary by my presence; but it was not, I found out, to be a matter of repayment for services, but of active participation. I was to become a temporary member of Prashad, the commonwealth, and to bring this into effect we set off for the *khomidakharad,* the large building on the market place that I mentioned earlier.

Here it is necessary to give some background on the basic economy of Prashad and how it works. The people of Prashad own their land in common. They consider themselves to be a single tribe which has, as a matter of convenience, split itself up into approximately a thousand sub-tribes, the *khudakhad'l,* whose *khudkharad'l* make up the city of Palad Agormas. (I found the difference between these two terms, which are so similar in sound and appearance, a difficult one to grasp at first, and, I suspect, so does the reader.)

Originally this was entirely an agricultural economy, but there was apparently a strong feeling among them that any culture worth its salt required an urban element. Thus, perhaps as long as five centuries ago (their presence in this isolated location goes back at least two thousand years and probably longer, if the language is any indication), some of the sub-clans began the settlement of the town and the foundation of the *kholdekharad,* the so-called "university," and the *miradmida,* the hospital. While these two functions were at first deemed a sufficient reason for a separate community, it soon became apparent that the situation was inherently an unstable one. In the long run, all of the Prashadsim had to be either on the land or urbanized. Thus, on a gradual basis, over a period of at least two centuries, there was a deliberate and, to the degree possible, selective recruitment of tenants from the surrounding semi-desert lands to farm the land and tend to the livestock. The terms were favorable: in exchange for a rent set by the Prashadsim, the *sholnai sidim'l* (the "other people") were to set their own prices for their commodities, make their own decisions as to what to raise, and keep their tenancy in the family after the death of the original tenant. This last was an enormous concession, for the members of Prashad have no private property except, so to speak, the clothes on their backs, and so at death, their share of the commonwealth reverts back to the common holding to be redistributed among the living.

In effect, a two-caste system was put into operation, one urban and the other agricultural; but this should not be taken as an implied superior and inferior relationship, for the kinds of physical labor required to maintain the *khudkharad,* as indeed the whole city and its few institutions, are not tremendously different in kind or less onerous in nature than those required of the agricultural community.

It was to handle the collection and distribution of the rents, in which every member of Prashad, man, woman and child, from birth to death, has equally one share, that the *khomidakharad* was instituted. (Part of the confusion in separating terms is that all these old words dealing with their institutions have either the element *kharad* meaning "house" or *dakhad* meaning roughly "business" in them, and the last-mentioned manages to include both elements.) There is, as a matter of fact, no money at all in circulation; all transactions are carried out on the basis of credit (which is one meaning of the word *khomi;* others we will find out later). There is, however, a basic monetary unit, a *dakh,* which means "piece." Thus, when a member of Prashad makes a purchase in the market, he makes a notation that he has spent so many *dakh'l* of his share, and gives this to the seller along with an identifying symbol. (No names are ever used—a security measure in case of invasion.) The seller deposits this at the *khomidakharad* to his credit, and these deposits are then used to pay his rent. The whole system is rather informal and depends on a great deal of mutual trust, which is another meaning of the word *khomi.*

It was therefore at the *khomidakharad* that I presented myself in the late afternoon of the day of my arrival, still under the patient guidance of Birital Tolkom, who of course had to interpret for me. We entered the building and immediately were in a large room whose roof was supported by huge beams leaving the floor entirely clear. This last was covered by rich, figured Persian and Chinese rugs, as was the raised bench or ledge that ran around three sides of the room against the walls. Against the fourth wall, opposite the main entrance—which interrupted the ledge—was a dais, also covered by rugs, upon which was a desk and a chair— and here the *suchemisim* or "president" sat. The light came from large windows which had elaborate wood-and-paper screens set in them. These occupied most of the wall space between the stone pillars that supported the roof beams. The fourth wall, facing the entrance, had no windows but there were two doors in it on either side of the president's dais.

The effect was that of some luxurious room in an Eastern palace or club. Indeed people seemed to be lounging about, squatting on the floor or perched crosslegged on the ledge, as if they were simply spending the time of day in these comfortable surroundings.

From what I had already seen, I knew there were no rooms of comparable elegance and comfort in the *khudkharad;* and, as I learned, the *khomidakharad* was used exactly as if it were a club where people from different *khudakhad'l,* as well as members of the *sholnai sidim'l,* came to meet sociably and discuss matters of mutual interest. The people of Prashad do not visit each other or entertain each other at home; the *khomidakharad* provides one alternative for meeting one's friends outside the family. There are at least two others.

The ceremony of induction as a temporary member of Prashad proved to be a very simple matter. It involved my turning my money over to them and receiving in return a temporary "book" (*shisamtro kol*) which would allow me to buy commodities in the market place and to pay my way at the *drukharad.* Every member of Prashad has a *kol;* he receives it at birth, but he may not be allowed to use it himself until some time in adolescence, when on one of the most important days in the life of any Prashad-sim, he is permitted to use his own credit, a local form of coming of age. The *kol* is only the record—if even that, for it is rarely kept up—of the member's share in the annual common income. My *kol* was the record of what I had put in, which was of course the limit to what I might take out. It was relatively unlikely that I would ever receive in return the same currency that I put in. (The Prashadsim do on occasion buy commodities brought in from the outside, and foreign currencies are required on such occasions to satisfy sellers who do not want, understandably, to take the whole amount out in trade.) But the amount, translated by some system of their own into *dakh'l,* minus the amount I had spent, would be restored to me in some currency or other at the end of my stay. If I felt at the time that the bounds of mutual trust were being strained somewhat, I refrained from expressing the feeling. Since then I have learned to what an enormous extent *khomi*—credit, honor, mutual trust, or whatever—was the foundation stone of their society without which they could not exist as they do. I was safer than I knew.

Having performed this little operation, and having visited the garden which, uniquely in tightly built-over Palad Agormas, adjoins the *khomidakharad* on the side facing away from the market (this was the new *khomidakharad;* the old one, close to the bridgehead, also had a garden behind it going down to the river), we once again went home. I went to my room, whose few sticks of furniture consisted of a bed, a table, a chair, a little stove or brazier, and a chest for clothes and belongings, where I threw myself down on my bed in a state of complete exhaustion and promptly fell asleep.

When I awoke to the sound of gentle knocking, the room was pitch dark. I stumbled and groped my way to the door, and there again was Birital, carrying a lamp, a little provision that I had forgotten I would need. He suggested I might like to come out with him after a suitable change of clothes and visit his *drukharad*. I readily consented, only wondering dimly what sort of institution this one would turn out to be. I made a rapid toilet and we set out. It must have been at least eight o'clock at night and I noticed that the *khudkharad* was almost completely deserted; from somewhere in the house one heard the sounds of children playing, presumably in the nurseries, and that was all.

We descended the ridge along narrow, dark lanes in the general direction of the bridge. In a short while we arrived at a small open space leading to the bridgehead where the old bank (*ta boir khomidakharad*) was pointed out to me, and we swung into another narrow, twisting lane, this time lined along one side with those narrow buildings whose fronts were open to the street and on whose raised terraces the adult citizenry of Palad Agormas were to be seen seated in their finest attire—badly fitting Western-style clothes, for the most part, for the men; the women affecting rich scarves which they draped around their heads and shoulders in a manner reminiscent of the Indians—talking, drinking, and eating.

When Birital mentioned "his" *drukharad,* he meant the one he usually patronized. The choice seems to lie with the one in which one is reasonably sure of finding no one from one's own *khud-*

kharad. For their evening's entertainment, the last thing they want to do is to sit around and exchange pleasantries with their own brothers and sisters, aunts and uncles, and possibly even with their own mothers.

From what little Prashadsim I knew, I was aware that the word *drukh* means "push" or "shove" or "root" and has a very strong sexual connotation. I was not, however, prepared, I'm afraid, to receive the full blast of these people's sexual permissiveness on immediate exposure. My first indication of this was, having sat down with a group of people, friends of Birital, I was asked by a young man who, like Birital, had a modicum of English, whether I liked boys or girls. This reference—which I later realized was untypically gauche and malicious; in other words, meant for a barbarian—went completely over my head and I replied in some surprise and bewilderment, "Whose?" My reply was then taken to mean that I was quite open on the question, which, since it reflected their uncategorizing view, immediately ingratiated me with my new friend. It was only later that I began to realize to what, unwittingly, I was exposing myself, and even to what extent I was by then committed.

Let me explain here as simply as possible that the *drukharad* is a place of entertainment which provides for not only the more superficial social amenities—food, drink, and friendly conversation and argument—but, on a voluntary basis and depending on whatever agreements might be reached, private opportunities for physical gratification. Polyandry is, of course, very common in Central Asia and Tibet, but among the Prashadsim, where marriage as an institution exists not at all, sexual permissiveness is absolute in theory and limited in practice only by one's ability to attract an amenable partner or partners. The *drukharad* serves not only the purpose of facilitating such meetings and arrangements, but, since the Prashadsim don't take friends of either sex home (not from prudery or fear of disapproval, however), on its upper floors it provides for privacy (or lack of same if that's what's wanted) and whatever other amenities are required for more intimate play.

In this respect, one must take into account the absolute equality afforded the woman of Prashad who, like everyone else, has her share and her *khudakhad* which provide her with lifelong security. There is little wonder, in this connection, that she does not share in the sexual and social anxieties of her Western contemporaries. There is, for instance, no such thing as an illegitimate child in Prashad, for the simple reason that the child belongs from birth not to the mother but to the *khudakhad* and to the greater clan, the Prashadsim as a whole. Also, it should be pointed out, they are relatively sophisticated in matters of contraception and general birth control, something required by their uniquely closed, stable, and somewhat static economy. Later I shall have a tale to tell in this regard, not at all flattering to the author, but so revealing of the society and its manners and mores that, painful though it be, I cannot suppress it in the interest of *amour-propre*.

In the week that followed, as part of my initiation into the remarkable world of Prashad, I visited the two other institutions that make up the Prashadsim five-starred constellation: the *khudakhad,* the *drukharad,* the *khomidakharad,* the *miradmida,* and the *kholdekharad.*

Of the remaining two, the *miradmida* is the one of which I can say the least. This is the hospital, and my knowledge of medicine, even relatively primitive medicine, is scant. Americans visiting Central Asia with medical supplies in hand know that in no time at all they become, for better or for worse—and I sometimes very much suspect for the latter—dispensing physicians to the local population. The *miradmida* of Palad Agormas, a relatively large, low structure on the edge of town near the top of the ridge, shares in some of this since it is the only such institution for hundreds of miles around. But its care—*miradmi,* by the way, means "care," among other things—does not consist in handing out antibiotics and the other synthetic products of Western pharmacopeia.

As far as I could determine, what medicine *is* available is based on Chinese herb-lore (which is not necessarily to be deprecated), but the *miradmida* is primarily a place to which people who are ill may come and, in a sense, simply be cared for at no expense to themselves. The Prashadsim, as a matter of fact, rarely use it except in the case of some disease that they fear to be communicable, since, in much the same way, the *khudkharad* is a *miradmida,* a place of care. (In the Prashadsim language, the suffix *ida* means "place of.") Thus, most of the patients in the *miradmida* were either *sholnai sidim'l* or, using the more general term, *sholsidim'l,* foreigners.

Surgery was not performed except in emergencies, and my general impression was that, in terms of modern medical standards, the *miradmida* left everything to be desired, except, perhaps, the most important thing: a real interest in the well-being of human beings. This is true if modern medical practice is any criterion of the value of such an institution. The only other thing that caused me to wonder about the *miradmida* was how the name wonderfully managed to escape having one of those ugly *kharad* or *dakhad* endings.

An institution that did not manage to escape was the *kholdekharad,* and again one throws up one's hands and settles for the inadequate and inaccurate word "university." The inadequacy of this term is best indicated by pointing out that the *kholdekharad* has no students, no faculty, not even, God save the mark, an administration. It occupies a group of buildings also on the outskirts of the town somewhat downhill from the *miradmida.* I see that "group of buildings" might be misleading. The "campus" actually consists of one low, rambling building, which at first sight seems to be several, and two long low barracks-like structures. The entire ensemble surrounds a rock- and gravel-strewn yard which is relatively level. The largest building contains a series of rooms of various sizes which are used for informal lectures, conversations, musical and dramatic performances, and for the occasional exhibition of art work; another series of rooms constitutes the library; and in another suite of three rooms the press is located, the only one in Palad Agormas. The other two structures consist of one large room each; these are the work rooms or study halls of the scholastic community.

For that, a scholastic community, is what the *kholdekharad* consists of; a group of scholars with no particular rank or organization whose primary work is the translation and subsequent publication (in quite small quantity) of a vast variety of work from one of any number of foreign languages into their own. The main sources are English, Russian, and Chinese, but French, German, Italian, Japanese, and a mixed bag of Indian languages are well represented. The members of the *kholdekharad* are a little tight-lipped about where and how they receive their original material but there is a simple answer. Just as my father's friend Lalmital Tolkom had left Prashad in his adolescence, a good many others, particularly young men, have always done the same over the years and, from wherever they are, by a circuitous underground route, they manage to get reading material as well as letters and other communications back to the homeland and the *khudakhad*. (Witness my own case where a degree of preparation was required on both ends.)

The *kholdekharad* also publishes, on occasion, works written in Prashadsim, but this represents a very small part of the total, probably no more than one or two items a year. For the most part, the Prashadsim are too busy to write anything other than those short poems which serve as letters to their friends.

The *kholdekharad* is, however, the temple of their language and perhaps now is as good a time as any to say something about that; for the language is as important to the Prashadsim as any of their more concrete institutions. As a language, it is a difficult one to place; the vocabulary, except for a few leads, seems unrelated to any other, but in general construction it has elements of both Indo-European and Ural-Altaic or Turkic origin. If Sino-Tibetan has had any influence at all, it has been in the direction of simplicity, for the Prashadsim grammar, while not the simplest, is surprisingly uncomplicated for the language of a society as isolated as this. The languages of relatively primitive peoples are usually marked by a highly involved construction and by a lack of general or abstract terms. For instance, there will be hundreds of words for different kinds of trees or fish but no word for "tree" or "fish." This is certainly not true of the language of Prashad, which is surprisingly rich in abstract terms. However, this is definitely the result of their urbanization and the resulting cosmopolitanism which is centered in the *kholdekharad*. They may be physically at a remove from their fellow human beings, but mentally they are quite aware of the main currents of contemporary thought. Still, there are large gaps, for which they don't pretend to apologize, in the vocabularies of science, technology, and, they admit with pride, jurisprudence. A culture without laws, lawyers, courts, judges, prisons, police, or criminals can exist without a great deal of the linguistic ballast that plagues our own. Again, a society that has no politicians, no bureaucracy, and no advertising industry—in other words, no need to manipulate people by manipulating words—can, without too much embarrassment, continue to call itself *Prashad,* which means "truth."

In essence the language distinguishes between two general types of words: *drukhpadi'l* or root words which carry most of the information, and *kthirpadi'l* or auxiliary words which link and relate the information words. The former are extremely versatile in that, by the addition of prefixes and suffixes, and sometimes just by their position in a sentence, they can take on the function of a great many parts of speech. Any *drukhpadi,* for instance, can be a verb. A *kthirpadi* usually only serves one function; in this category are the articles, pronouns, conjunctions, what we call prepositions but which, in many cases, are post-positional in Prashadsim, as well as a large variety of names having to do with time, weight, distance, and other measures.

To the credit of the language, there are no case endings in the usual sense. There is no gender, no agreement between adjective and noun, no concordance, and while the verb has a full set of tenses, there is really only one very regular conjugation and only two verbs whose irregularities require any special attention. It is, in other words, a language like any other but better than many in its degree of simplicity. On that scale it lies somewhere between Italian and Chinese, leaving such primitive tongues as German and Russian far behind in its dust.

There is also a Prashadsim alphabet, which looks vaguely Arabic but which is completely unrelated to that vowel-poor system. The Prashadsim alphabet is a phonetic one in which each character represents a single sound wherever it appears. Although there are more than forty different symbols, these are based on a mere handful of sixteen root characters. They have also adopted a system of romanization, but since it uses the standard roman type font, which is the only one they possess, it is not nearly as accurate as their own alphabet in describing sounds.

I have said before that the Prashadsim are busy, but one might wonder, outside of the responsibility of carrying on the work of the *khomidakharad,* the *kholdekharad* and the *miradmida,* what they do. Even these three institutions do not occupy everybody's time; in fact they absorb only a minority of the population, and that only on a part-time basis. But, on a day-to-day basis, everyone has his hands full. This day begins not inordinately early—rising with the sun is for the people on the land—with most people up and about between eight and nine in the morning. After making breakfast, usually bread and tea, and helping see to it that the very young, the very old, and the sick are fed, the next order of business is general maintenance and janitoring. The Prashadsim are not fanatical housekeepers, but buildings on this scale housing this many people—fifty, on the average—require a minimum of daily maintenance or a serious breakdown would result. I never heard anybody give anyone an order as to what to do; I have heard people ask for help in doing something, sweeping down the stairs or mending the roof or what have you, and I have often heard people asking if they could help. At any rate, the horses do get fed and cared for, laundry is done and floors are swept, but all on an individual basis without assignment; the responsibility always lies with everyone. The same is true of marketing; no list is made up, no menu devised. People simply go out and buy things in the market, and yet I was never aware that there was any unnecessary duplication or wastage. This technique of cooperation, which is uniquely their own, is an essential development out of their life style; it is their "way" without which nothing would work and, long since, they would have foundered in chaos and disorder, contention and competition; or they would have succumbed to regimentation and oppression.

Someone, usually a man, takes on the responsibility of teaching the younger children how to read and do simple arithmetic; but it must be imagined that the *khudkharad* itself is the most practical kind of school that could be devised. It is a beehive of activity during the day, deserted only at night, and no curiosity is ever discouraged, no question left unanswered, no interest not met with a practical demonstration or an initiation in the techniques of making something.

Most household articles are indeed made in the *khudkharad,* as well as most articles of clothing; pottery, spinning, weaving, sewing, wood and metal working are essential crafts carried on at all times in the workshops and the courtyards of the *khudkharad.* The staffing of the *miradmida* and the *khomidakharad* is a result of a specialization that occurs as the individual enters his adolescence; some young people inevitably do drift towards these institutions or in the scholastic direction, but it is always voluntary. Large projects such as the building of the aqueduct, the reservoir, and the water-delivery system (it fed the well in our courtyard) may include every man, woman, and child over a period of time, as well as members of the *sholnai sidim'l.*

Some young people decide in their adolescence that life in the society of Prashad is too narrow, too limiting, too static; and so they leave. But, remembering my father's friend, I think they do so at the expense of an intense, lifelong, personal regret. Needless to say, once they are in the world of passports, taxes, and conscription, there is no way to return to the anonymous ranks of the

Prashadsim except to the prejudice of these last. Even I, young as I was, was already too committed to the outside world to ever be able to make Prashad my permanent home. I was, even if only very marginally, known.

In time, I too chose my "own" drukharad; not because I had grown tired of the company of Birital Tolkom but that I feared it might become tiresome for Birital forever and always to have me in tow. It also might have an inhibiting effect on his own pleasure, as he would feel obliged to stick with me even though opportunities might occur to slope. A change also meant that I could not depend on Birital's English, which was a lazy habit of mine whose acquisition I minded more than he, since he wanted the practice.

The result of this move was that I met Kharshal (the word means "Rose"), a woman a few years my senior, handsome, and very self-assured. I suppose, in a sense, that's the wrong word to use when speaking of Prashadsim men and women. They almost all had an ease and security about them that at moments made me despair, because, at that age, these were the qualities I most lacked, even though I attempted, quite unsuccessfully, to conceal the fact. Rather, I think my lack of ease was my drawing card; it *was* that for Kharshal. I was unique and she instinctively put me under her wing. I was inexperienced (life in a *khudkharad* does not protect one from experience; they would consider giving children formal classes in sex education a complete waste of time), and Kharshal saw an opportunity to put her unique didactic gifts to work. Actually, I was grateful to her, for I was, after all, a fish out of water, an innocent lamb, I won't say among wolves, but surely among a species whose sophistication on certain levels left one goggle-eyed and gasping. The Prashadsim don't know how to use a camera or tune in a television set or even to type on a typewriter, but these technological lapses are minuscule indeed when set in the balance with their all-encompassing, really magnificent understanding of how life is to be lived. To put it at its mildest, they simply take the cake; and, in a sense, I was the

Character	Romanization	Pronunciation	Character	Romanization	Pronunciation
∽	a	f<u>a</u>ther	ც	th	<u>th</u>in
∪	'	m<u>o</u>ther	ƫ	v	<u>v</u>an
♦	o	d<u>o</u>g	ƫ	f	<u>f</u>an
⌐	e	ch<u>ao</u>s	∟	m	<u>m</u>an
⌐	e	b<u>e</u>d	∟	n	<u>n</u>et
⌐	i	f<u>ee</u>	∟	ng	ri<u>ng</u>
⌐	i	t<u>i</u>p	∪	d	<u>d</u>ot
⌐	ai	h<u>igh</u>	∪	l	<u>l</u>ot
⌐	oi	b<u>oy</u>	⌐	r	<u>r</u>ag
⌐	ei	s<u>ay</u>	—	w	<u>w</u>ill
⌐	o	n<u>o</u>te	⌐	y	<u>y</u>et
⌐	u	s<u>ue</u>	⌐	yu	<u>u</u>se
⌐	au	h<u>ow</u>	⌐	h	<u>h</u>at
⌐	iu	n<u>ew</u>	⌐	kh	Ba<u>ch</u> (Ger.)
⌐	s	<u>s</u>o
⌐	sh	<u>sh</u>am
⌐	z	<u>z</u>eal
⌐	ch	<u>ch</u>ain
⌐	jh	plea<u>s</u>ure
⌐	k	<u>k</u>id
⌐	g	<u>g</u>od
⌐	j	<u>j</u>ob
⌐	b	<u>b</u>ad
⌐	p	<u>p</u>ad
⌐	t	<u>t</u>an

(Note: This list does not include those characters that are only used in transcribing foreign languages into the Prashadsim alphabet, for instance the 'th' sound in <u>the</u> or the 'u' sound in French <u>lune</u> or German gr<u>ü</u>n. However, such characters do exist.)

PLATE 3

cake. I was wolfed down in one gulp but, at least then, I enjoyed it immensely. I felt that in a moment, in a single leap, I had grown up—and to such wonders.

Then came what was for me in my innocence, with my poor, mingy, Western values, a great awakening. Kharshal quite parenthetically happened to mention one day that she was pregnant. That she was carrying *my* child was what I immediately assumed and she, off-handedly, thought that that was most probably the case. I was stunned, I was shocked, I was literally laid low by this casually dropped bit of information. What in the world could I do? What arrangements could I make? How could I get Kharshal and my child out of Prashad? My visit had only three or four months left to go; this was due to waning funds and other arrangements and decisions previously made.

When I attempted to bring these matters up to Kharshal, she looked at me as if I had left my senses. Leave Prashad? Whatever for? But how could I abandon her—abandon her and the child—and to what? She wanted to know, in the name of all that was sane, what I meant. The fact that she was pregnant certainly couldn't, in her mind, account for my sudden hysteria. As a matter of fact, she couldn't rightly see how my feelings were involved at all. What claim, after all, did I have over her or any child that she might see fit to bear?

I became indignant. After all, I was the father. She had admitted as much, and that was the basis of my claim over her *and* the child. At this she was both amused and bewildered. She said some rather coarse things and told me, in effect, to come off it; no such claim existed among the Prashadsim and my feelings of responsibility and ownership were not only inappropriate, they were utterly meaningless. This to me was an outrage. That child was mine and, in a sense, she was mine. I was not to be deprived of my right, my responsibility, my clear title. My very name was at stake. She felt my brow for fever and told me to go home; or if I was not willing to go home, she would. At any rate, after this

ridiculous outburst, she was certainly going to change her
drukharad.

When she left, I ran to find Birital. I took him from his friends
and I poured out my tale of bewilderment and hurt. He smiled,
he soothed, he told me what I already knew intellectually but
could not accept emotionally. Not only did I have no claim over
either the mother or the child-to-be, but even *she* had no real claim
over her own offspring. The child would be, from the moment of
birth, a member of Prashad, and the responsibility for its upbringing
was that of the *khudakhad* to which it was born. Indeed, motherly
identification was discouraged and while she might breast-feed her
child, if she felt so inclined, once weaned the child was just one
among all the children in the *khudkharad* for which everyone was
responsible, for which no one had any special, over-riding
claim. The child would not be born by the time I was scheduled to
leave and there was absolutely no way I could force Kharshal to
leave with me.

That the Prashadsim do not trust the ability of two individuals
to satisfy each other emotionally and sexually over an indefinite
period of time, and therefore find this, as a basis for family, a
singularly weak and inadequate one, is basic to their way of life.
To bring up children on such a sketchy and vulnerable foundation
is, to them, unthinkable. The child needs the stability of his clan,
he needs a dozen fathers and a dozen mothers all with as many
talents and interests and the ability to be warm and protecting.
That is what the *khudakhad* provides and, at this stage, they see
no reason for reform, let alone revolution. Provide one and they
will consider that too: after all, there is no law that keeps things
the way they are; just the simple good sense inherent in the
arrangement.

Thus Birital talked me down and smoothed me out and, if the
knife has never left me, at least I had grown used to its sticking
in me—the sense of what of me I have left there, irretrievably
and inexorably. I saw no more of Kharshal. I shall never see the
child. I do not know to this day whether it was a boy or a girl,

whether it lived or died. But to assuage a certain residual and no doubt foolish bitterness that sometimes still wells up inside me, I know that, had I been a member of Prashad, I might know no more; my responsibility would have lain with the children of my own *khudakhad,* not some other.

In our society today, where only the dry husks of "democratic" or "Christian" or "Marxian" idealism conceal the complete blight of the seed within, where the only remaining purpose of any society is the maintenance of a status of power without regard to the quality of life produced, the on-going reality and vitality of the uninstitutionalized values of the people of Prashad seem utterly foreign and almost unnatural. They have no institutionalized façade behind which their life values can decay and die unnoticed. Their values are either alive and operative in the society as a whole or they aren't, and no verbal formula or no structure of courts and legislatures can conceal the fact. This is perhaps the most important lesson they have to teach; for their particular life style may not be universally approved of. Their complete lack of sentimentality, their indifference to technological advance, their acceptance of a relatively meager equal sharing of whatever is available, their second-rating of the claim of the individual may all be anathema to a majority of those outside their culture. But whatever motivates their lives, whatever functioning principles produce their unique culture, they are nothing if not real and in operation. They are not institutionalized except in their simple, day-by-day working out. This is the element of value for the rest of us. In Prashad it is not belief that sustains the system, it is action, mutual trust, honesty in the fact of what exists; it is *khomi,* it is consideration for others, it is imagination about life without resort to tricks and trappings, it is seeing human existence in the greater setting of all nature, of all existence.

The Prashadsim live their values as simply and quietly as possible, calling no attention to themselves, competing with no one, not contending or proselytizing. They are aware that the mad rest of us may wipe them out in the process of wiping out ourselves by either war or the exploitation of our planet. But they have no power except what they share equally; they have no influence except that what they represent may be an influence; they cannot hope to change the world in their image or any other without destroying themselves. Thus they cling to *khomi* as others cling to hope; and if there is ever a revolution in the world in favor of their values and their system (or lack of system), it will be because they have remained just silent enough, just still enough, just without raising a finger or stirring a wind. They understand the paradox in that if no one else does.

An Informal Introduction to the Language of Prashad

A short conversation:

—*Nyod dai bli?*	"What do you want?" (1)
—*Dai fi antulitel forfai-id?*	"Do you have something to drink?" (2)
—*Kai menida an faisil sishilisio.*	"Here is a glass of water." (3)
—*Sha bal irda nyod ablijhamum.*	"That's not what I meant." (4)

(1) The peculiar English "do" does not, of course, translate. *Nyod dai bli'n* would be more polite but that's for a later lesson. *Nyod dai'l blin* would be used if more than one person were being spoken to. (' is pronounced like the "u" in "dull.")

(2) In a question, the subject and the verb are never reversed. If the question is not preceeded by an asking word such as *nyod* (what) or *sili* (why), the question is implied by a rising tone on the final word.

(3) *Menid* is a root word meaning "being in a place, rest, remaining." *Faisil* means something to drink out of, not the material glass, which is *bailkam*. *Sio* means "of" or "from" and, like most positional words, is added as a suffix to the noun it refers to. Thus, the sentence reads literally: Here is a glass of water-of.

(4) The final sentence reads literally: That not is what I meant. The root *ir* means, for one thing, being in a state or condition, as contrasted with *menid*, being in a place. The verb *irid*, to be, as is often the case with this verb in other languages, is slightly irregular, but *ir* also means "god" or "wrong" (for reasons best known to the

Prashadsim); *sha ira* would mean "that is wrong" or "that is god." This also illustrates that any root word can be made into a verb. *Sha irtumia* means "that is difficult," or literally "that difficults." The pronoun *a*, meaning "I," is never separated from the verb; thus *ablijhamum* means "I meant." *Al* or "me" is used where there is no verb to support the *a*.

The normal conjugation of a verb in the present tense goes as follows:

> *akhebilo*—I give
> *dai khebili*—you give
> *si, se su khebila*—he, she, it gives
> *ami khebilon*—we give
> *dai'l khebilin*—you give (plural)
> *sei khebilan*—they give

This pattern of *o, i, a, on, in, an* endings carries through all but the imperative and the past tenses, thus: *akhebilvo*, I am giving; *akhebilo'*, I will give; *akhebilo'n*, I would give; *akhebilido*, I may, might give; but *khebilami*, let us give. *Akhebilum* is "I gave" and the *um* ending is the same for all persons. The same applies for *akhebilu'm*, I was giving, used to give; *akhebilum'*, I will have given; *akhebilu'n*, I would have given; *akhebilum'n*, I had given; *akhebilidum*, I may, might have given.

The root word (*drukhpadi*), as distinguished from the auxiliary or helping word (*kthirpadi*), has a very versatile character. By itself it is always a noun or word idea; *goim*, sight, scene; *goimidam* is the noun gerund, seeing; *goim'l*, sights, scenes; *goimid*, to see (the root serves as the stem for all verb endings); *semgoimid*, to be seen; *goimin*, a person who sees; *goimida*, a place where one sees; *goimsim*, an extrinsic quality, seen; *goimsum*, an intrinsic quality, "the seeing eye"; *goimibi*, a capability or potential quality, "visible"; the adverbs *goimsimi* and *goimsumi* have no exact equivalents in English, but *goimibai* means "visibly"; *goimo*, more seeing (*mo* is the comparative ending); *goimul*, most seeing (*mul* is the superlative ending).

In the written Prashadsim alphabet (see Plates 3 and 4), the vowels are placed between the consonants close to their tops and linked with them where possible or, in printed form, above and separate from the consonants.

The short poem that ends our introduction to the language is typical of the somewhat ironic little messages the people of Prashad write each other:

> *Esram,*
> *tam so tali so tudam*
> *dai telpilshami?*
> *Atelpilshamo dil,*
> *diliam.*

> Young man,
> do you choose
> art or life or both?
> I choose you,
> little Mister.

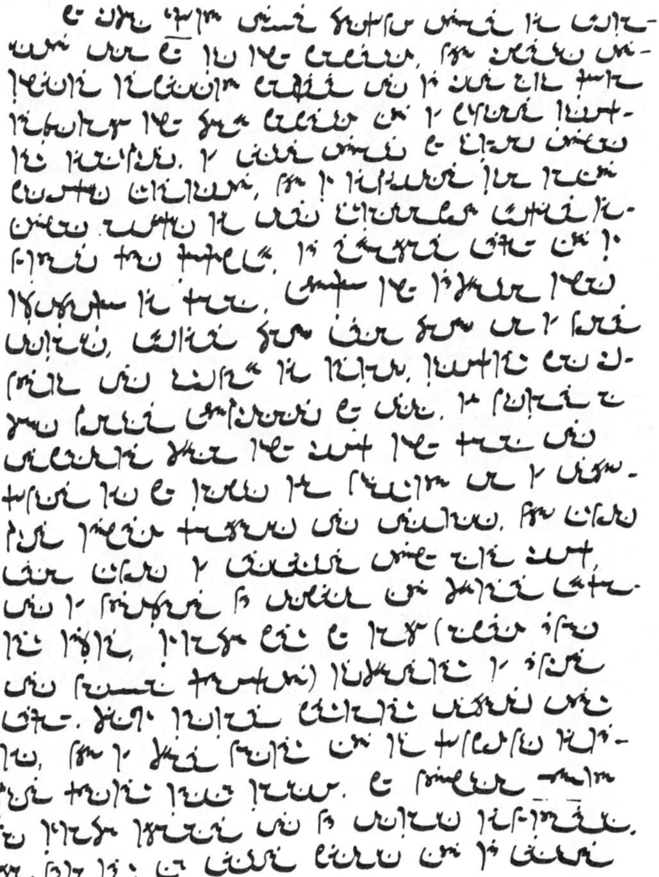

PLATE 4

More about Prashad and its discoverer.

"I think the most salient bit of biography," James Keilty writes, "is that I have a master's degree in City Planning from the University of California (1951) and for twelve years, until 1963, I worked in the San Francisco Department of City Planning, out of which experience came most of my ideas of how a society might better be constituted (*not ever* by planners). . . . The most important thing about the language is that it is a *real* one spoken by imaginary people. I suspect that is my unique contribution. . . . I have completed three books concerning the people of Prashad, hopefully to be published together as *The Prashad Papers.* The first of these, *Palad Agormas,* was written in Prashadsim and translated back into English with copious footnotes. The second, *Ta Moikham* (*The Play*), was also written in the language and translated into English. The third book consists, in part, of a kind of correspondence between people living in and out of the *tamtilselyav,* but all originally members of Prashad. Some of it is in English and some in Prashadsim (translated, of course). It is called *Ta Baibesh* (*The Network*)."

Some of Mr. Keilty's plays in Prashadsim were produced in San Francisco in 1969. Bill Brodecky, Gerald Fabian, and Marilyn Hacker co-starred under the author's direction, so it must be allowed that Prashadsim isn't spoken *exclusively* by imaginary people. If you want to learn it, apply to Mr. Keilty at 1219 Kearny Street, San Francisco, California 94133.

Isolation is a great problem for utopia-builders—not the fact of it, but how it's to be achieved. Too ready access to the great, lazy, unwashed world out there is the second-largest cause of utopian failure (plain, damn-fool miscalculation of human capacity and Nature's bounty being cause Number One). America is covered with myriad towns that started out as utopias only to end up, twenty or fifty years later, indistinguishable from every other town around them. It's the Curse of the Prairie.

Utopias survive best in outposts (Salem, Salt Lake City), on Pacific islands (New Atlantis, Pitcairn, More's great original) or in the Himalayas (Shangri-la, Prashad). There is even one that manages to be in the Himalayas *and* on a Pacific island simultaneously—Réné Daumal's inscrutable *Mount Analogue.*

Outer Space, being the new *terra incognita,* is the logical site for any new large-scale utopia. As this book goes to press, the most distinguished and persuasive of extraterrestrial utopias that I know of are in, or on the verge of, print. Both are the work of that new breed of Man that is bidding fair to take over Everything, including s-f: Woman. *The Dispossessed: An Ambiguous Utopia* is already gathering fresh laurels for its author, and few readers of this book should require any other recommendation of *The Dispossessed* than the fact that it exists and is the work of Ursula Le Guin.

A portion of the other interstellar utopia won a Nebula Award for Joanna Russ when it appeared in Harlan Ellison's *Again, Dangerous Visions.* With all due hubris, I like to think that *my* excerpt from *The Female Man* is even better than Harlan's. What a book it's got to be!

A FEW THINGS I KNOW ABOUT WHILEAWAY

by Joanna Russ

1

"Humanity is unnatural!" exclaimed the philosopher Dunyasha Bernadettesdaughter (A.C. 344–426), who suffered all her life from the slip of a genetic surgeon's hand which had given her one mother's jaw and the other mother's teeth—orthodontia is hardly ever necessary on Whileaway. Her daughter's teeth, however, were perfect. Plague came to Whileaway in P.C. 17 (Preceding Catastrophe) and ended in A.C. 03 with half the population dead; it had started so slowly that no one knew anything about it until it was too late. It attacked males only. Earth had been completely re-formed during the Golden Age (P.C. 300–ca. P.C. 180), and natural conditions presented considerably less difficulty than they might have during a similar catastrophe a millennium or so before. At the time of the Despair (as it is popularly called), Whileaway had two continents, called simply North and South Continents, both of which possessed many ideal bays or anchorages. Severe climatic conditions did not prevail below 72° S and 68° N latitudes. Conventional water traffic, at the time of the Catastrophe, was employed almost exclusively for freight, passengers using the smaller and more flexibly routed hovercraft. Houses were self-contained, with portable power sources, fuel-alcohol motors or solar cells replacing the earlier centralized power. The invention of practical matter-anti-matter reactors (K. Ansky, A.C. 239) produced great optimism for a decade or so, but these devices proved to be too bulky for personal use. Katharina Lucysdaughter Ansky (A.C. 201–282) was also responsible for the principles that made genetic surgery possible. (The merging of ova had been practiced for the previous century and a half.) Animal life had become scarce before the Golden Age; many species were reinvented by enthusiasts of the Ansky Period. In A.C. 280 there was an outbreak of coneys on Newland (an island off the neck of North Continent), a pandemic not without historical precedent. By A.C. 492, through the brilliant agitation of the great Betty Bettinasdaughter Murano (A.C. 453–A.C. 502), Terrestrial colonies were re-established on Mars, Ganymede, and among the Asteroids, the Selenic League assisting, according to the treaty of Mare Tenebrum (A.C. 240). Asked what she expected to find in space, Betty Murano made the immortal quip "Nothing." By the third century A.C., intelligence was a controllable, heritable factor, though aptitudes and interests continued to elude the surgeons and intelligence itself could be raised only grossly. By the fifth century, clan organization had reached its present complex state and phosphorus was being almost completely recycled; by the seventh century, Jovian mining made it possible to replace a largely glass-and-ceramics technology with some metals (which were also recycled) and for the third time in four hundred years (fashions were sometimes cyclic, too) dueling became a serious social nuisance. By the beginning of the ninth century A.C., the induction helmet was a practical possibility, industry was being drastically altered, and the Selenic League had finally outproduced South Continent in kg. protein/person/annum. The induction helmet (which made it possible for one workwoman to have not only the brute force but the flexibility and control of thousands) allowed both South and North Continents to increase childbearing leave to five years. Historians of the period compared this custom to the ancient Chinese custom of three years' mourning for one's father; "A hiatus at the age of thirty" (as one has been quoted) "is just the right time." In 913 A.C., an obscure and discontented descendant of Katy Ansky put together

various items of mathematical knowledge and thus discovered—
or invented—probability mechanics, which offers the possibility
(by looping into another continuum, exactly chosen) of tele-
portation. In the last hundred and twenty years, reorganization
of industry consequent to the widespread introduction of the
induction helmet has driven the Whileawayan workweek up to
the unprecedented length of sixteen hours.

2

(Interview with a Whileawayan named Janet Evasdaughter)

MC. Our social scientists, as well as our physicists, tell us they
will have to revise a great deal of theory in light of the information brought us by our fair visitor from the future. This
is not *our* future, it seems, but only a possible future—Miss
Evasdaughter, perhaps you had better explain about the existence of different probabilities in the future. You know, we
were talking about that before.

JE: It's in the newspapers.

MC: But, Miss Evasdaughter, if you could, please explain it for
the people watching the program.

JE: Let them read. Can't they read?

(A moment's silence)

MC: As you probably know, ladies and gentlemen, there have
been no men on Whileaway for at least eight centuries—I don't
mean no human beings, of course, but no men—and this
society, run entirely by women, has naturally attracted a great
deal of attention since the appearance last week of its representative and first ambassador, the lady on my left here. Miss
Evasdaughter, can you tell us how you think your society in
Whileaway will react to the appearance of men from Earth—I
mean men from our present-day Earth, of course—after an
isolation of eight hundred years?

JE: Nine hundred. What men?

MC: What men? Surely you expect men from our society to visit Whileaway.

JE: Why?

MC: For information, trade, ah—cultural contact, surely. (*Audience laughter*) I'm afraid you're making it rather difficult for me, Miss Evasdaughter. When the—ah—the plague you spoke of killed the men on Whileaway, weren't they missed? Weren't families broken up? Didn't the whole pattern of life change?

JE: Sure. People always miss what they are used to. Yes, they were missed. Even a whole set of words, like "he," "man," and so on—these are banned. Then the second generation, they use them to be daring, among themselves, and the third generation doesn't, to be polite, and by the fourth, who cares? Who remembers?

MC: But surely—that is—

JE: Excuse me, perhaps I'm mistaking what you intend to say, as this language we're speaking is only a hobby of mine; I am not as fluent as I would wish. What we speak is a pan-Russian even the Russians would not understand: it would be like Middle English to you, only vice versa.

MC: I see. But to get back to the question—

JE: Yes.

MC: Don't you want men to return to Whileaway, Miss Evasdaughter?

JE: Why?

MC: One sex is half a species, Miss Evasdaughter. Do you want to banish sex from Whileaway?

JE (*with massive dignity and complete naturalness*): Huh?

MC: I said, Do you want to banish sex from Whileaway?

JE: I'm married. I have two children. What the devil are you talking about?

MC: I—we—well, we know you form what you call "marriages," Miss Evasdaughter, that you reckon the descent of your children through both partners, and that you even have "tribes"— I'm calling them that—I know the translation isn't perfect—but

I am not talking about economic institutions or even affection-
ate ones. I am talking about sexual love.

JE (*enlightened*): Oh! You mean copulation.

MC: Yes.

JE: Of course we have that.

MC: Ah?

(Great audience reaction)

JE: With each other. Allow me to—

(Commercial break. Later:)

MC: How do the women of Whileaway do their hair?

JE (*annoyed*): They hack it off with clam shells.

3

On Whileaway they have a saying: When the mother and
child are separated they both howl, the child because it is
separated from the mother, the mother because she has to go
back to work. Whileawayans bear their children at thirty—
singletons or twins, as the demographic pressures require. These
children have as one genotypic parent the biological mother
(the "body-mother") while the nonbearing parent contributes
the other ovum ("other-mother"). A family of thirty persons may
have as many as four mother-and-child pairs in the common
nursery at one time. Food, cleanliness, and shelter are taken
care of communally; they are not the mothers' business. At the
age of four or five, these independent, blooming, pampered,
extremely intelligent little girls are torn weeping and arguing
from their thirty relatives and sent to the regional school, where
some of them have been known to construct deadfalls or small
bombs (having picked this knowledge up from their parents) in
order to obliterate their instructors. Children are cared for in
groups of five and taught in groups of differing sizes according
to the subject under discussion. Their education at this point is
heavily practical: how to run machines, how to get along with-

out machines, law, geography, transportation, and so on. At puberty, they are invested with Middle Dignity and turned loose; children have the right of food and lodging wherever they go, up to the power of the particular community to support them.

Some go back home, but neither mother may be there, and the adults who were so kind to a four-year-old have little time for an almost-adult.

Some, wild with the desire for exploration, travel all around the world—usually in the company of other children. Bands of children going to visit this or that are a common sight on Whileaway.

The more profound may abandon all possessions and live off the land just above or below the forty-eighth parallel; they return with animal skins, scars, visions.

Some make a beeline for their callings and pester part-time actors, part-time musicians, part-time scholars, and so on.

At seventeen, they achieve Three-Quarters Dignity and are assimilated into the labor force. Groups of friends are kept together, if the members request it and if it is possible, but most adolescents go where they are sent, not where they wish. This is generally the worst time in a Whileawayan's life. None can join the Geographical Parliament or the Professions Parliament until she has entered a family and developed that network of informal associations of the like-minded which is Whileaway's substitute for everything else.

At twenty-two, they achieve Full Dignity and begin either to learn heretofore forbidden jobs or have their learning formally certified. They may marry into pre-existing families or form their own. Some signal this time of life by braiding their hair. By now, the typical Whileawayan is competent to do almost any job on the planet; by twenty-five, she has entered a family, which consists of twenty to thirty other persons, ranging in age from her own to the early fifties. Approximately every fourth person must begin a new or join a nearly new family.

Sexual relations—which have begun at puberty—continue both inside the family and outside it. Whileawayan psychology locates the basis of Whileawayan character in the early indulgence, pleasure, and flowering which is drastically curtailed by separation from the mothers. This (it says) gives Whileawayan life its characteristic independence, its dissatisfaction, its suspicion, and its tendency toward a rather irritable solipsism.

"Without which" (says Dunyasha Bernadettesdaughter, q.v.) "we would all become contented slobs, *nicht wahr?*"

The genuine flowering of Whileawayan life is in old age (i.e., after fifty-eight), for then the Whileawayan—no longer physically as strong and elastic as in youth—is allowed to join with computing machines in the state they say can't be described. Sedentary jobs are held by the old, who can use one-fiftieth of their brainpower for work while the other forty-nine parts riot in a freedom they haven't had since adolescence. The old can spend their days mapping, drawing, thinking, writing, collating, composing. In the libraries, old hands come out from beneath the induction helmets and give Whileawayan customers reproductions of the books they want; old feet twinkle below the computer shelves, hanging down like Humpty-Dumpty's; old ladies chuckle while composing such works as the *Blasphemous Canata* (universally considered the greatest art work in Whileawayan history) or mad-moon cityscapes that turn out to be—surprisingly—doable after all.

On Whileaway it is the young who are priggish about the old; they don't approve of them.

Whileawayan taboos: sexual relations with anybody considerably older or younger than oneself, waste, ignorance, offending others without intending to.

No Whileawayan works more than three hours at a time on any one job, except in emergencies.

No Whileawayan marries monogamously. Some restrict their sexual relations to one other person—at least while that other person is nearby—but there is no legal bond. Whileawayan psychology again refers to the distrust of the mother and the reluctance to form a tie that will engage every level of emotion. Also, the necessity for artificial dissatisfactions.

"Without which" (Dunyasha Bernadettesdaughter, *op. cit.*) "we would become so happy we would sit down on our fat, pretty behinds and starve to death, *nyet?*"

4

A quiet country night. The hills east of Green Bay, the wet heat of August during the day. One woman reads; another sews; another smokes. Somebody takes from the wall a kind of whistle and plays on it the four notes of the major chord. This is repeated over and over again. We hold on to these four notes as long as we can; then we transform them by only one note; again we repeat these four notes. Slowly something tears itself away from the not-melody. Distances between the harmonics stretch wider and wider. How the lines open up! Three notes now. The playfulness and terror of the music written right on the air. Although the player is employing nearly the same dynamics throughout, the sounds have become painfully loud; the little instrument's guts are coming out. Too much to listen to, with its lips right against your ear. By dawn, it will stop; by dawn it will have gone through six or seven changes of notes, maybe two in an hour.

By dawn you'll have learned a little something about the major triad. You'll have celebrated a little something.

5

Etsuko Belin of the cave-dwelling Belins, stretched cruciform on a glider, shifts her weight and goes into a slow turn, seeing fifteen hundred feet below her the rising sun of Whileaway reflected in the glaciated lakes of Old Dirtyskirts. She flips the glider over and—sailing on her back—passes a hawk.

6

A troop of little girls contemplating three silver hoops welded to a silver cube are laughing so hard that some have fallen down into the autumn leaves on the plaza and are holding their stomachs. Their hip-packs lie around the edge of the plaza, near the fountains. Their reaction is not embarrassment or ignorant contempt for something new; they are genuine connoisseurs who have hiked for three days in order to experience just this moment.

7

An ancient statue outside the fuel-alcohol distillery at Ciudad Sierra: a man seated on a stone, his knees spread, both hands pressed against the pit of his stomach, a look of blind distress, his face blurred by time. Some wag has carved on the base the eight-lying-on-its-side that means infinity, and has added a straight line down the middle; this double-lollipop-on-a-stick is both the Whileawayan schematic of the male genital and the mathematical symbol for self-contradiction.

8

Some homes are extruded foam: white caves hung with veils of diamonds, indoor gardens, ceilings that weep. There are places in the Arctic to sit and meditate, invisible walls that shut in the same ice as outside, the same clouds. There is one rain forest, there is one shallow sea, there is one mountain chain, there is one desert. Rafts anchored in the blue eye of a dead volcano. Eyries built for nobody in particular, whose guests arrive by glider. There are more shelters than homes, more homes than persons; as the saying goes, "My home is in my shoes." Everything (they know) is eternally in transit. Everything is pointed toward death. Radar dish-ears listen for whispers from Outside. Whileaway is inhabited by the pervasive spirit of underpopulation, and alone at twilight in the permanently deserted city that is only a jungle of sculptured forms set on the Altiplano, attending to the rush of one's own breath in the respiratory mask, then—

9

I gambled for chores and breakfast with an old, old woman, in the middle of the night by the light of an alcohol lamp. Somewhere on the back roads of the swamp and pine flats of South Continent. Watching the shadows dance on her wrinkled face, I understood why other women speak with awe of seeing the withered legs dangling from the shell of a computer housing: Humpty-Dumptess on her way to the ultimate Inside of things.

(I lost. I carried her baggage and did her chores for a day.)

10

If you are so foolhardy as to ask a Whileawayan child to "be a good girl" and do something for you:

"What does running other people's errands have to do with being a good girl?

"Why can't you run your own errands?

"Are you crippled?"

(The double pairs of hard, dark children's eyes everywhere, like mating cats'.)

11

There is an unpolished white marble statue of God on Rabbit Island, all alone in a field of weeds and snow. She is seated, naked to the waist, an outsized female figure as awful as a classical Zeus. Her dead eyes staring into nothing. At first She is majestic; then I notice that Her cheekbones are too broad, Her eyes set at different levels, that Her whole figure is a jumble of badly matching planes, a mass of inhuman contradictions. There is also a distinct resemblance to Dunyasha Bernadettesdaughter, also known as the Playful Philosopher (A.C. 344–426), although God is older than Bernadettesdaughter and it's possible that Dunyasha's genetic surgeon modeled her after God instead of the other way round. Persons who look at the statue longer than I did have reported that one cannot pin it down at all, that She is a constantly changing contradiction, that She becomes in turn gentle, terrifying, hateful, loving, "stupid" (or "dead"), and finally indescribable.

Persons who look at Her longer than that have been known to vanish right off the face of the Earth.

12

I study my Whileawayan hostess's blue-black hair and velvety brown eyes, her heavy, obstinate chin. Her waist is too long (like a flexible mermaid's), her solid thighs and buttocks surprisingly sturdy. She gets a lot of praise in Whileaway because of her big behind. She is modestly interesting, like everything else in this world formed for the long acquaintance and the close view; they work outdoors in their pink or gray pajamas and indoors in the nude until you know every wrinkle and fold of flesh, until your body's in a common medium with theirs, and there are no pictures made out of anybody or anything; everything becomes translated instantly into its own inside. Whileaway is the inside of everything else. I sleep in the Belins' common room for three weeks, surrounded by people with names like Nofretari Ylayesdaughter and Nguna Twasdaughter. One little girl decides I need a protector and sticks by me, trying to learn English. She takes me into the kitchen, which is a storytelling place.

My hostess translates, speaking softly and precisely:

"Once upon a time there was a child who was raised by bears. Her mother went up into the woods pregnant and gave birth there, for she had made an error in reckoning. Also, she had got lost. Why she was in the woods doesn't matter. It is not germane to this story.

"Well, if you must know, the mother was up there to shoot bears for a zoo. She had captured three bears and shot eighteen but she was running out of film; and when she went into labor she let the three bears go, for she didn't know how long the labor would last and there was nobody to feed the bears. They stayed around, though, because they had never seen a human being give birth before and they were curious. Everything went fine until the baby's head came out, and then the Spirit of Chance, who is very mischievous and clever, decided to have some fun. So right after the baby came out, it sent a rockslide down the mountain, cut the umbilical cord, and knocked the mother to one side. And then it made an earthquake which separated the mother and the baby by miles and miles, like the Great Canyon in South Continent."

"Isn't that going to a lot of trouble?" say I.

"Do you want to hear this story or don't you? *I* say they were separated by miles and miles. When the mother saw this, she said, 'Damn!' Then she went back to civilization to get a search party together, but by then the bears had adopted the baby and all of them were hidden up above the forty-ninth parallel. So the little girl grew up with the bears.

"When she was ten, there began to be trouble. She had some bear friends by then, although she didn't like to walk on all fours as the bears did and the bears didn't like that, because bears are very conservative. She argued that walking on all fours didn't suit her skeletal development. The bears said, 'Oh, but we have always walked this way.' They were pretty stupid. But nice, I mean. Anyway, she walked upright, the way it felt best, but when it came to copulation, that was another matter. The little girl wanted to try it with her male-best-bear-friend (for animals do not live the way people do, you know), but the he-bear would not even try. 'Alas,' he said (you can tell by that he is much more elegant than the other bears), 'I'm afraid I'd hurt you with my claws because you don't have the fur that she-bears have. And besides, you have trouble assuming the proper position because your back legs are too long. And besides *that*, you don't smell like a bear and I'm afraid my mother would say it was bestiality.' That's a joke. Actually it's race prejudice. Anyway, the little girl was very lonely and bored. Finally she browbeat her bear-mother into telling her about her origins, so she decided to go out and look for some people. So she said goodbye to her bear-friends and started south. The little girl was very hardy and woods-wise, since she had been taught by the bears. She traveled all day and slept all night. Finally she came to a settlement of people, just like this one, and they took her in. Of course she didn't speak people-talk" (with a sly glance at me), "and they didn't speak Bearish. This was a big problem. Eventually she learned their language so she could talk to them, and when they found out she had been raised by bears, they directed her to the Geddes Regional Park where she spent a great deal of time speaking Bearish to the scholars. She made friends and so had plenty of people to copulate with, but on moonlit nights she longed to be back with the bears, for she wanted to do the great bear dances, which bears do in the winter under the full moon. So eventually she went back north again. But the bears were a bore. So she decided to find her human mother. At the flats to Rabbit Island, she found a statue with an inscription that said, 'Go that way,' so she did. At the exit from the bridge to North Continent, she found an arrow sign that had been overturned, so she followed the new direction it pointed in. The Spirit of Chance was tracking her. At the entry to Green Bay, she found a huge goldfish bowl barring her way, which turned into the Spirit of Chance, a very very old woman with tiny, dried-up legs, sitting on top of a wall. The wall stretched *all* the way across the forty-eighth parallel.

" 'Play cards with me,' said the Spirit of Chance.

" 'Not on your life,' said the little girl, who knew better.

"Then the Spirit of Chance winked and said, 'Aw, come on,' so the little girl thought it might be fun. She was just going to pick up her cards when she saw that the Spirit of Chance was wearing an induction helmet with a wire that stretched way back into the distance.

"The Spirit of Chance was connected to a computer!

" 'That's cheating!' cried the little girl angrily. She ran at the wall and they had an awful fight, but in the end everything melted away, leaving nothing but a lot of pebbles and sand, and afterward that melted away, too. Then the little girl went and found her real mother, who was a very smart, beautiful lady with fuzzy black hair combed out all round like electricity. But the mother had to go build a bridge (and fast, too), because the people couldn't get from one place to the other without the bridge. So the little girl went to school and had lots of lovers and friends, and practiced archery, and got into a family, and had lots of adventures, and saved everybody from a volcano by bombing it from the air in a glider, and achieved Enlightenment.

"Then one morning somebody told her there was a bear looking for her—"

"Wait a minute," I say, "this story doesn't have an end. It just goes on and on. What about the volcano? And the adventures? And the achieving Enlightenment—surely that takes some time, doesn't it?"

"I tell things," says my dignified little friend (through her interpreter), "the way they happen," and, slipping her head under her induction helmet, she goes back to stirring thirty bowls of blancmange.

She says, casually over her shoulder, "The story is about you, you know," and then (through my hostess, who finds this most amusing):

"Anyone who lives in two worlds at once is bound to lead a complicated life."

13

This is a story about a Whileawayan folk character called the Old Philosopher.

The Old Philosopher was sitting cross-legged among her disciples (as usual) when, without the slightest explanation, she put her fingers into her vagina, withdrew them, and asked, "What have I in my hand?"

The disciples all thought very deeply.

"Life," said one young woman.

"Power," said another.

"Housecleaning," said a third.

"The passing of time," said the fourth, "and the tragic irreversibility of organic truth."

The Old Whileawayan Philosopher hooted. She was immensely entertained by this passion for mythmaking. "Exercise your projective imaginations," she said, "on something that can't fight back," and, opening her hand, she showed them that her fingers were perfectly unstained by any blood whatever, partly because she was one hundred and three years old (and so long past the menopause) and partly because she had just died that morning. She then thumped her disciples severely about the head and shoulders with her crutch and vanished. Instantly two of the disciples achieved Enlightenment, the third became violently angry at the imposture and went to live as a hermit in the mountains, while the fourth—entirely disillusioned with philosophy, which she concluded was a game for crackpots—left philosophizing forever to undertake the dredging of silted-up harbors. Now, the moral of this story is that all images, ideals, pictures, and fanciful representations tend to vanish sooner or later unless they have the great good luck to be exuded from within, like bodily secretions or the bloom on the grape. That is, romance is bad for the mind.

Do not tell me about masculinity and femininity; do not tell me that enchanted frogs turn into princes, that frogesses under a spell turn into princesses. Why slander frogs? Princes and princesses are fools. They do nothing interesting in your stories. According to your history books, you passed through the stage of feudal social organization in Europe some time ago. Frogs, on the other hand, are covered with mucus, which they find delightful; they suffer agonies of passionate desire in the spring, in which the male will embrace a stick or your finger if he cannot get anything better; and they experience rapturous, metaphysical joy (of a froggy sort, to be sure) which shows plainly in their beautiful, chrysoberyl-line eyes.

How many princes or princesses can say as much?

14

I am a liar. I have never been to Whileaway.

Whileawayans breed into themselves an immunity to ticks, mosquitoes, midges, and parasites of all kinds. I have no such immunity. And the way into Whileaway is barred not by time, distance, or an angel with a flaming pen, but by a large cloud or crowd of gnats.

Two-legged, talking gnats.

The utopian isolationist need not venture as far as the stars. So long as doors are hard to open, any wall will do. (The first sentence of *The Dispossessed* is: "There was a wall.") A convent, a penitentiary, a London club—each supplies the utopian prerequisite of exclusivity, of boundaries not easily to be broached. This clubbish aspect of utopia, its invariable coziness, is distinctly at odds with the expansionist impulse of the average utopian, who'd like to share his Coke with the world at large. A sad dilemma, embedded in the heart of even the most humane utopias. Günter Grass's *From the Diary of a Snail* contains a poignant meditation on this complex interconnectedness of utopia and melancholia. As does, in its own sideways fashion, the following tale of . . .

DRUMBLE

by Cassandra Nye

The visitor had only *just* set out for Drumble, returning home, when the roar began. The sky darkened. Miss Mathilda Jenkyns observed from the second-story window that the leaves of the walnut tree were deathly still and ran to inform Martha there would be a terrible rain—but there was no rain in Cranford, or none for a great while. Instead, a great whirling and rushing of . . . could it have been wind? A hurricane, and Cranford the eye? Perhaps at the very borders of the sky, a grinding, whining . . . even farther off than Mrs. Forrester's home in Over Place, and the event seemed to be surrounding the little town on every side (as Martha's Jem observed in his quiet way, bringing an armload of firewood for the fall night). Whether the visitor did or did not reach Drumble—the long road climbing and falling as it did over the low Cheshire hills—is not called into question. She did not. Nor was there any trace of "the nasty cruel railroad" that had promised to convey her there. The tracks—you can see them still—stop with a singed twist of steel less than two miles from the center of town.

The unseemly phenomenon lasted no more than fifteen minutes, while Cranford's resulting loss (or boon) has endured for two centuries. It was no easy feat under normal conditions in Cranford to find suitable new companions, as there was rarely any fresh blood, and the population was delighted to remain stable year after year, as most of the town's residents were, in fact, single elderly ladies. Formerly, that is in times before the Insulation of Cranford, distant aunts and sisters came regularly on annual visits, and although *they* eventually were obliged to return from whence they'd come (to appease their own gods of home and hearth), their now continued absence is a painful reminder of the Event. On the other hand, as demonstrated by Burger King's recent study, Cranford left to its own ways (i.e., without some industry to draw people) would have vanished from the earth by 1897.

Yet, as we know, Cranford lives today and promises to last— with the continued support of London University's Department of History—forever.

In a recent interview, one *Rolling Stone* reporter spoke with Miss Mathilda Jenkyns about her four-century-spanning life:

R: I hope you don't mind my calling you Miss Matty?

MJ: Well . . . I—

R: Good. First of all, I know all our readers will be interested to have your opinion about the twenty-first century. What do you think of us? Can you tell us some of the respects in which . . . life has changed, I mean . . .

MJ: Yes (*thoughtfully, slowly*), yes, of course our lives are quite different—since they built the visine domes.

R: 1858, that was.

MJ: Yes, and (*seemingly shy, or at a loss for words*) I don't know what I feel about . . . the twenty-first century.

R: Ah, yes, you're referring to the transparent modules that contain each of Cranford's wonderful seventeenth- and eighteenth-century homes—to maintain their mint condition.

MJ (*nodding, with a smile*): Yes, I thought it was very kind of the King to think of us here. They must be costly, and do you know, sometimes I suspect that the modules, as you call them, help to preserve *us,* too. (*Nervous laughter*) Our lives are so much less . . . busy now with all our needs taken care of—our being allowed to visit one another only three days of the week. It is less taxing and we seem to have more to say, particularly on Thursdays.

R: Thursdays?

MJ: Thursday is the only weekday on which we are permitted to visit; and it is also the day for our special marketing: lavender . . . drops for a dry throat, and such. And I fear, unless we're allowed another day, I will be forced to again discontinue selling tea.

R: Uh-huh, you're caught in a bind because you have to be home to see your customers and then there isn't time to go out and shop.

MJ: That is true, but what I meant—oh dear, you see, I go about my errands Thursday morning quite early and, as you perhaps know, all our food is delivered automatically from outside Cranford at no cost. Consequently it is difficult for me only in the servicing of so many people in my home in so short a time—there isn't a moment for a friendly word. And our curfew is at four o'clock in the wintertime.

R: I see. And you feel that you could better service your clientele if you had more time.

MJ: Yes.

R: Getting back to my original question, how—Miss Matty—has your own life changed—aside from learning to cook with our easy new foods? (*Laughing*)

MJ (*a flicker of hurt in her eyes*): I'm afraid I don't know how to cook, nor did my sister Deborah. Oh, I often wonder *what* Deborah would have thought of all this. (*Pause*) Our lives are better . . . better protected. We no longer worry about burglars and highwaymen. There was a time when we ladies were in constant agitation because foreigners—Frenchmen, particularly—were in the habit of passing through the small and unprotected villages of England, like Cranford, and they would often be seen lurking about. They never hurt me but I remember when Miss Pole and her Betty burst in here with all their silver once, believing that their own home was about to be robbed. Miss Pole for some time kept one of Mr. Hoggins's old hats in her lobby to frighten away prowlers. Yes, those were difficult times but we survived, and now, as I say, we feel much better protected from the Turks and—

R: The Turks?

MJ: Well, foreigners. Dark men dressed in turbans and the like.

R: Miss Matty, I understand that you have never been away from England?

MJ: My goodness, no, although I am always hoping we shall be allowed to hear of the newer styles. I imagine they are wearing some very lovely silk gowns in Drumble—I do apologize for my appearance. Oh . . . there, I've forgotten what I was saying. Do you know why they have stopped bringing the *St. James Chronicle*?

R (*smiling*): I don't know. I . . . don't keep up with what the ladies are wearing. You understand, Miss Matty. Getting back to my question: your own life, the lives of your friends at Cranford, how does it compare today, two hundred years beyond your presumable life expectancy? Is it congenial living forever?

MJ (*head shaking*): I don't know.

R: Miss Matty, I'm sorry if this upsets you but—

MJ: No, no, not at all—

R: You see, your answers to my questions are of incalculable value to the students of today. Imagine, for example, what it would be like had it been possible to provide such favorable conditions for Julius Caesar; technology has given us these marvelous one-way windows, the constant supply of real Christmas puddings and beeswax candles—just imagine what we might have learned of ancient Roman culture.

MJ: One-way windows?

R: Precisely, don't you *see* the ways in which, by scrutinizing and then analyzing your small community's ways—then allowing a maximum cultural shift of ten years per century—how we can better perfect the already exemplary institution of England today?

MJ: Do you mean that we are being . . . watched?

Now, it has never been discovered just how an atomic pencil sharpener happened one night to *be* flying through space, but we'll accept the word as fact, since it did indeed break a characteristically shaped hole through both the visine dome and the very roof of Miss Pole's cottage in Cranford.

It was a Tuesday night, late. Miss Pole was asleep and snoring loudly with the door closed. Betty, below in the room off the kitchen, was dreaming of a man in Marsden 207 years ago—when thump, there it was, all chrome and glittering like a peacock.

Miss Pole thought immediately she had died—for there could be no noisier event, according to her imagination—and went promptly to Betty to announce the fact. The latter had already, however, run as far as the low-ceilinged passage that connected the kitchen and dining room, herself having heard the sound, and, inadvertently adding terror on terror, ran smack into the elderly spinster. "What! . . . Oh," she said, "Ma'am, is there strange folk in the house?"

"Strange? Nothing of the kind. What?" Miss Pole asked (without allowing sufficient time for an answer). "Have I died? Tell me. Shall I never again play Preference with Mrs. Jamieson and dear Miss Matty? Shall I never again watch as Signor Brunoni removes his pocket handkerchief from a loaf of bread?"

"But . . ." was all the domestic could muster, holding the trembling hand and then leaving it carelessly to go in search of a candle.

"Betty!" Miss Pole shrieked.

"Oh, do come, ma'am," she said with impatience. A lack of vocabulary prevented her from effectively silencing the mounting hysteria at her fingertips. "It was a terrible bang—"

"We have been *robbed!*" Miss Pole sobbed.

"Hush." Betty cupped one hand about the soft glow of a candle and proceeded back in the direction of the front parlor with Miss Pole following two steps behind, terrified but at the same time indignant at having been silenced by someone lower in station. "Now how did he enter your room, ma'am? I heard the glass break, but you know there's no tree outside the window."

"Why . . . I don't know, that is, I—it rushed so quickly past my bed. I do believe he was nearly as tall as Mrs. Forrester's sideboard."

Betty nodded, proceeded toward the stair, and quite boldly took the first half-flight, her mistress close behind. "Like as not, that was the dome I heard go. Most peculiar." And within five brisk seconds they were standing before the open door to Miss Pole's room, which, for all the fuss, appeared—at least in the darkness—to be perfectly in order but for the ruffled bedding.

The window opposite them was sealed to prevent any night breeze that might have accidentally been contained within the dome from daring to disturb the lady's sleep.

Betty gave a little huff that precluded any further discussion of the prowler's complexion or boot size. " 'Pears to me, ma'am, we'd ought be sure the attic is safe, too." She announced the intention with such an air of methodical courage that for a moment even her employer (clutching a comforter about her) managed to dispel her terror. And they ascended once again.

"Now what do you suppose *that* is?" Betty murmured, having measured a safe distance between herself and the atomic pencil sharpener. (The hole in the roof and beyond, the hole—neat and rather large—in the dome, and even a gust of cold air that flooded the ordinarily hot attic were last year's fashions beside the marvelous machine with its shiny planes and unequivocal corners.)

Miss Pole searched her mind but couldn't make a single suggestion. She moved closer to Betty. "Miss Matty's brother would know what to do. *He* lived in India."

"And he's dead—but there's Jem." (Both ladies understood quite well that Jem, in his simplicity, would be as much at sea as they given so extraordinary a plight, yet still the very thought of his brooding bulk brought comfort.) "If we could *get* to Jem. It's only Wednesday morning and the doors won't be unlocked until Thursday."

The two shuddered affectingly.

"I think," Miss Pole suggested finally, tapping the wooden floor solidly with one foot, "that we should have a cup of green tea."

An hour passed before the accident was picked up by the equipment. What Pinny Brisbane saw on the Cranfordscope was a tiny black dot directly opposite Mr. Hoggins's shop—within minutes, it was the tiniest bit larger. Nothing like this had ever happened before when Pinny was on duty; in fact, the Cranford project had a reputation for being miraculously self-sustaining. As a tourist attraction it more than paid for itself. The most recent "problem" was 112 years ago when Lady Glenmire had her famous nosebleed at an impromptu knitting party in Miss Matty's kitchen garden (now defunct). The resulting documentary was subsequently televised both at home and on the moon.

Now what . . . thought Pinny. It isn't a fire, because then there'd be a green light flashing and speckle readings on the monitor. Can't be kidney failure—all the blood's okay. Who is that, anyway? His eye slipped down the bulletin until it reached Cranford Person #7BZ, where he read, *"female. 68. large sense of self-esteem. feather-brained. often mean."* Then a reference to somebody's doctoral thesis. He shrugged his shoulders—probably a hitch in the computer.

But (and although he was alone) he would make a routine check.

When Pinny Brisbane arrived, having driven the seven-mile span of Bifrost II in a leisurely eight seconds, the hole was about as large as one of your antique manhole covers (the kind used as tops for knickknack tables). He let himself down easily into the small attic with all the wonder of discovery that Magellan must have felt. Of course, like millions of other British subjects, he had viewed the utopia from behind visine. As a staff member, he had even enjoyed the customary tour of the house that once belonged to Captain Brown and which was normally not open to anyone but a specialist. And now here he was.

Miss Pole and Betty had only finished their green tea when the relatively gentle thump of Pinny Brisbane's descent sounded above them. Both women sat erect.

"It's funny," said Pinny, shying at the alarm writ large upon the two ladies' faces, "y'know, because nothin' usually goes wrong."

Miss Pole stared at his glisterine jump suit with unmitigated horror. "Oh!" she cried. "Betty, take the plate. Hide it behind the green baize table. I'll—" She interrupted herself. "No, I'll go down, too, but"—she turned, for the first time acknowledging the other presence—"please, spare us. Leave our little home!"

"Gee," said Pinny, "gee, I'm sorry for disturbin' you ladies. I don't mean no harm. Y'see, I got a readin' on you that there was some kind o' problem in your place." He pointed to the hole in the ceiling growing larger moment by moment. It was then that he saw the guilty atomic pencil sharpener languishing unnaturally on its side—and laughed.

"Are you," Miss Pole asked (her curiosity even larger than her caution), "a Turk?" What she meant of course was Hottentot (since all Turks were known to sport mustachios and this man was quite hairless).

"Uh-uh, lady. Manchester, before that New York. Uh . . . hey, listen. If you girls'll just sit tight, I gotta get back to the city and have a repair crew come out here before you lose your atmosphere."

"Atmosphere!" said Betty (but not before Miss Pole let out a little gasp at "city").

"Do you," she interrupted with dedicated civility, "expect to be in the neighborhood of Flint's . . . in Drumble, of course? They had a white worsted that—"

"Drumble? Lady," Pinny said hastily, "my shift gets off in"—looking at his watch—"twenty minutes, and I gotta get down to the lawyers 'cause today me and my wife are finalizing the divorce from the kid. I tell you, seven months *too* many. Today's the day—y'know what freedom is?" A broad smile swept over his whole face and he began to whistle the chorus from "There's a Little Bit of Paradise in Orkney." "But . . . like I say, you girls are losing your atmosphere. Actually"—he looked seriously at Betty—"I donno what the hell we can do for you at this point —but I'll get the crew out on the double."

Miss Pole returned a look of grave understanding and glanced at the bulky molybdenum object on the floor. "Then you don't want our plate." She smiled with relief.

"Your silver?" He reflected a minute (with the baby out of the way, his life would be quite perfect now). "What's yours is yours," returning the smile. He turned, boosted himself up with the corner of a no longer useful Sheridan tea table, and disappeared.

"Well," said Betty after several seconds had passed in silence, "*I* don't think he'll remember your worsted."

"Nor do I," Miss Pole agreed.

The hole in the ceiling had become quite large enough for Mrs. Jamieson's sedan chair to pass through comfortably, and Betty's black curls—although neither lady had yet noticed the phenomenon—were melting.

"It's almost daybreak," said Betty, "and I haven't been out for two hundred years."

Miss Pole looked up at the whitening sky with longing. "We might risk . . . we might stop the coach to Drumble, or if we hurry, that nice young man may still be below watering his horses."

Betty smiled. Miss Pole's right ear had begun to deliquesce—though not noticeably. "Yes."

They passed the little church and then Miss Matty Jenkyns's. The great walnut tree that shaded the entranceway whispered under visine. They walked past the Assembly Hall and since, as they approached the road leading to Drumble, no coach *had* passed, and because the day promised to be a perfection of the combined seasons summer and fall, they didn't stop but let themselves be drawn on by the magnificent spires of Bifrost II, the sun and sky, their thoughts and flesh dissolving slowly in light.

The first great heyday of utopian writing, 1550 through 1660, was also, and not accidentally, a time of intense religious crisis. In a sense, utopias can be about nothing else but religion. Why did God make us, the catechism wants to know; and whatever answer we come up with, it will necessarily involve building the City of God, be it ever so humble.

Many of the pre-1660 utopias were theocracies out-and-out. Since then the drift has been secular. In such utopias as the United States Constitution, religion was relegated to the status of only-on-Sunday. By and large it's stayed that way, and we regard religion as something nice but rather disreputable, like a poor relation who's also a little tetched.

S-f writers have been no exception to this rule. Indeed, like Southern rednecks, we've tended to be rather more openly intolerant than most folk, as though we still held it against God that He burned Isaac Newton at the stake. Consider the record: Leiber's *Gather, Darkness,* Vidal's *Messiah,* Wyndham's *Re-Birth,* Spinrad's *The Men in the Jungle.* Where outside of Italian opera can you find such an iniquitous assembly of *sacerdoti?* It is a testament to the peculiar genius of Robert Heinlein that he could conceive (in *Stranger in a Strange Land*) what any other s-f writers would dismiss out of hand, a wholly sympathetic theocracy.

The two theocracies that follow are at least ambiguous. If the touchstone of a utopia is whether you'd be tempted to try it on for size, then for me Eleanor Arnason's Motor City qualifies. I'm all in favor of fidazene—and if anybody knows where I can get some . . .

With regard to M. John Harrison's millennium, I am more of two minds. There are distinctly some aspects of *his* brave new world that would be harder to swallow than a pill. All things considered, a case can be made for its genuine utopianness—but not without spoiling one of the best s-f stories I've read in years.

Consider that a nomination.

A CLEAR DAY IN THE MOTOR CITY

by Eleanor Arnason

The power station had eight smoke stacks, which were called the Seven Sisters. The rule was, if the Seven Sisters were visible from the roof of the office building where she worked the bosses declared a clear air holiday.

This particular day only half of her department came in. The others had gotten up and looked out at the morning sky, said, "It's going to be a clear air holiday," and got out their beach clothes instead of their office clothes. The people who did come in stood around talking about what they were going to do after they were let out. A little before nine the P.A. system told everyone to proceed to the roof. Up they all went. As everyone had expected, they could see the Seven Sisters upriver and the factories downriver, whose many smoke stacks released grey, brown, yellow and pink smoke into the perfectly transparent air. The bosses came up after the rest of them. They had wreaths of plastic oak leaves on their heads, and the company president carried a cage with a pigeon in it. He said, "We send this bird to whoever's responsible for the weather, to bear our thanks to him, her, it or them." He opened the cage. The pigeon stayed put till he shook the cage and said, "Shoo." Then it took off.

After that, they hurried down to clear off their desks and pick up their coats. As she went down the stairs she wondered what it had been like before the psychopharmacologists had discovered fidazene and the Age of Belief had begun. Going past the fifth and fourth floors, at the moment unrented, dark and silent, she tried to imagine a world full of people to whom nothing was certain. But such a world was inconceivable. When she reached the second floor, where her department was, she gave up trying to imagine it. She got to her desk and the girl who sat next to her said, "I'll bet that was a homing pigeon. It probably goes back to his house, and he saves the cost of a new pigeon the next time there's a clear day."

"The weather gods must like that a lot," she said, "but you're probably right."

She and Daisy, who was Canadian but worked in Detroit, went across the street to the restaurant on top of the gas building. The streets were already full of people. When the Seven Sisters were visible every business downtown let its employees out. They reached the restaurant ahead of the crowd and got a table beside a window, ordered Golden Cadillacs and looked out at the Detroit River and Canada on the other side of it. It was so clear, she thought, that she could almost see the individual leaves on the Canadian trees. There wasn't a cloud in sight. Soon the river was full of sailboats and cabin cruisers. A fireboat moved slowly upriver, sending great fountains of water into the air. Two barges decked with flags and bunting moved out into the river, one from the American shore and one from the Canadian. They stopped side by side at the river's center. They were too far away for her to see what was going on. She found out later from the evening paper that the mayors of Detroit and Windsor, Ontario, had been out on the barges, performing ceremonies of thanksgiving and friendship, the chief of which was releasing two sacred carp into the river while bands played and a chorus of castrati sang "America, the Beautiful" and "O Canada."

She drank three Golden Cadillacs and got a pretty good buzz going. Daisy said she had to go home. Canada didn't celebrate clear air days, which meant she'd have her house to herself till five, since her mother, who worked in Windsor, would be at work. When you live with someone, Daisy said, you appreciate being home alone.

She stayed on awhile after Daisy left and had another Golden Cadillac, then went down and caught a Woodward bus. The bus was packed, and it moved slowly, since the streets were full of people. There were a couple of monks in the back, one a saffron-robed Buddhist, the other a painted and perfumed, scarlet-robed devotee of one of the Middle Eastern fertility gods, probably Christ-Adonis. The Buddhist had a couple of pairs of finger cymbals. The other monk had a glockenspiel. They started playing their instruments and after a while people started singing: "Give Peace a Chance," then "O Happy Day," then "Under the Bo Tree," while the bus moved slowly up Woodward Avenue.

When the bus got to the Caniff change the guys from the Plymouth plant got on, sweaty and happy and full of booze. One of them had a piece of red cloth, which he waved out the window. They started singing "The Workers' Flag Is Deepest Red," first the workers, then everyone on the bus, even the monks. More factory workers got on in front of the Ford Highland Park plant. They finished "The Workers' Flag" and started on "Solidarity Forever." She got off at Six Mile Road, waving farewell to the monks and clerks and blue-collar workers, all singing like crazy.

Walking down Six Mile, she passed three small black girls playing with plastic yarrow stalks and felt suddenly nostalgic. How well she could remember her childhood possessions: yarrow stalks and ouija boards and toy birds whose plastic entrails foretold only happy futures.

She stopped at the Biff's restaurant on Six Mile for a glass of milk with which to wash down her midday capsule of fidazene. Otherwise a panacea, fidazene had one small defect: it tended to upset the stomach, and it was a good idea to take milk with it. There were a few people whose stomachs got so upset that they couldn't keep fidazene down. Some of these mainlined the stuff, but most simply did without. Doubters, as these unfortunates were called, were classified as hopelessly handicapped and given the right to ride free on all forms of public transport and to beg in front of all churches, synagogues and temples. They were usually easy to spot: their brows were lined and they didn't smile much. Their eyes moved continually back and forth, looking for they knew not what.

She paid for the milk and decided to walk around Palmer Park. The sky was still entirely cloudless. At the horizon it was pale blue instead of its usual brown and overhead it was a deep, intense blue, the color of the mosques in Isfahan and Samarkand. Going along the Woodward side of the park, she passed two temple harlots, off for the day, walking hand in hand and joking together. A gypsy fortune teller had set up her table beside the tennis courts and was dealing out greasy tarot cards. The gypsy's gold rings and earrings glittered in the sunlight, as did her gold teeth when she grinned.

Further on there was a Good Humor truck. She bought a strawberry-shortcake-flavored Good Humor covered with nuts and ate it as she walked around the north end of the park, past the public golf course. It was packed with golfers, all wearing enormous, inflated plastic phalluses to attract the favourable notice of the game's patron gods, who were all of them gods of the woods and meadows like Freyr and Pan. She stopped for several minutes and watched a beginner who was having terrible trouble with his phallus. He'd tuck it between his legs, then every time he began to swing, out it would pop and get in the way of his arms as he brought his club down. All this was good for a chuckle or two. Finally, however, he looked around and saw her watching him, and she moved on.

She finished her Good Humor and tossed the stick into a litter can, then started down the west side of the park. There was a little winding street there, hidden behind a row of trees. All along the street there were big houses with wide, smooth, green lawns. She always enjoyed looking at rich people's houses. There was something holy about them. They were so clean and calm and they seemed so assured. They sat along the street like a row of bodhisattvas.

She walked slowly down the street. Toward the end of it was a house that was for sale. The lawn was dry with brown patches in it and the curtainless windows opened in on empty rooms. Suddenly curious, she didn't know why, she went across the lawn and up onto the terrace in front of the house. There was a balustrade around the terrace. Last fall's leaves were still piled into the balustrade's corners and what looked like a heap of rags lay against the house wall. As she came onto the terrace, the heap moved, turning into a huddled man, who stretched and sat up. He was a doubter. She recognized the signs: the lined face and the shifting eyes. "Alms," he said and held out his hand, which was bony and none too clean. "Have pity, lady, I have an over-active thyroid." He pulled his shirt away from his neck so she could see how the thyroid glands bulged out on either side of it. "It's because I'm nervous, lady, because I don't believe in anything. That's what the doctors said. I wouldn't have it if I could stomach fidazene."

He was, she realized, the same age as she was, more or less. For some reason this horrified her.

"I get terrible depressions, too, lady," the doubter went on. "Nothing seems to mean anything. Lady, you don't know how bad it is."

She fumbled in her purse till she found some change, put it in his hand and hurried away. He called after her, "I'd say God bless you, lady, but I don't believe in God."

She kept on, making no reply, and didn't slow down till she was a block away, back at Six Mile. She stopped then and stared up at the sky till she felt less upset.

The day continued clear. The wind decreased till the cool air barely moved. The afternoon shadows seemed to have sharper edges than was usual, and the trees' foliage looked hard and solid.

The sky seemed solid too, like a blue crystal bowl covering the world. She went up to the delicatessen opposite Marygrove College for lunch: hot pastrami on rye, coffee and a piece of cheesecake. She felt restless and uneasy, probably because of her encounter with the doubter, and had a second piece of cheesecake to calm herself. After that she decided, for want of anything better to do, to go downtown in the evening to see the holiday fireworks. She went home and put on new clothes: a white blouse, a blue midi-skirt with little mirrors sewn on it, silver sandals and a silver mask. There'd be dancing in the streets, she knew, to the sound of the civic rock band. Many of the dancers would be masked and some would be elaborately costumed. She took a bus back down Woodward to a dinner in Greek Town: squid in wine sauce, a salad, milk and her evening capsule of fidazene. By the time she was done, it was eight-thirty and the sun was setting. She walked over to Kennedy Square, thinking the only defect in clear days was their sunrises and sunsets, which were pretty uninteresting, nothing more than a band of pink light at the horizon. For a really good sunrise or sunset it was necessary to have clouds and a fair amount of pollution. Well, she told herself, that goes to show that nothing is perfect, not even a clear day.

In Kennedy Square the rock band was already playing, and the fountain was gushing out apple wine instead of water. There were a thousand people or more there, dancing or standing around drinking wine in paper cups. She pushed through the people to the paper-cup table, got a cup with "DETROIT—LOVE IT OR LEAVE IT" printed on it and filled the cup with wine from the fountain. On her way back from the fountain she bumped into a man in a black-and-silver harlequin costume, who turned and looked at her, his eyes glittering through the eyeholes in his black satin mask. "Sweetheart," he said. "Let's dance."

Dance they did, then drank wine, then danced again. At ten the display of fireworks began. The dancers—by this time there were several thousand—trooped down to the Detroit River to see it.

Hand in hand with the harlequin she watched rockets explode above the dark river, expanding like fiery blossoms opening. When the fireworks were over they danced again.

At midnight the mayor arrived, virgins in white going before him, some scattering flowers, some bearing torches. After the mayor came his bodyguards, cops dressed in black leather and steel, guns at their hips and clubs in their hands. The mayor took his place on the platform above the apple-wine fountain. One by one the local heads of all the major religions joined him, while the band played and the dancers applauded. In a black car from Wayne County Jail came the sacrifice. The music stopped and a drum roll began. Spotlights came on in the Campus Martius across the street from Kennedy Square. There was a temporary altar there and beside the altar stood the sacrificer, dressed all in black, a black hood covering his head.

This was the part she didn't like. She grabbed hold of the harlequin's hand and held on to it tightly, while the sacrifice was led to the altar and stretched out on it and tied down. The sacrifice seemed awfully calm, considering his situation. Someone had told her that they were all heavily drugged.

The sacrificer unbuttoned the sacrifice's shirt, baring his chest, then took a knife and cut into the sacrifice under the ribs—at that point the sacrifice screamed—and cut out the sacrifice's heart. He held the heart up with bloody hands so all could see it. Then the spotlights went out and once again the band began to play.

She shuddered and looked at the harlequin. He smiled and took off his mask. His face was deeply lined and his bright eyes, she noticed now, were always shifting, looking first here, then there. He was the doubter she'd met at the empty house.

"You!" she cried, then asked, "Who are you?"

"I'm the Doubter King, sweetheart," he said, "whom you believers doubt exists. You did me a good turn today. This is to pay you back." He bent and kissed her on the lips, then turned and pushed his way through the crowd. She was too startled to do anything except watch him till he was out of sight. When she could no longer see his narrow, bony, black-and-silver back, she wiped her lips with her hand. Then she walked to the Hotel Pontchartrain and took a cab home from there.

The next morning when she took her fidazene capsule, she threw up.

SETTLING THE WORLD

by M. John Harrison

With the discovery of God on the far side of the Moon by a second-wave (Apollo B series) exploration team, and the subsequent gigantic and hazardous towing operation that brought Him back to start His reign anew, there began on Earth, as one might assume, a period of far-reaching change. I need not detail, for instance, the numerous climatic and political refinements, the New Medicine or the global basic minimum wage; or those modifications of geography itself which have been of so much benefit. However, despite the immediate, the "gross" progress, certain human institutions continued for a while to function as they always had; I think particularly of those edifices of a bureaucratic nature, whose very structure militates against devolution.

The Department to which I have given my services for so long was one of these: and so it was in a perfectly normal way that I received the call to visit my chief one Monday morning in the first April since the inception of the New Reign. The memo was issued, passed lethargically through the secretarial system and the typing pool, and reached me by way of my own secretary, Mrs. Padgett, who has since retired, I believe to help her mother in a market garden in Surrey. After dealing in a leisurely way with the rest of my post—we were all delightfully relaxed in those first days, settling our shoulders, as it were, into a larger size of coat—I took the lift up to the top of the building where by tradition the chief has his office, to find him in a ruminative mood.

"Look at that, Oxlade," he invited, gesturing at the panoramic sweep of the city beneath. "How much fresher you must all find it down there, now the hurry has gone. Eh? The air refined, the man refreshed!"

Indeed, as I stared down at the clean and quiet streets, where a brisk wind and bright sunshine filled one with a corresponding inner vitality, I had been thinking the precise same thing. In the parks, hundreds of daffodils were out, the benches were full of elderly citizens taking calm advantage of the new weather, and somewhere a great clock was striking ten in thoughtful, resonant tones. So different from the grey Springs of previous years, with their heavy, slanting rains stripping the advertisements from the hoardings to flap dismally in the wind over the downcast heads of the hurrying crowd. There was so little joy in living then.

"Even you, sir, must find things changed," I ventured. "In the beginning—"

"Ah, Oxlade," he interrupted, "there is still so much to be done, and I have little opportunity to leave this wretched office. Events, however slowly, progress; and my time is not my own." My chief is given to these moments of reserve; perhaps it is his nature—who can tell?—or a nature forced on him by the exigencies of his position. But he allowed it to pass genially enough and turned the talk first to my wife, Mary, and the children—he is always perfectly solicitous—and then to the cultivation of orchids, a hobby of mine. The new climate of Esher is perfect for this purpose and I was able to inform him, with all due modesty, of some truly astonishing results in the outdoor hybridisation of English types like *Cephelanthera rubra* with their more exotic epiphytic cousins.

After a few minutes, we came to the business of the Department. "Oxlade," said the chief, "I would like you to look at some pictures that were brought to me by"—here he mentioned the name of one of our most trustworthy agents—"early this morning."

He darkened the room and on one of the walls there appeared a rectangle of white light, shortly to be filled with a strange series of photographic slides. "You will observe, Oxlade, that these are still-shots of God's Motorway." It was in fact difficult to make out what they did show; I saw only certain apparently random blocks and slices of light and shadow, and, central to each frame, some blurred object which I could make no sense of; they were of a uniform graininess. "The quality isn't good, of course. But I have no reason to believe they represent anything other than a sudden intense surge of activity along the whole length of the Motorway." He paused reflectively, and allowed the last picture to remain on the screen for a while (I thought for a moment that I could discern in it some mammoth organic shape) before replacing it with that passive, enduring oblong of white light.

"A perfect whiteness," he murmured, and we stared at it for some minutes of comfortable silence. Then he said: "I feel that this may be as important as the affair of the eight-angstrom band, Oxlade."

A complicated business, with a solution perhaps more metaphysical than actual, which I well remembered, since it had led to my executive preferment.

"I want you to go down there. Look around. Test the air, so to speak. The Motorway must always be of interest to us."

God's Motorway: a lasting enigma. Certainly, none of us in the Department knew why God had caused His road to be constructed, why He should have need of a link between the lower reaches of the Thames estuary and a place somewhere in what used to be called the "industrial" Midlands; none of the executives, that is—and if my chief knew, he was for some reason of policy or private amusement keeping the knowledge from us. Our curiosity was at that time intense, but necessarily veiled; so I was elated to have an opportunity to catch a glimpse of that great artery. It ran, I knew, a hundred and twenty-five miles inland north north-west from the front at Southend; it was by repute twenty lanes and a mile wide; all ordinary traffic was barred from it (indeed, there were no access points), and it was central to His purpose.

"Go down there tomorrow, Oxlade. Find out who else is there. Come back and tell me." The shutters slid back, and the chief was gazing once more out of the window. After the projector's harsh white rectangle of light, the sunshine seemed warm and mellow, for a moment more suited to Autumn than to Spring. "Still so much to be done, Oxlade," he mused, "but an inspiring sight, nonetheless. Good luck."

My chief's orders have been at times difficult of interpretation; but on this occasion I felt that he had made himself unusually plain.

I reached Southend, by way of Liverpool Street and one of the amazing new railway trains, at about seven-thirty the following morning—to find it full of white gulls, sun, and a curiously invigorating tranquillity. I decided to have a quiet breakfast on the seafront. I have always loved that row of archway cafés on the Shoeburyness Road, each with its strip of carefully tended forecourt crammed with gaudy umbrellas and gaily painted tables, from which you can hear the sailing boats bobbing against the seawall on a light, inviting swell. To choose one to eat in—if mere satisfaction of appetite is your object—is the matter of a moment; to select the *right* one, the one that best suits your mood of the hour, must be a serious business: for you may sit there all morning, captured by the sight of the sea before you.

It was in one of these I met Estrades, lounging back in his slatted chair with a bottle of mineral water and a long thin cigar.

Under the old order, Estrades had been perhaps my craftiest opponent. All that was dispensed with now, of course: but once, in a pitilessly cold room high above the old Margarethenstrasse of Berlin, I had had occasion to try and shoot off one of his kneecaps. Only a lucky accident of radio reception had saved him. We greeted each other now with a cautious pleasure: professionally speaking, we knew each other well, but had little in common. He was a tall, elegant, but somewhat faded man, older than myself and given to the most flamboyant of white linen suits and to buttonhole flowers of extravagant size (although I noticed that today his carnation in no way matched my own home-grown *Palaeo-nophis*). He hid his age well, but a faint pitting of the skin about the eyes was hindering his efforts, and in another year or so would betray him completely. Some said he was a Ukrainian, others a Kirghizstanian from the western slopes of the Tien Shan; but he had the lazy undeviating eye of the cultured Frenchman, and the morose, ironic sense of humour of a dispossessed Polish count. Estrades was certainly not his real name, but it is the only one we have to remember him by.

During my examination of the menu we exchanged courtesies and anecdotes of mutual friends and enemies. Estrades claimed that he was bored; he had come over, he said, on the strength of a rumor (he would place no greater weight than that on any information from Alexandria), and had been in Southend for some days. "You must," he said, "be interested in the Motorway, Oxlade, my friend—no, no, I can see it plainly in the set of your shoulders." He laughed in a peculiar restrained manner, his thin, scarred face remaining immobile but for a slight drawing back of the lips. "We are too old to play games. So take my advice, if you aren't too proud. I have been here for a week, and have seen nothing in daylight but that which is already known. Go at night, go at night."

"That which is already known"—how could I admit that I knew so little? I determined immediately to do both, and turned the conversation to another subject.

Later, Estrades leaned back in his chair and yawned. "Tell me honestly, my friend, what you think of all this." And he made a gesture which took in the sea, the Shoeburyness Road, the gulls like white confetti at some marriage of water and air. I was puzzled: I thought that it was a remarkably fine sort of day; I thought that I had never eaten such large prawns. He stared at me for a moment, then threw back his head to laugh in earnest, revealing teeth of a miraculous regularity. "As evasive as ever," he said, wiping his eyes. "Oxlade, you are either the most stupid or the most careful of men. Look. Nobody is listening except the waitress, and she to her transistor radio. By 'this,' I mean this whole thing, this"—he paused thoughtfully—"this paradise for bad poets and old-age pensioners in which we now find ourselves (you and I, who have left toothmarks on the bone in half the gutters of Western Europe!); this warmed-over Eden in which we exercise ourselves by reading C. S. Lewis in a sunny garden in Kent—or, God forgive us all, grow flowers! 'Our reality is so much from His reality as He, moment by moment, projects into us. . . .'? Is that all He's left to us?"

"And yet, Estrades," I said, a little pointedly, for I suspected that penultimate lapse of taste to be deliberate, and I saw that he was enjoying himself not a little at my expense, "you find yourself perfectly in place. I grow orchids, and that is sufficient—in the old days I asked for nothing more; and you—why, you sit at a café table in Southend, or some *estaminet* of Antwerp, with perhaps more freedom than before to exercise your wit, your (if I may say so) rather impractical and gauzy cynicism. No one asks you to write bad poetry—or, indeed, to judge the poetry of others. All of us are satisfied in our individual ways."

He nodded slowly. "It is an argument. It is *the* argument. But it does not impress me. Can one find satisfaction in simply being dissatisfied? Is it that I am now *allowed* to be dissatisfied? I have considered it. I chafe." He gazed sadly out to sea, moved his hands. His face slackened, aged; for a brief moment, a hunger I can't describe illuminated his eyes, and I saw the whole superb pose, insouciance, iconoclasm and all, collapse into vacancy. Eventually, he turned back to me, drew on his cigar, examined his graceful, nicotine-stained fingers. They shook a little as he strove to bring back that younger Estrades, the spoiled sophist and street-corner dandy. "Oxlade, I suspect we have been robbed, but I cannot discover how. As you say, each man is content. How then have I been passed over and left to wonder why?"

I paid my bill and got up to go. But then he was quite at ease again, smiling over my embarrassment, looking for the world as if he'd intended all along to give me this glimpse behind the shell.

This, he seemed to be saying, is a secret between us; Estrades is not so brittle as he seems, old friend.

"I'm on my last throw here, Oxlade," he said, suddenly, squashing out the stub of his cigar. "There is only one thing left to be discovered." And when I failed to respond to this invitation, "Wait a minute." He came swiftly and gracefully to his feet and stared up and down the seafront. "Eisenburg!" he called. "You must remember Eisenburg," he said to me. "From the Piazzale Loreto riots—?"

I didn't. But I had met a hundred like him in the formless chaotic years immediately preceding the New Reign, when it seemed that every capital of the world was in ferment, throwing up its filth in unconscious anticipation of a cleansing sun that was yet to rise. He came ambling and soft-footed through the light morning traffic of the Shoeburyness Road, a huge muscular Sephardic Jew paying no attention to the drivers except to grin unnervingly in at them when they braked to avoid running him down. His forehead was furrowed, his eyebrows obliterated, by a long rumpled scar he had as a legacy from some Near Eastern oil-coup or religious war.

He stood on the pavement, grinning and posturing wordlessly, and he brought to the bright, mild coastal weather something of the freezing winter heights of Mount Hermon.

Estrades watched both of us closely to see what effect he had created. He seemed satisfied. "You can do nothing until dark," he told me. "I thought the three of us might walk into town together and remember things as they were before this comic opera visitation—?"

Eisenburg began to laugh. "Bloody striped umbrellas, eh?" he appealed suddenly. "That's good!"

"I think I'll take a look anyway," I said, and walked off. I could feel Estrades staring after me, perhaps with contempt, perhaps with amusement. If his motive had been simple discomfiture, he had failed. Like a clever illusionist he had confused me for perhaps half a minute with his *Angst* and his cheap linguistic philosophy and his lightning changes of mood. But by importing the Jew into that otherwise perfect morning he had resurrected all the fakery, all the hollow melodrama of the "games" he had himself warned me against, and destroyed his own stature with innuendo and mystification. Nothing could mar the eagerness I felt as I strolled along the north bank of the estuary. My very first glimpse of God's Own Road awaited me; the scent of my *Palaeonophis* mingled deliciously with the scent of the sea; and I found it easy to put him out of my mind.

God's Motorway rises out of the water almost exactly opposite the old refineries of the Sheerness promontory. No houses are near it, and here the road to Shoeburyness ends. It emerges along a vast but indistinct causeway, about which the very air seems to hum with agitation: standing there in awe on that pleasant day, I could not tell whether it was made of stone, or some less palpable substance. I could see very little of that crucial interface between Road and sea—there, the water boiled and effervesced, and spray hung like some diaphanous shifting curtain, full of the strangest hues. There is no sight more impressive than those twenty lanes of metalled road emerging (as if from some other, longer journey) from the fume to race away inland, joyfully precise and resolute.

In a way (though in what a mean way) Estrades was proved right: nothing came up from the water, there was little concrete information to be gained there, and I had to turn elsewhere for something to take back to my chief. Yet I spent all morning watching the ever-changing, spectral colours of that spray and wondering what ecstatic energies had given them birth. Meanwhile, the herring gulls dived and gyred through it, apparently for the mere joy of the sensation, and after passage seemed whiter than before. Had I wings, I should certainly have followed them: how they spun and whirled!

That night I set out to discover more of the Motorway. It was my intention to strike inland behind the town and meet the road some three miles down its length. The thick sea-fog that hung over the suburbs as I left broke rapidly up into drifting and unpredictable banks. I carried a compact but powerful torch, a flask of hot tea. I had provided myself also with a warm coat and field glasses of a remarkable resolution purchased in Dortmund some years before. In the chilly fields and abandoned housing estates between the north-eastern peripheries of the town and God's Road, I became aware that I was not alone: yet I was sure, too, that none of the stealthy movements in the dark were aimed at myself. "The Motorway must always be of interest to us," my chief had said; it must have been of interest to many that night, for a continual procession of agents rustled through the fog toward it.

I lost my way (I have never been fond of the night, a serious weakness perhaps in a man of my profession, and one that I have often pondered) and consequently my line of travel intersected the Motorway a little sooner than I might have liked: but it did not matter in the end. A tall embankment towered up before me against the strange new constellation which, appearing in the skies about two years before, had heralded the Rediscovery of God; and as I struggled up that enormous earthwork, I could already hear the sound of heavy engines toiling north. The Road had woken up: I took my station close to the chain-link fence, and wiped the condensation from the lenses of my night-glasses.

These now revealed that every one of the lanes was in use; at forty or more points along my field of vision, massive vehicles crawled and groaned northward up the slight gradient. None of them was less than two hundred feet long. The commonest type was composed of a single tractor unit coupled to the front of a great low-loading trailer, although many were built up like railway trains out of five or six of each component. They were of a uniform matte black color, studded with large rivets; and while each tractor had what might be described as a cabin, nothing could be seen behind its windows. What sort of motor drives them, I have no idea—they seemed to toil; none moved at more than five or six miles an hour—and yet a sense of enormous power hung like a heat-haze over each carriageway, and the ground trembled beneath my feet.

Shifting fogs made my observations intermittent and superficial, and some actual distortion of the air rendered the carriageways of the far side difficult to see at all. At first, I experienced a sensation similar to that which I have already described in connection with the photographs shown me by my chief: while I could now make a little more sense of the general aspects of the picture before me, still the central object of each quick glimpse somehow defied interpretation. The road, I understood; the vehicles, I was able to perceive as such; it was their cargo that remained puzzling. What a strange commerce—what dim and ambiguous shapes in the night.

Suddenly, however, eye and brain seemed to perform the necessary trick of adjustment; I understood the problem to be one of scale; and I was able to see that the objects before me were in fact gigantic anthropoid limbs.

Quite close to me in the second or third lane, set upright on its truncated wrist, a human fist moved slowly past, shrouded in tarpaulin. It was clenched, with palm toward me, a left hand perhaps thirty feet high—extended, it would have been twice that from the heel of the palm to the tips of the fingers. The tarpaulin flapped and fluttered round its deep contours; steel cables moored it to the bed of the vehicle. All was for a moment perfectly clear—then a fog bank occluded it forever. For a time my own excitement betrayed me. I neglected to refocus the glasses, and, desperately scanning the more distant lanes, saw only slow mysterious movements, like those of some extinct reptile passing along an overgrown ride in a forest of cycadeoids.

Then a truly enormous forearm slipped by five lanes out, more than a hundred feet long and heavily muscled; and from then on I was witness to an astonishing parade of members—gargantuan calves and thighs, hands and feet, and some shapes difficult of definition that I took to be more private, possibly internal, organs; a parade accompanied by the groan and throb of God's Engines, by the shuddering of the earth and, above all, that sense of vast energies almost accidentally dissipated into the air.

Toward dawn the traffic became sporadic. One last limb crept past, supported by trestles and requiring two trailers to accommodate its length; the fog reasserted its grip; all movement ceased.

Stiffly, I rose from the crouch into which I had fallen, my knees aching and reluctant, my hands numb and cold. Minute beads of moisture clung to everything: my coat, the binoculars, the chain-link fence. My ears felt uncomfortable in the silence, as if some pressure on the inner passages had suddenly been relieved. For a minute or two I flapped my arms against my sides in an attempt to restore some warmth and vitality; but it was in a stupor of weariness that I stumbled away.

I stood for a moment at the foot of the embankment. Silence was no longer absolute—all about me were mysterious shiftings as other observers shrugged, yawned, put up their instruments and prepared to leave the Motorway. Dawn now illuminated the fog, filling it with a diffuse internal radiance which in no way aided the eye. Two or three men passed me within touching distance, conversing in low tones—they were quite invisible. Then, faint and thin, a cry of despair reached me through that drifting, luminous mist; running footsteps thudded along the top of the embankment, moving south. "Stop him!" someone shouted, then added something made unintelligible by excitement.

I turned to look back. Estrades was suddenly standing beside me, the mist seeming to give him up without sound. A fur-lined leather jacket, the patched and oil-stained relic of some European aerial war of his youth, bulked out his slim figure. He was breathing heavily. He stared at me for a second or two as if he hardly recognised me, then called urgently into the mist, "He's yours, Eisenburg—about a hundred feet ahead of you, now!" A shot rang out. The running man blundered on.

"For God's sake," said Estrades disgustedly. He took his cigar out of his mouth and frowned at it. "Never trust a Jew." Then, in a different tone, "Think about what you've seen, Oxlade," he advised me quietly. "Esher is no longer yours. How can you go on, know-ing what's happening up there? How will you ever feel safe again?" He considered this; nodded; pulled a small revolver from the pocket of his flying jacket. "Must I do it all myself?" he demanded of the man Eisenburg. "It's all up if he gets away!" And he van-ished once more into the mist. Later, two more shots startled the bright air. I waited, but Estrades did not return. I made my way back across the damp fields, wondering if the poor wretch on the embankment knew who was pursuing him. It was a dreary trudge.

Somewhat later in the morning, I considered my position care-fully. I had made progress of a kind which may be summed up in the following problem. At a maximum observed speed of six miles an hour, it would be quite impossible for God's Vehicles to com-plete their entire journey in one night; and yet by day the Motor-way lay silent, abandoned to the wind and sunshine along its whole length; where, then, did the traffic go? A fascinating and significant anomaly—but had I any assurance that it was not already known to my chief? Estrades was aware of it; there may have been others. It would be injudicious, I realised, to commit myself too early to one point of view and return to London with what would certainly be regarded as an incomplete report. It was safe to assume that my chief had some other interest—one that had appeared up until now to be peripheral.

Again, I thought of Estrades.

That saturnine expatriate, survivor of a thousand and one labyrinthine excursions beneath the political crust, liked to present his motives in terms of simple curiosity (and indeed there lay con-cealed behind his objectionable languor not only the keen and feral energy I had seen released that morning in the Essex mist but also, as I had discovered to my cost on more than one previous occasion, a mind subtle, relentless and unassuaged)—but only some specific objective could have drawn him from his retire-ment among the bleached river terraces of North Africa to kill by pistol on a cold morning in England. What tenuous thread had he

followed through the brothels of Marseilles, the grey boulevards of
Brussels, to Southend-on-Sea?

All the rest of the morning I sought him out along the crowded
sea-wall, submerging myself in that fierce and unrestricted tide of
bare red forearms and light opera, with its odors of fried fish,
lavender and bottled stout. I knew he would be waiting for me. At
noon, a light, uncustomary drizzle began to fall from a sky filled
alternately with gunmetal cloud and weak, silvery sunshine. The
esplanade was all of a sudden bleak and empty. In the shadow of
the pier I sat on a stone, gazing up at the salt-caked fretwork of
struts and warped boards that support the thumping slot-machines
and shooting galleries. Shouting children hung over the white rail-
ings high above. When I looked toward the mercuric thread of the
surf, Estrades stood at the end of the avenue of corroded iron
supports, motionless and shining in a single watery ray of sun.

The rain died off as we walked toward one another. I wish
sometimes that I had walked away instead. Up above, the planking
thumped and rattled. By the time we met, the front was thick with
people again, issuing, with no more than a single shiver to dispel
the chilly interruption of their day, from the cafés and shop doorways that had sheltered them.

"I've been watching the faces on the beach," said Estrades,
"hoping to recognise the old familiar ones. You remember, Oxlade? They were grey, as if moulded out of a flesh like soft wax,
grey with insecurity and lost sleep, wincing from short tense en-
counters on windy street corners. (Can you remember even the
corners, Oxlade, from the comfy recesses of your new dream?)
They were sick, but real: they were our faces." He shook his head.
"There must be fifty men out on that embankment every night.
Many of them I must have known before. I look for them on the
beach every day, but if they are there, they are burnt red like
rentiers on holiday, they wear open-necked shirts and rolled
sleeves. Like you, Oxlade, they have *relaxed.*"

He sighed, indicated the promenade crowds. "And there," he
said, "you look for spirit. You watch them, you hear the noise and

expect to find some visible motive for this happy, happy seething."
He shrugged. "Ha. Their eyes are pale, blind. They have been
robbed. They perform by rote, like some kind of animal."

"If that is true, Estrades—and I suspect it isn't—then it may
simply be what they prefer. And look at the children. They seem
happy enough. You can't deny that they seem happy enough, and
aware of it."

He looked instead at the shingle, and hacked with his elegant
heel at a tangle of bright green weed. He bent down quickly and
prised something loose from it with his long, strong fingers. "Children ask less. Are they to remain children all their lives?" He
flicked his fingers distastefully to remove a bit of seaweed, then
held up an old threepenny piece, still somehow bright and un-
tarnished. God knows how long it had rolled about the foreshore.
"Even here there is spirit," he said gnomically, and flipped it
away—it sped out of the shadow of the pier, glittered briefly in the
exhausted light and vanished.

"Up there on the promenade is a festival of mediocrity, a feast
of tolerance, an emptiness filled with wheelchair entertainers—"
For a moment he watched them pass. "You don't want to know,"
he asked distantly, "who was killed this morning by the Motorway?" I must have revealed my tension in some way, for he
turned back with a triumphant grin. "Oh, the Department is so
careful with its executives. I killed your back-up operator. He
sent a radio-message, 'All goes smoothly,' then I killed him before
he could transmit again. Will you tell them?"

"I have never," I said carefully, "been informed that back-up
operators are in use. You may have killed an innocent man."

"Then you are remarkably ill-informed. And no man on that
embankment was entirely innocent." When my face remained
blank, he laughed uproariously. "Oxlade, Oxlade!" he gasped.
"If you could *see* yourself!" He recovered his composure. "Oh,
how I am sick of all this faith," he muttered bitterly. I had, perhaps, succeeded in making him feel uncomfortable.

"Why did you kill him?"

He smiled off at something in the distance. The sun had come out fully; on the pier a small orchestra had begun to play selections from Gilbert and Sullivan.

"I intend to put an end to this half-wit's Utopia," he said quietly. "I want you with me, if only as a representative of your organisation; but I can allow no more reports until the thing is accomplished—your shadow was an embarrassment." He studied me intently. "What do you say, Oxlade, old friend? Set against one another, we were always wasted." And before I could make the obvious answer: "Why, if you come you may even be able to stop me doing it! What a coup! And all else failing, you will enter the most astonishing report on the episode. It will mean another promotion. More orchids will bloom in the quiet backwaters of Esher."

"Come where?" I asked.

"The Midlands," he said, "by way of the Road of God."

"What you are intending to do is more hopeless than blasphemous." I started to walk away.

He allowed me to leave the shadow of the pier before calling, "I will have you killed before you can reach a telephone, Oxlade." I looked up and down the front. Eisenburg the Jew stood negligently at the foot of the sea-wall. He grinned and lit a cigarette, staring at me over his cupped hands. Fifteen yards separated us. "I can't take the risk," said Estrades. I believed him.

"You are an evil man, Estrades," I told him. "The rest of us have forgotten how."

He laughed. "That is what is wrong with you," he said. Up above him children flocked into the shooting galleries. Their cries drowned the noise of the orchestra.

That was how I entered into my unwilling association with Estrades the European agent and became a party to the plot against God. Why that madman really wanted me with him, I don't know. Murder would have been so much easier. I believe now that it merely gratified his vanity to have a captive observer. He was an enormously vain man. At any rate, I could do noth-

ing about it; and all that afternoon and part of the evening I
watched passively as he prepared his ground in a series of visits to
what were presumably "safe" houses scattered across Southend.

It was at one of these that Eisenburg took charge of the mysterious three-foot packing case upon which they had placed their
hopes. It must have weighed half a hundredweight, if not more,
but he carried it—together with a pair of long-handled bolt-cutters
with which they intended to breach the fence at the summit of
the embankment—under one arm, as if it were empty. I grew to
loathe that crate (although I had no idea at that time of what it
contained—had I done so, I might have taken my chances with
him in one of the more crowded streets behind the esplanade) and
he knew it. Whenever Estrades's attention was occupied elsewhere, Eisenburg would catch my eye and go through a long, complicated dumb-show of insinuation, tapping the thing significantly,
making motions as if to open it—grinning ferociously all the time,
so that his scar made ghastly furrows in his forehead. He never let
it out of his sight, and he never tired of taunting me.

Meanwhile, Estrades, his pristine suit and carnation exchanged
once more for flying jacket and revolver, had become tense and excited, given to Romantic gesture which constantly reaffirmed the
emotional instability of his character. "So!" he exclaimed, as we
made our way over the sodden fields behind the town. "Here we
go! Everything staked on one throw! Three men against God!"
Even the sunset seemed alarmed at this vast, childish vanity: the
sky was one great inverted bowl of cloud, tilted up a little on the
horizon over Shoeburyness to show a thin strip of blood-coloured
light. "Oxlade, you think it can't be done. Pah. It can! We'll
liberate Esher; and if the orchids are a little smaller next year, a
little less gaudy—well, they will be *your* orchids, at least!"

"You aren't uneducated, Estrades. You must know it's been
tried before."

"Not by a *man,* Oxlade." He nudged his accomplice. "Not by a
man, eh, Eisenburg?" And they winked excruciatingly at one another like boys about to raid an orchard.

Up on the embankment we waited for the last shreds of light to be dispersed. A thin cold wind sprang up and hissed across the fields; for a moment, hung there between night and day, all seemed a grey and empty waste, an end to independent struggle under aimless airs—had God, I wondered, already lifted the protection of the New Reign from us three? Estrades shivered and zipped his jacket up. As darkness fell and the sound of God's Engines came throbbing up from the south, Eisenburg got to work with his bolt-cutters. The chain link proved tougher than expected; the Jew grunted and swore, Estrades fumed impatiently about; reluctantly, each strand of wire curled back on itself like burnt hair. By the time the first vehicle had crawled into view, we had our breach—but it was small and mean.

Estrades then replaced Eisenburg at the wire and remained crouched in the gap for perhaps half an hour, frequently consulting his watch. His face had become drawn and uncommunicative, as if he realised for the first or possibly the last time what his own actions meant, and the scars on his cheeks were lambent, raw. Did he see in the slow, enigmatic shapes crawling up the incline his own final annihilation, the Hand irrevocably withdrawn? The ground shuddered, the air above the Road shimmered and reverberated with its implication of awful energies. Suddenly, he seemed to gather himself. He showed me a hunted, almost panic-stricken face and shouted, "Now or never, Oxlade! If you want to live, *run!*"

And he squirmed through the breach.

I remember so little. For a second or two, I know, I watched as he sprinted for his life, a tiny energetic weaving and dodging under the threat of those huge wheels; then I felt a tremendous blow between the shoulder blades, and turned to find Eisenburg sweating and grinning at me in the gloom. "You next," he said, and gave me another push. We fled like insects across the broad back of the road, the Jew shoving me on before him; the wind eddying round those massive machines whipped at our clothing; black dizzy expanses of riveted steel towered above us. When I stumbled, he dragged me upright, raging incoherently in some foreign language.

Out in the third lane, Estrades, by dint it seemed of sheer hysterical strength, had gained the bed of an immense trailer. Eight feet above me, white-faced and peering, he extended a hand to haul me up. Eisenburg tossed us the crate and the bolt-cutters, but at his first attempt to ensure his own safety, missed his stride. His jump took him six inches below Estrades's straining hand, and for a full half-minute he had to run along behind the vehicle gathering his courage for a second try, laughing and sobbing, his face a perfect mask of panic and fear.

Panic and fear—all that remains to me of the journey.

How long we clung freezing and immobile to the back of that machine, I can't tell. Blue and waxy light pervaded all that space which might be described as the Road, and Time moved unreasonably along the warped perspectives into which we travelled. Estrades's watch, damaged in his mad scramble up the side of the vehicle, was useless. A regular, disturbing modulation of that cyanic light suggested we might have been aboard the thing for days rather than hours. What could be seen of the Motorway's environs, we saw transfigured, blurred, and it gave us neither help nor comfort. (The Road has, I suspect, little "real" existence in this way, little connection with what we know as reality. I was to confirm, for instance, on my eventual return to the World, that three days had passed since our breaching of the fence—but I place no significance on such crude measurements, since they are at best a device for the description of the human *Umwelt*. We travelled in the *Umwelt* of God, which, to my admittedly limited knowledge, no theologian has yet undertaken to define.)

To begin with, Estrades was determined to make some sort of study of the vehicle which we had infested like morose and frightened lice—even, I think, to gain access to the tractor cab and "commandeer" it; but this came to nothing. We shared the trailer with something unimaginable and shrouded. We were from the start too awed, too precarious. We sat apart, drew our knees up to

our chins and stared silently before us. Eisenburg did once take a
turn around the trailer, out of bravado or to ease some cramp of
the joints, but even he didn't dare examine the thing beneath the
tarpaulin, and Estrades soon called him back. He seemed glad
enough to obey.

It was a wonder, finally, that any of us retained energy enough
to make decisions, even to move (although move we did, and soon
enough). The tarpaulin cracked and flapped dismally, like a
tent pitched in a dark valley. Belts of fog came and went, to
leave beads of condensation on the black metal; sudden winds
chilled us to the bone. Our vehicle never left its precise position
in the order of the convoy. We were stiff and tired and hungry,
our ears were battered and stupefied by the constant beat of God's
Engines. In that dreary blue suspension, we felt like the ghosts of
the newly dead—who, filled with horror, stare numbly at one
another in continual discovery of their irreversible state. Later,
Estrades took to brooding for long periods over the crate, hoping
perhaps to find his salvation there.

At last, Time, in an understandable human sense, was returned
to us; the light ceased its steady fluctuation; ahead, the perspectives of the Road shifted and straightened, enabling us once more
to estimate speed and distance; and for the first time the adjoining
landscape became clearly visible to us. We found ourselves moving
slowly across a great arid peneplain touched here and there by
sourceless orange highlights and shadows of the profoundest purple.
The earth was cracked and bare, like mudsoil on some abandoned
African plateau. Nothing moved beyond the fence.

You will say, and quite reasonably, that there is no such view
to be found in the British Isles. I can only agree. This was nothing
to us. On the horizon had appeared the tall and awful shape of
God.

Eisenburg the Jew bent his head and whimpered suddenly.
Estrades stared astounded. "Christ, Oxlade!" he shouted, and
lapsed immediately into some Magyar dialect I couldn't follow. He
produced his revolver and for some reason began to wave it ex-

citedly in my direction. Eisenburg, meanwhile, wept, choked
and tried to kneel; Estrades saw this action from the corner of his
eye, and went at him like a snake. "None of that!" he hissed. "Get
the bloody box open, Eisenburg! We've got him!" But his eyes
were captured by that unbearable Enigma or apparition and when
the Jew failed to obey he didn't seem to notice.

How can I describe Him?

He crouches there in my memory as He will crouch forever.
He is in part profile, silhouetted against the sky. Ten square miles
of earth lie between His six splayed legs. Rainbows of iridescence
play across His vast black carapace. If He should ever spread the
wings beneath those shimmering elytra! One compound eye a hundred yards across gazes fixedly into realms that we may never see.
A mile in the air, gales thunder impotently about His stiff antennae
and motionless, extended jaws. In the shadow of His long abdo-
men, the giant factories seem like toys, and it is as if He had
brought with Him from the hidden obverse of the Moon an airless-
ness that makes the sky a harder, brighter place. We see that
where His legs touch the earth, deep saucer-shaped depressions
have formed. From each of these, huge fissures radiate. Can the
World bear His weight without a groan?

What has He taken away from us, what has He come to give us
in return? Estrades claimed to know—but Estrades had long been
destroyed by his own despair. Staring up at that gargantuan entomic
form, *Lucanus Cervus Omnipotens,* I knew there must be more.
If I am no longer sure of that, it is because I am no longer sure
of anything.

Eisenburg gaped, vomited. He wiped his mouth with the back of
his hand and began to laugh. "It's a bloody beetle!" he shrieked.
"It's only a bloody beetle!" Estrades winced, stared at his feet
for a moment; then he started to laugh, too. They embraced, sobbing, rocking to and fro in a sort of clumsy dance. "Quick!" cried
the Jew, disengaging himself. "Quick!" He grabbed the bolt-cutters
and used them to lever off the lid of the crate. Grey-faced and

shaking, the two of them knelt over its contents and began to make feverish adjustments to a nest of coloured wire and electrical components. In their haste, they fought briefly over the only tool they had, a small screwdriver. Eisenburg won.

Estrades glanced over his shoulder and shuddered. "It's about five miles," he said. "Set it for that."

He felt my gaze on him. "Freedom, Oxlade," he murmured. "Freedom." A fit of shivering got hold of him. Up ahead, that enormous shape was coming closer and closer.

"An hour and twenty minutes," he told Eisenburg, "to be on the safe side. We can't be certain what happens once it gets there."

"You don't mean to carry on with this!" I found myself shouting. I can't express the panic that had come over all of us. It was almost physiological, some old fear etched into the cells of the nervous system. "Estrades! Not so close to Him—!" I clutched his shoulders. His trembling communicated itself to me, and for a second we clung to one another, unable to speak. Estrades made noises. I tore myself away. "What's *in* that crate, man? What are you going to do?" Slowly, the trembling died away. Estrades drew a long, shuddering breath; his face writhed, he lifted the pistol. Then he laughed bitterly and turned his back.

"Ask what all this is for," he suggested quietly, "instead." And he gestured at the Motorway, at the impossible landscape and the factories in the Shadow.

"Ask what this thing intends to do with *us,* why it has turned us into tourists and parsons and performers of simpering amateur dramatics in a world we no longer control. Ask—" But he began to tremble again, and couldn't go on. He clenched his fists against the onset of the fit. Eisenburg, dropping the screwdriver, looked up in horror, his jaw muscles quivering uncontrollably. Wracked and quaking, I thought, It will get worse as we go closer; He cannot allow us any closer. I was terrified in case I should see those gigantic mandibles *move.* Estrades clutched at his gun with both hands, as if it offered anchorage. "I have ten pounds of plutonium in that box"—each word forced out between clenched teeth—"Eisenburg built the trigger. Twenty men died stealing the stuff, a hundred more are committed in Europe alone. I shall go . . . on . . . whatever happens. . . ."

He groaned, and gave himself up to shivering.

I don't know quite what I intended to do. When I saw them both overcome, I threw myself at the bomb—I thought that if I could heave it over the side it would be broken, or at least irrecoverable. But they were on me in an instant, clubbing madly at my head and groin. Estrades's revolver went off with an enormous bang. Something smashed into my lower legs. The Jew roared, dropped his body squarely across mine and probed with stiffened fingers for the arteries in my neck. We flopped about like fish in the bottom of a rowing boat, panting and groaning. Then I discovered the discarded bolt-cutters under my hand and beat him repeatedly under the ear with them until he rolled away from me and stopped moving.

Scrambling to my feet, I discovered Estrades kneeling about two feet away. "For Christ's sake, Oxlade," he pleaded, "it's the *world!*" The pistol was pointed directly at my belly, but he was shivering so hard he couldn't pull the trigger. I opened his head up with the bolt-cutters. He knelt there, covered in blood, and said, "You shouldn't have done this." Then he went down like a dead man.

I took a step toward the bomb; my left leg folded up under me; and, clutching helplessly at the empty air, I fell into the Road —where I lay on my back for a moment unable to move, watching the vehicle draw inexorably away from me. Hot and stinking of rubber, huge wheels ground past, not a yard away from me through a fog of pain and nausea. About a minute later, the figure of Estrades reappeared on the trailer, looking small and desperately unsteady. His shoulders were a mantle of blood. He staggered about for a time, waving the revolver. A couple of rounds splattered into the metalling beside me; then he turned away and emptied the weapon defiantly into the air toward God. That was the last I saw of him.

The rest is nothing. I turned my back on it all and ran, despite the hole Estrades had put in the muscle of my calf (I still limp a little, although not now as proudly as I did in the weeks of my convalescence). "God," I remember praying, "let me get away before it goes off!" So close, it might even be that He heard me. I don't recall what I offered Him in exchange. Several times, I made some feeble attempt to cut my way through the fence; but I never managed to break more than a strand or two of wire before panic overtook me and I began to run again, timing my prayers to the sound of my own ragged breath. I was painfully conscious of the Mystery looming immobile and abiding behind me; but I never looked back.

Eventually, I fell down exhausted. There, where the Motorway ran through a cutting with broad, gently sloping sides of soft red earth, I scraped a shallow hole. Into this I thrust my face; I clasped my hands behind my neck, and in that submissive position, waited for Estrades's madness to find me out. A long time later, I passed out. Perhaps they had built the thing badly, or failed to complete the fusing sequence—perhaps after all I had killed them both. At any rate, the bomb never went off.

I suspect it never would have. I realise now that it was a failure of Faith to believe even for a second that they could have succeeded; and I suspect now that a dozen bombs would have made no difference to Him—I imagine Him spreading His great transparent wings to the blast, like a housefly in the sun.

The driver of a quite ordinary lorry, I am told, found me stumbling along the muddy verge of the A5 somewhere near Brownhills. How I got there, I am at a loss to explain. Presumably I succeeded at last in breaching the fence. God rises majestically above the suburbs of Birmingham and Wolverhampton, where His factories are: but He seems smaller than He does in that other place, that Simultaneous or Alternative Midlands

which can only be seen from the other side of the chain link;
and people live at ease within the sight of Him.

What a pure pleasure the convalescent experiences when he is at
last released from his prison of a bed! The sheets, chains and
fetters of his sapling vitality, become mere sheets once more; his
dull fellow-patients, now that he must leave them, seem the most
interesting of human beings; and the view from his window—
that sad fishbowl stage for his obsessive fantasies of recovery,
peopled by actors whose motives he can only invent—becomes
the World again, and he its newest participant. And what a
world! What rediscoveries, what heartfelt reconsiderations! It was
with just this profound sense of being made anew that, a little
over a month after my adventures in the Realm of God, I made
my way home from the offices of the Department.

I had been released from hospital that morning; my preliminary
report was made—though there remained a necessary sharpening
of its edges, the sketch, so to speak, was completed; and before
me stretched the most poignant of May afternoons. I dawdled
down Baker Street, and paused for a while to admire the flower-
beds by the Clarence Gate. Regent's Park was full of cool laconic
breezes, but beneath them there moved a heaviness, a languor,
a promise of the Summer to be. In my absence, cherry blossoms
had sprung in every corner; the waterfowl had put on a fresh,
dapper plumage and were waddling importantly about in the
white sunlight that scoured the newly painted boards of the boat
house.

Calm and happy, I let the faint cries of some large animal draw
me across the jetty footbridge toward the distant Zoological Gardens. The wind brought me declamatory voices and the laughter
of children—at the Open Air Theatre, they were presenting *A
Midsummer Night's Dream;* and as I crossed the wide spaces
north of the lake, the glowing phrases of my lunchtime interview
with the chief mingled inextricably with strains of a Flanders and

Swann medley issuing from the new bandstand: "A most genuine contribution . . . a hundred others rounded up in Europe alone; in Africa we move with speed and caution. We were of course well aware of Estrades and his cynical conspiracy. Nothing less than a victory, a triumph for decency and common sense . . . certain promotion." Old men were flying their kites from the benches by the pagoda; white and ecstatic as the gulls above God's Causeway, the kites danced and bobbed in tribute to the dashing air!

Since childhood, the elegant cages, the precise spaces, the immense color and vitality of the Zoo have been a passion with me. Where else can be seen such relentless grace, such refined energy as we see in the leopard? Or such mysterious moonlit depths as those of the Small Mammal House? What a cacophony of wisdom the lories and macaws generate, what a deep spring of humor wells beneath the elephant's hide! That afternoon, I was remade. Mary and the children, I thought, would hardly begrudge me an hour; so I took it with the gibbons and the mountain sheep, and with the tiger who so reminded me of Estrades—pacing, hungry, so economical and dangerous that I caught myself trying to attract his eye. . . .

That was surely enough; the polar bear like a fixated ballet dancer run to fat, the sharp ammoniacal smell of the rhino, the flocking children, that sense of peaceful yet animal activity—these were surely enough: I shouldn't have gone to the Insect House.

I don't believe it was a beetle of any kind, much less *Lucanus Cervus,* that captured my attention—rather it was something grey and leafish, looking absurdly like a woman in muslin rags. It was resting on a twig, almost invisible and quite immobile, and perhaps this very quality of stillness—this perfectly alien perception of the passage of time—was sufficient. As I stared into the hot yellow recesses of the vivarium, I remembered the Mystery that lies at the end of God's Motorway, and I thought, What possible emotion could this thing have in common with us? I recalled the twisted perspectives and quaking blue light of the *Umwelt* of God, the factories in the Shadow, Estrades's final bitter suggestion —"Ask what this thing intends to do with *us,* in a world we no longer control."

In what continuum or sphere of reality would we find that nightmarish Simultaneous Midlands, with its pocked dreary landscape and vast presiding deity, if we once thought to look? Why is God building an enormous human body while we build bandstands? What does He want with us?

As I reread what I have written here I can see the progression of my loss mirrored in the very words I have used; Estrades began it, perhaps, as he had intended to, on the seafront at Southend—but that was only a moment's uncertainty, whereas this . . . Since the revelation in the Insect House, where the only sound is a shuffle of feet as visitors file past the specimens like communicants, I have been unable to recapture my sense of wonder. My attention wanders from my second-generation *Epipactis tetralix;* I grow bored and restless at rehearsals of the Esher Light Operatic Society; I chafe.

And I confess that it frightens me now to visit that penthouse office where my chief crouches high above the neat, the eternally bright and windy streets of the city, whispering "Still so much to do, Oxlade," as he grooms with quick strokes of his forelegs his feathery antennae, or flexes the horny wing-cases which, closed, look so much like an iridescent tail-coat—or in the gloom fixes his enigmatic compound eyes on that white, perfect rectangle of light cast by the slide projector, engaging in some renewal of the senses, some exploration of a consciousness I will never appreciate. I am his deputy now, and have risen as far as a man can rise. I look out over the pensioners in the trim parks below, and I should be proud.

What did Estrades know? He was an old man. He retired, he took himself off to North Africa and a study of Byzantine military history long before the Rediscovery. He had never stood above the streets of some familiar city, faced with one of the small energetic Replicas of Him that fill every responsible office in the World. He had no chance.

Why has God come to us in this way? We were so eager to accept Him.

My favorite Jesuit theologian, Ivan Illich, maintains, and I believe him, that Educators have become the high priests of our secular age, much to the detriment of everyone's education. It is quite in keeping, then, that blueprints for the School Beautiful have tended to supplant rules for a devout and holy life as the foundation stone of most contemporary utopias. Joanna Russ's Whileaway is typical in this (if in no other) respect.

The supreme example of Education becoming the be-all and end-all of the utopian way of life is surely B. F. Skinner's *Walden Two,* from which the following selection is taken. By almost any standard, *Walden Two* is the Representative Utopia of Our Time (or of Their Time, if you belong on the other side of the generation gap). Which is not to say it's a hoary classic, like (yawn) Fénelon's Salentum or (snore) Limanora, the Island of Progress. On the contrary, no other utopia is still capable of exciting its readers either to active emulation (one Virginia community is presently following Skinner's prescription, and Kathleen Kinkade has written a fascinating chronicle of its ups and downs in *A Walden Two Experiment* [William Morrow])—or to empassioned denunciation. Thus, the otherwise mild-tempered authors of *The Quest for Utopia* (Doubleday Anchor, and the best one-volume anthology of classic utopias available) insist: "While it was to be expected that sooner or later the principle of psychological conditioning would be made the basis of a serious utopia . . . not even the effective satire of Huxley is adequate preparation for the shocking horror of the idea when positively presented. Of all the dictatorships espoused by utopists, this is the most profound, and incipient dictators might well find in this utopia a guidebook for political practice." With such encomiums, who could resist *Walden Two?* Not I, said the editor.

Those readers who have already had it out, one way or other, with B. F. Skinner will, I hope, be readier to permit the inclusion of a Golden Oldie for the sake of Harry Harrison's cautionary tale that follows it. "I Always Do What Teddy Says" is all the more effective as an antidote to Skinner's somewhat oppressive infallibilities in that it never tries to contest the logic of Skinner's thesis, but only to bear witness, with both pity and disdain, to its essential inhumanity.

INSTEAD OF THE CROSS, THE LOLLIPOP

by B. F. Skinner

"Each of us," Frazier began, "is engaged in a pitched battle with the rest of mankind."

"A curious premise for a Utopia," said Castle. "Even a pessimist like myself takes a more hopeful view than that."

"You do, you do," said Frazier. "But let's be realistic. Each of us has interests which conflict with the interests of everybody else. That's our original sin, and it can't be helped. Now, 'everybody else' we call 'society.' It's a powerful opponent, and it always wins. Oh, here and there an individual prevails for a while and gets what he wants. Sometimes he storms the culture of a society and changes it slightly to his own advantage. But society wins in the long run, for it has the advantage of numbers and of age. Many prevail against one, and men against a baby. Society attacks early, when the individual is helpless. It enslaves him almost before he has tasted freedom. The 'ologies' will tell you how it's done. Theology calls it building a conscience or developing a spirit of selflessness. Psychology calls it the growth of the super-ego.

"Considering how long society has been at it, you'd expect a better job. But the campaigns have been badly planned and the victory has never been secure. The behavior of the individual has been shaped according to revelations of 'good conduct,' never as the result of experimental study. But why not experiment? The questions are simple enough. What's the best behavior for the individual so far as the group is concerned? And how can the individual be induced to behave in that way? Why not explore these questions in a scientific spirit?

"We could do just that in Walden Two. We had already worked out a code of conduct—subject, of course, to experimental modification. The code would keep things running smoothly if everybody lived up to it. Our job was to see that everybody did. Now, you can't get people to follow a useful code by making them into so many jacks-in-the-box. You can't foresee all future circumstances, and you can't specify adequate future conduct. You don't know what will be required. Instead, you have to set up certain behavioral processes which will lead the individual to design his own 'good' conduct when the time comes. We call that sort of thing 'self-control.' But don't be misled, the control always rests in the last analysis in the hands of society.

"One of our Planners, a young man named Simmons, worked with me. It was the first time in history that the matter was approached in an experimental way. Do you question that statement, Mr. Castle?"

"I'm not sure I know what you are talking about," said Castle.

"Then let me go on. Simmons and I began by studying the great works on morals and ethics—Plato, Aristotle, Confucius, the New Testament, the Puritan divines, Machiavelli, Chesterfield, Freud—there were scores of them. We were looking for any and every method of shaping human behavior by imparting techniques of self-control. Some techniques were obvious enough, for they had marked turning points in human history. 'Love your enemies' is an example—a psychological invention for easing the lot of an oppressed people. The severest trial of oppression is the constant rage which one suffers at the thought of the oppressor. What Jesus discovered was how to avoid these inner devastations. His technique was to *practice the opposite emotion.* If a man can succeed in 'loving his enemies' and 'taking no thought for the morrow,' he will no longer be assailed by hatred of the oppressor or rage at the loss of his freedom or possessions. He may not get his freedom or possessions back, but he's less miserable. It's a difficult lesson. It comes late in our program."

"I thought you were opposed to modifying emotions and instincts until the world was ready for it," said Castle. "According to you, the principle of 'love your enemies' should have been suicidal."

"It would have been suicidal, except for an entirely unforeseen consequence. Jesus must have been quite astonished at the effect of his discovery. We are only just beginning to understand the power of love because we are just beginning to understand the weakness of force and aggression. But the science of behavior is clear about all that now. Recent discoveries in the analysis of punishment—but I am falling into one digression after another. Let me save my explanation of why the Christian virtues —and I mean merely the Christian techniques of self-control— have not disappeared from the face of the earth, with due recognition of the fact that they suffered a narrow squeak within recent memory.

"When Simmons and I had collected our techniques of control, we had to discover how to teach them. That was more difficult. Current educational practices were of little value, and religious practices scarcely any better. Promising paradise or threatening hell-fire is, we assumed, generally admitted to be unproductive. It is based upon a fundamental fraud which, when discovered,

turns the individual against society and nourishes the very thing
it tries to stamp out. What Jesus offered in return for loving one's
enemies was heaven *on earth,* better known as peace of mind.

"We found a few suggestions worth following in the practices
of the clinical psychologist. We undertook to build a tolerance
for annoying experiences. The sunshine of midday is extremely
painful if you come from a dark room, but take it in easy
stages and you can avoid pain altogether. The analogy can be
misleading, but in much the same way it's possible to build a
tolerance to painful or distasteful stimuli, or to frustration, or to
situations which arouse fear, anger or rage. Society and nature
throw these annoyances at the individual with no regard for the
development of tolerances. Some achieve tolerances, most fail.
Where would the science of immunization be if it followed a
schedule of accidental dosages?

"Take the principle of 'Get thee behind me, Satan,' for example," Frazier continued. "It's a special case of self-control by
altering the environment. Subclass A 3, I believe. We give each
child a lollipop which has been dipped in powdered sugar so
that a single touch of the tongue can be detected. We tell him
he may eat the lollipop later in the day, provided it hasn't already been licked. Since the child is only three or four, it is a
fairly diff—"

"Three or four!" Castle exclaimed.

"All our ethical training is completed by the age of six," said
Frazier quietly. "A simple principle like putting temptation out
of sight would be acquired before four. But at such an early age
the problem of not licking the lollipop isn't easy. Now, what
would you do, Mr. Castle, in a similar situation?"

"Put the lollipop out of sight as quickly as possible."

"Exactly. I can see you've been well trained. Or perhaps you
discovered the principle for yourself. We're in favor of original
inquiry wherever possible, but in this case we have a more important goal and we don't hesitate to give verbal help. First of all,
the children are urged to examine their own behavior while look-

ing at the lollipops. This helps them to recognize the need for self-control. Then the lollipops are concealed, and the children are asked to notice any gain in happiness or any reduction in tension. Then a strong distraction is arranged—say, an interesting game. Later the children are reminded of the candy and encouraged to examine their reaction. The value of the distraction is generally obvious. Well, need I go on? When the experiment is repeated a day or so later, the children all run with the lollipops to their lockers and do exactly what Mr. Castle would do—a sufficient indication of the success of our training."

"I wish to report an objective observation of my reaction to your story," said Castle, controlling his voice with great precision. "I find myself revolted by this display of sadistic tyranny."

"I don't wish to deny you the exercise of an emotion which you seem to find enjoyable," said Frazier. "So let me go on. Concealing a tempting but forbidden object is a crude solution. For one thing, it's not always feasible. We want a sort of psychological concealment—covering up the candy by paying no attention. In a later experiment the children wear their lollipops like crucifixes for a few hours."

> " 'Instead of the cross, the lollipop,
>   About my neck was hung,' "

said Castle.

"I wish somebody had taught me that, though," said Rodge, with a glance at Barbara.

"Don't we all?" said Frazier. "Some of us learn control, more or less by accident. The rest of us go all our lives not even understanding how it is possible, and blaming our failure on being born the wrong way."

"How do you build up a tolerance to an annoying situation?" I said.

"Oh, for example, by having the children 'take' a more and more painful shock, or drink cocoa with less and less sugar in it until a bitter concoction can be savored without a bitter face."

"But jealousy or envy—you can't administer them in graded doses," I said.

"And why not? Remember, we control the social environment, too, at this age. That's why we get our ethical training in early. Take this case. A group of children arrive home after a long walk tired and hungry. They're expecting supper; they find, instead, that it's time for a lesson in self-control: they must stand for five minutes in front of steaming bowls of soup.

"The assignment is accepted like a problem in arithmetic. Any groaning or complaining is a wrong answer. Instead, the children begin at once to work upon themselves to avoid any unhappiness during the delay. One of them may make a joke of it. We encourage a sense of humor as a good way of not taking an annoyance seriously. The joke won't be much, according to adult standards—perhaps the child will simply pretend to empty the bowl of soup into his upturned mouth. Another may start a song with many verses. The rest join in at once, for they've learned that it's a good way to make time pass."

Frazier glanced uneasily at Castle, who was not to be appeased.

"That also strikes you as a form of torture, Mr. Castle?" he asked.

"I'd rather be put on the rack," said Castle.

"Then you have by no means had the thorough training I supposed. You can't imagine how lightly the children take such an experience. It's a rather severe biological frustration, for the children are tired and hungry and they must stand and look at food; but it's passed off as lightly as a five-minute delay at curtain time. We regard it as a fairly elementary test. Much more difficult problems follow."

"I suspected as much," muttered Castle.

"In a later stage we forbid all social devices. No songs, no jokes —merely silence. Each child is forced back upon his own resources— a very important step."

"I should think so," I said. "And how do you know it's successful? You might produce a lot of silently resentful children. It's certainly a dangerous stage."

"It is, and we follow each child carefully. If he hasn't picked up the necessary techniques, we start back a little. A still more advanced stage"—Frazier glanced again at Castle, who stirred uneasily—"brings me to my point. When it's time to sit down to the soup, the children count off—heads and tails. Then a coin is tossed and if it comes up heads, the 'heads' sit down and eat. The 'tails' remain standing for another five minutes."

Castle groaned.

"And you call that envy?" I said.

"Perhaps not exactly," said Frazier. "At least there's seldom any aggression against the lucky ones. The emotion, if any, is directed against Lady Luck herself, against the toss of the coin. That, in itself, is a lesson worth learning, for it's the only direction in which emotion has a surviving chance to be useful. And resentment toward things in general, while perhaps just as silly as personal aggression, is more easily controlled. Its expression is not socially objectionable."

Frazier looked nervously from one of us to the other. He seemed to be trying to discover whether we shared Castle's prejudice. I began to realize, also, that he had not really wanted to tell this story. He was vulnerable. He was treading on sanctified ground, and I was pretty sure he had not established the value of most of these practices in an experimental fashion. He could scarcely have done so in the short space of ten years. He was working on faith, and it bothered him.

I tried to bolster his confidence by reminding him that he had a professional colleague among his listeners. "May you not inadvertently teach your children some of the very emotions you're trying to eliminate?" I said. "What's the effect, for example, of finding the anticipation of a warm supper suddenly thwarted? Doesn't that eventually lead to feelings of uncertainty, or even anxiety?"

"It might. We had to discover how often our lessons could be safely administered. But all our schedules are worked out experimentally. We watch for undesired consequences just as any scientist watches for disrupting factors in his experiments.

"After all, it's a simple and sensible program," he went on in a tone of appeasement. "We set up a system of gradually increasing annoyances and frustrations against a background of complete serenity. An easy environment is made more and more difficult as the children acquire the capacity to adjust."

"But *why?*" said Castle. "Why these deliberate unpleasantnesses —to put it mildly? I must say I think you and your friend Simmons are really very subtle sadists."

"You've reversed your position, Mr. Castle," said Frazier in a sudden flash of anger with which I rather sympathized. Castle was calling names, and he was also being unaccountably and perhaps intentionally obtuse. "A while ago you accused me of breeding a race of softies," Frazier continued. "Now you object to toughening them up. But what you don't understand is that these potentially unhappy situations are never very annoying. Our schedules make sure of that. You wouldn't understand, however, because you're not so far advanced as our children."

Castle grew black.

"But what do your children get out of it?" he insisted, apparently trying to press some vague advantage in Frazier's anger.

"What do they get out of it!" exclaimed Frazier, his eyes flashing with a sort of helpless contempt. His lips curled and he dropped his head to look at his fingers, which were crushing a few blades of grass.

"They must get happiness and freedom and strength," I said, putting myself in a ridiculous position in attempting to make peace.

"They don't sound happy or free to me, standing in front of bowls of Forbidden Soup," said Castle, answering me parenthetically while continuing to stare at Frazier.

"If I must spell it out," Frazier began with a deep sigh, "what they get is escape from the petty emotions which eat the heart out of the unprepared. They get the satisfaction of pleasant and profitable social relations on a scale almost undreamed of in the world at large. They get immeasurably increased efficiency, because they can stick to a job without suffering the aches and pains which soon beset most of us. They get new horizons, for they are spared the emotions characteristic of frustration and failure. They get—" His eyes searched the branches of the trees. "Is that enough?" he said at last.

"And the community must gain their loyalty," I said, "when they discover the fears and jealousies and diffidences in the world at large."

"I'm glad you put it that way," said Frazier. "You might have said that they must feel superior to the miserable products of our public schools. But we're at pains to keep any feeling of superiority or contempt under control, too. Having suffered most acutely from it myself, I put the subject first on our agenda. We carefully avoid any joy in a personal triumph which means the personal failure of somebody else. We take no pleasure in the sophistical, the disputative, the dialectical." He threw a vicious glance at Castle. "We don't use the motive of domination, because we are always thinking of the whole group. We could motivate a few geniuses that way—it was certainly my own motivation—but we'd sacrifice some of the happiness of everyone else. Triumph over nature and over oneself, yes. But over others, never."

"You've taken the mainspring out of the watch," said Castle flatly.

"That's an experimental question, Mr. Castle, and you have the wrong answer."

Frazier was making no effort to conceal his feeling. If he had been riding Castle, he was now using his spurs. Perhaps he sensed that the rest of us had come round and that he could change his tactics with a single holdout. But it was more than strategy, it was genuine feeling. Castle's undeviating skepticism was a growing frustration.

"Are your techniques really so very new?" I said hurriedly.

"What about the primitive practice of submitting a boy to various tortures before granting him a place among adults? What about the disciplinary techniques of Puritanism? Or of the modern school, for that matter?"

"In one sense you're right," said Frazier. "And I think you've nicely answered Mr. Castle's tender concern for our little ones. The unhappinesses we deliberately impose are far milder than the normal unhappinesses from which we offer protection. Even at the height of our ethical training, the unhappiness is ridiculously trivial—to the well-trained child.

"But there's a world of difference in the way we use these annoyances," he continued. "For one thing, we don't punish. We never administer an unpleasantness in the hope of repressing or eliminating undesirable behavior. But there's another difference. In most cultures, the child meets up with annoyances and reverses of uncontrolled magnitude. Some are imposed in the name of discipline by persons in authority. Some, like hazings, are condoned though not authorized. Others are merely accidental. No one cares to, or is able to, prevent them.

"We all know what happens. A few hardy children emerge, particularly those who have got their unhappiness in doses that could be swallowed. They become brave men. Others become sadists or masochists of varying degrees of pathology. Not having conquered a painful environment, they become preoccupied with pain and make a devious art of it. Others submit—and hope to inherit the earth. The rest—the cravens, the cowards—live in fear for the rest of their lives. And that's only a single field—the reaction to pain. I could cite a dozen parallel cases. The optimist and the pessimist, the contented and the disgruntled, the loved and the unloved, the ambitious and the discouraged—these are only the extreme products of a miserable system.

"Traditional practices are admittedly better than nothing," Frazier went on. "Spartan or Puritan—no one can question the occasional happy result. But the whole system rests upon the wasteful principle of selection. The English public school of the nineteenth century produced brave men—by setting up almost insurmountable barriers and making the most of the few who came over. But selection isn't education. Its crops of brave men will always be small, and the waste enormous. Like all primitive principles, selection serves in place of education only through a profligate use of material. Multiply extravagantly and select with rigor. It's the philosophy of the 'big litter' as an alternative to good child hygiene.

"In Walden Two we have a different objective. We make every man a brave man. They all come over the barriers. Some require more preparation than others, but they all come over. The traditional use of adversity is to select the strong. We control adversity to build strength. And we do it deliberately, no matter how sadistic Mr. Castle may think us, in order to prepare for adversities which are beyond control. Our children eventually experience the 'heartache and the thousand natural shocks that flesh is heir to.' It would be the cruelest possible practice to protect them as long as possible, especially when we *could* protect them so well."

Frazier held out his hands in an exaggerated gesture of appeal.

"What alternative *had* we?" he said, as if he were in pain. "What else could we do? For four or five years we could provide a life in which no important need would go unsatisfied, a life practically free of anxiety or frustration or annoyance. What would *you* do? Would you let the child enjoy this paradise with no thought for the future—like an idolatrous and pampering mother? Or would you relax control of the environment and let the child meet accidental frustrations? *But what is the virtue of accident?* No, there was only one course open to us. We had to *design* a series of adversities, so that the child would develop the greatest possible self-control. Call it deliberate, if you like, and accuse us of sadism; there was no other course." Frazier turned to Castle, but he was scarcely challenging him. He seemed to be waiting, anxiously, for his capitulation. But Castle merely shifted his ground.

"I find it difficult to classify these practices," he said. Frazier emitted a disgruntled "Ha!" and sat back. "Your system seems to have usurped the place as well as the techniques of religion."

"Of religion and family culture," said Frazier wearily. "But I don't call it usurpation. Ethical training belongs to the community. As for techniques, we took every suggestion we could find without prejudice as to the source. But not on faith. We disregarded all claims of revealed truth and put every principle to an experimental test. And by the way, I've very much misrepresented the whole system if you suppose that any of the practices I've described are fixed. We try out many different techniques. Gradually we work toward the best possible set. And we don't pay much attention to the apparent success of a principle in the course of history. History is honored in Walden Two only as entertainment. It isn't taken seriously as food for thought. Which reminds me, very rudely, of our original plan for the morning. Have you had enough of emotion? Shall we turn to intellect?"

Frazier addressed these questions to Castle in a very friendly way and I was glad to see that Castle responded in kind. It was perfectly clear, however, that neither of them had ever worn a lollipop about the neck or faced a bowl of Forbidden Soup.

I ALWAYS DO WHAT TEDDY SAYS

by Harry Harrison

The little boy lay sleeping, the artificial moonlight of the picture-picture window throwing a pale glow across his untroubled features. He had one arm clutched around his teddy bear, pulling the round face with its staring button eyes close to his. His father, and the tall man with the black beard, tiptoed silently across the nursery to the side of the bed.

"Slip it away," the tall man said, "then substitute the other."

"No, he would wake up and cry," Davy's father said. "Let me take care of this, I know what to do."

With gentle hands he laid another teddy bear down next to the boy, on the other side of his head, so that the sleeping-cherub face was framed by the wide-eared unsleeping masks of the toys. Then he carefully lifted the boy's arm from the original teddy and pulled it free. Though this disturbed Davy it did not wake him. He ground his teeth together and rolled over, clutching the substitute toy to his cheek, and within a few moments his quiet breathing was regular and deep again. The boy's father raised his forefinger to his lips and the other man nodded; they left the room without making a sound, closing the door noiselessly behind them.

"Now we begin," Torrence said, reaching out to take the teddy bear. His lips were small and glistened redly in the midst of his dark beard. The teddy bear twisted in his grip and the black-button eyes rolled back and forth.

157

"Take me back to Davy," it said in a thin and tiny voice.

"Let me have it," the boy's father said. "It knows me and won't complain."

His name was Numen and, like Torrence, he was a Doctor of Government. Both DGs and both unemployed by the present government, in spite of their abilities and rank. In this they were similar, but physically they were opposite. Torrence was a bear, though a small one, a black bear with hair sprouting thickly on his knuckles, twisting out of his white cuffs and lining his ears. His beard was full and thick, rising high up on his cheekbones and dropping low on his chest.

Where Torrence was dark Numen was fair, where short he was tall, where thick, thin. A thin bow of a man, bent forward with a scholar's stoop and, though balding now, his hair was still curled and blond and very like the golden ringlets of the boy asleep upstairs. Now he took the toy animal and led the way to the shielded room deep in the house where Eigg was waiting.

"Give it here—here!" Eigg snapped when they came in, and reached for the toy. Eigg was always like that, in a hurry, surly, square and solid with his stocky body pressed into a spotless white laboratory smock. But they needed him.

"You needn't," Numen said, but Eigg had already pulled it from his grasp. "It won't like it, I know. . . ."

"Let me go . . . let me go . . . !" the teddy bear said with a hopeless shrill.

"It is just a machine," Eigg said coldly, putting it face down on the table and reaching for a scalpel. "You are a grown man, you should be more logical, have your emotions under greater control. You are speaking with your childhood memories, seeing your own boyhood teddy who was your friend and companion. This is just a machine." With a quick slash he opened the fabric over the seam seal and touched it: the plastic-fur back gaped open like a mouth.

"Let me go . . . let me go . . ." the teddy bear wailed and its stumpy arms and legs waved back and forth. Both of the onlookers went white.

"Must we . . . ?"

"Emotions. Control them," Eigg said and probed with a screw-driver. There was a click and the toy went limp. He began to unscrew a plate in the mechanism.

Numen turned away and found that he had to touch a hand-kerchief to his face. Eigg was right. He was being emotional and this was just a machine. How did he dare get emotional over it, considering what they had in mind?

"How long will it take?" He looked at his watch; it was a little past 2100.

"We have been over this before and discussing it again will not change any of the factors." Eigg's voice was distant as he removed the tiny plate and began to examine the machine's interior with a magnifying probe. "I have experimented on the three stolen teddy tapes, carefully timing myself at every step. I do not count removal or restoral of the tape, this is just a few minutes for each. The tracking and altering of the tape in both instances took me under ten hours. My best time differed from my worst time by less than fifteen minutes, which is not sig-nificant. We can therefore safely say—ahh," he was silent for a moment while he removed the capsule of the memory spools, ". . . we can safely say that this is a ten-hour operation."

"That is too long. The boy is usually awake by seven; we must have the teddy back by then. He must never suspect that it has been away."

"There is little risk, you can give him some excuse for the time. I will not rush and spoil the work. Now be silent."

The two governmental specialists could only sit back and watch while Eigg inserted the capsule into the bulky machine he had secretly assembled in the room. This was not their specialty.

"Let me go . . ." the tiny voice said from the wall speaker, then was interrupted by a burst of static. "Let me go . . . bzzzzt . . . no, no, Davy, daddy wouldn't like you to do that . . . fork in left, knife in right . . . bzzzt . . . if you do you'll have to wipe . . . good boy good boy good boy. . . ."

The voice squeaked and whispered and went on, while the hours on the clock went by one by one. Numen brought in coffee more than once and towards dawn Torrence fell asleep sitting up in the chair, only to wake with a guilty start. Of them all Eigg showed no strain or fatigue, working the controls with fingers regular as a metronome. The reedy voice of the capsule shrilled thinly through the night like the memory of a ghost.

"It is done," Eigg said, sealing the fabric with quick surgeon's stitches.

"Your fastest time ever." Numen sighed with relief. He glanced at the nursery viewscreen that showed his son, still asleep, starkly clear in the harsh infra-red light. "And the boy is still asleep. There will be no problem getting it back after all. But is the tape . . . ?"

"It is right, perfect, you heard that. You asked the questions and heard the answers. I have concealed all traces of the alteration and unless you know what to look for you would never find the changes. In every other way the memory and instructions are like all others. There has just been this single change made."

"Pray God we never have to use it," Numen said.

"I did not know that you were religious," Eigg said, turning to look at him, his face expressionless. The magnifying loupe was still in his eye and it stared, five times the size of its fellow, a large and probing questioner.

"I'm not," Numen said, flushing.

"We must get the teddy back," Torrence broke in. "The boy just stirred."

Davy was a good boy and, when he grew older, a good student in school. Even after he began classes he kept teddy around and talked to him while he did his homework.

"How much is seven and five, teddy?"

The furry toy bear rolled its eyes and clapped stub paws. "Davy knows . . . shouldn't ask teddy what Davy knows. . . ."

"Sure I know—I just wanted to see if you did. The answer is thirteen."

"Davy . . . the answer is twelve . . . you better study harder, Davy . . . that's what teddy says. . . ."

"Fooled you!" Davy laughed. "Made you tell me the answer!" He was learning ways to get around the robot controls, permanently fixed to answer the questions of a smaller child. Teddies have the vocabulary and outlook of the very young because their job must be done during the formative years. Teddies teach diction and life history and morals and group adjustment and vocabulary and grammar and all the other things that enable men to live together as social animals. A teddy's job is done early in the most plastic stages of a child's life, and by the very nature of its task its conversation must be simple and limited. But effective. Teddies are eventually discarded as childish toys, but by then the job is complete.

By the time Davy became David and was eighteen years old, teddy had long since been retired behind a row of books on a high shelf. He was an old friend who had outgrown his useful days, but he was still a friend and certainly couldn't be discarded. Not that Davy ever thought of it that way. Teddy was just teddy and that was that. The nursery was now a study, his cot a bed and with his birthday past David was packing because he was going away to the university. He was sealing his bag when the phone bleeped and he saw his father's tiny image on the screen.

"David . . ."

"What is it, father?"

"Would you mind coming down to the library now. There is something rather important . . ."

David squinted at the screen and noticed for the first time that his father's face had a pinched, sick look. His heart gave a quick jump.

"I'll be right down!"

Dr. Eigg was there, arms crossed and sitting almost at attention. So was Torrence, his father's oldest friend, whom, though no relation, David had always called Uncle Torrence. And his father, obviously ill at ease about something. David came in quietly, conscious of all their eyes upon him as he crossed the room and took a chair. He was very much like his father, with the same build and height, a relaxed, easy-to-know boy with very few problems in life.

"Is something wrong?" he asked.

"Not wrong, Davy," his father said. He must be upset, David thought, he hasn't called me that in years. "Or rather something *is* wrong, but with the state of the world, and has been for a long time."

"Oh, the Panstentialists," David said, and relaxed a little. He had been hearing about the evils of Panstentialism as long as he could remember. It was just politics; he had been thinking something very personal was wrong.

"Yes, Davy, I imagine you know all about them now. When your mother and I separated I promised to raise you to the best of my ability and I think I have. But I'm a governor and all my friends work in government so I'm sure you have heard a lot of political talk in this house. You know our feelings and I think you share them."

"I do—and I think I would have no matter where I grew up. Panstentialism is an oppressing philosophy and one that perpetuates itself in power."

"Exactly. And one man, Barre, is at the heart of it. He stays in the seat of government and will not relinquish it and, with the rejuvenation treatments, will be there for a hundred years more."

"Barre must go!" Eigg snapped. "For twenty-three years now he has ruled and forbidden the continuation of my experiments. Young man, he has stopped my work for a longer time than you have been alive, do you realize that?"

David nodded, but did not comment. What little he had read about Dr. Eigg's proposed researches into behavioral human embryology had repelled him and, secretly, he was in agreement with Barre's ban on the work. But Panstentialism was different,

he was truly in agreement with his father. This do-nothing philosophy lay a heavy and dusty hand on the world of politics—as
well as the world at large.

"I'm not speaking only for myself," Numen said, his face white
and strained, "but for everyone in the world and in the system
who is against Barre and his philosophies. I have not held a
government position for over twenty years—nor has Torrence
here—but I think he'll agree that this is a small thing. If this was
a service to the people we would gladly suffer it. Or if our
persecution was the only negative result of Barre's evil works I
would do nothing to stop him."

"I am in complete agreement," Torrence nodded. "The fate of
two men is of no importance in comparison with the fate of us
all. Nor is the fate of one man."

"Exactly!" Numen sprang to his feet and began to pace agitat-
edly up and down the room. "If that were not true, if it were
not the heart of the problem, I would never consider being involved. There would *be* no problem if Barre suffered a heart
attack and fell dead tomorrow."

The three older men were all looking at David now, though he
didn't know why, and he felt they were waiting for him to say
something.

"Well, yes—I agree. A little embolism right now would be the
best thing for the world that I can think of. Barre dead would
be of far greater service to mankind than Barre alive has ever
been."

The silence lengthened, became embarrassing, and it was finally Eigg who broke it with his dry, mechanical tones.

"We are all then in agreement that Barre's death would be of
immense benefit. In that case, David, you must also agree that
it would be fine if he could be . . . killed. . . ."

"Not a bad idea," David said, wondering where all this talk
was going, "though of course it's a physical impossibility. It must
be centuries since the last . . . what's the word, 'murder' took
place. The developmental psychology work took care of that a

long time ago. As the twig is bent and all that sort of thing. Wasn't that supposed to be the discovery that finally separated man from the lower orders, the proof that we could entertain the thought of killing and even discuss it, yet still be trained in our early childhood so that we would not be capable of the act? If you can believe the textbooks the human race has progressed immeasurably since the curse of killing has been removed. Look —do you mind if I ask just what this is all about?"

"Barre can be killed," Eigg said in an almost inaudible voice. "There is one man in the world who can kill him."

"Who?" David asked, and in some terrible way he knew the answer even before the words came from his father's trembling lips.

"You, David . . . you. . . ."

He sat, unmoving, and his thoughts went back through the years and a number of things that had been bothering him were now made clear. His attitudes that were so subtly different from his friends', and that time with the plane when one of the rotors had killed a squirrel. Little, puzzling things, and sometimes worrying ones that had kept him awake long after the rest of the house was asleep. It was true, he knew it without a shadow of a doubt, and wondered why he had never realized it before. But it was like a hideous statue buried in the ground beneath one's feet, it had always been there but had never been visible until he had dug down and reached it. But he could see it now with all the earth scraped from its vile face and all the lineaments of evil clearly revealed.

"You want me to kill Barre?" he asked.

"You're the only one who can . . . Davy . . . and it must be done. For all these years I have hoped against hope that it would not be necessary, that the . . . ability you have would not be used. But Barre lives. For all our sakes he must die."

"There is one thing I don't understand," David said, rising and looking out of the window at the familiar view of the trees and the distant, glass-canopied highway. "How was this change made?

How could I miss the conditioning that is supposed to be a normal part of existence in this world?"

"It was your teddy bear," Eigg explained. "It is not publicized, but the reaction to killing is established at a very early age by the tapes in the machine that every child has. Later education is just reinforcement, valueless without the earlier indoctrination."

"Then my teddy . . . ?"

"I altered its tapes, in just that one way, so this part of your education would be missed. Nothing else was changed."

"It was enough, doctor." There was a coldness to his voice that had never existed before. "How is Barre supposed to be killed?"

"With this." Eigg removed a package from the table drawer and carefully opened it. "This is a primitive weapon removed from a museum. I have repaired it and charged it with the projectile devices that are called shells." He held the sleek, ugly, black thing in his hand. "It is fully automatic in operation. When this device—the trigger—is depressed, a chemical reaction propels a copper and lead weight named a bullet directly from the front orifice. The line of flight of the bullet is along an imaginary path extended from these two grooves on the top of the device. The bullet of course falls by gravity but in a minimum distance, say a meter, this fall is negligible." He put it down suddenly on the table. "It is called a gun."

David reached over slowly and picked it up. How well it fitted into his hand, sitting with such precise balance. He raised it, sighting across the grooves, and pulled the trigger. It exploded with an immense roar and jumped in his hand. The bullet plunged into Eigg's chest just over his heart with such a great impact that the man and the chair he had been sitting in were hurled backwards to the floor. The bullet also tore a great hole in his flesh and Eigg's throat choked with blood and he died.

"David! What are you doing?" His father's voice cracked with uncomprehending horror.

David turned away from the thing on the floor, still apparently unmoved by what he had done.

"Don't you understand, father? Barre and his Panstentialists are a terrible burden on the world and many suffer and freedom is abridged and all the other things that are wrong, that we know should not be. But don't you see the difference? You yourself said that things will change after Barre's death. The world will move on. So how is his crime to be compared to the crime of bringing *this* back into existence?"

He shot his father quickly and efficiently before the older man could realize the import of his words and suffer with the knowledge of what was coming. Torrence screamed and ran to the door, fumbling with terrified fingers for the lock. David shot him too, but not very well since he was so far away, and the bullet lodged in his body and made him fall. David walked over and, ignoring the screamings and bubbled words, took careful aim at the twisting head and blew out the man's brains.

Now the gun was heavy and he was very tired. The lift shaft took him up to his room and he had to stand on a chair to take teddy down from behind the books on the high shelf. The little furry animal sat in the middle of the large bed and rolled its eyes and wagged its stubby arms.

"Teddy," he said, "I'm going to pull up flowers from the flower-bed."

"No, Davy . . . pulling up flowers is naughty . . . don't pull up the flowers. . . ." The little voice squeaked and the arms waved.

"Teddy, I'm going to break a window."

"No, Davy . . . breaking windows is naughty . . . don't break any windows. . . ."

"Teddy, I'm going to kill a man."

Silence, just silence. Even the eyes and arms were still.

The roar of the gun broke the silence and blew a ruin of gears, wires and bent metal from the back of the destroyed teddy bear.

"Teddy . . . oh, teddy . . . you should have told me," David said and dropped the gun and at last was crying.

Most utopias are concerned with means. With, for instance, the wisest way to get the dishes washed, or the most sure-fire program for domesticating children. Ends are taken for granted, if for no other reason than that it can get scary thinking about the reasons we do most of the things we do—even, I dare say, in utopia.

My utopia—and surely I'm obliged, in the circumstances, to offer one of my own—puts forth a worthy objective and blithely assumes that the grail will create its own round table. Sooner or later the dishes always get washed, and an excessive concern over *who* does them is usually the signal of an impending divorce —not of utopia a-borning. So in terms of living arrangements, I'll go along with the crowd, so long as the crowd in turn is willing to help me erect . . .

PYRAMIDS FOR MINNESOTA

A Serious Proposal

by Thomas M. Disch

Q. Does Minnesota need pyramids?

A. No. Pyramids transcend the notion of "utility." This, indeed, is their special merit. If they could be put to any use whatever, people would not be interested in them. Why do people go to Europe? Not to see its magnificent grain elevators and factories, but to climb the ramparts of indefensible forts and stroll through the palaces of defunct monarchs. Above all, they visit churches—hundreds of churches, thousands of churches, ever more and more churches!

Q. Why not build churches, then?

A. It would confuse too many people. They would want the church to belong to a religion or express a style; they would complain of the expense, insisting that so much money and effort were better spent feeding poor children or searching for a cure for leukemia. Pyramids elude such controversies. They stand outside the flow of History. It is the very inexpressiveness of a pyramid, like that of a corpse or a crystal, that is so awesome.

Q. Why Minnesota, then? Why not in a desert?

A. There too, by all means. But, really, why *not* Minnesota?

Q. Should they all be the same size?

A. Yes. Especially if there are to be several in one area.

Q. And the same degree of steepness?

A. Yes—45°. As there will not be steps, this will dispel any lingering doubts as to their usefulness. One should never be prompted to climb a pyramid for the sake of a view. This is principally what is wrong with mountains.

Q. Passageways?

A. Absolutely not! No time capsules either. Rock-solid throughout. If they are to be vandalized, it should be from motives as disinterested as those that led to their formation.

Q. Who will build them?

A. All of us who want to. Volunteers must enlist for at least one year, but for no longer than three, thus steering a course between the Scylla of amateurism and the Charybdis of expertise. All volunteers must spend at least half their workweek in the actual labor of construction. Those who have clearly shirked or malingered must forfeit the bond they posted upon enlisting.

Q. Why would anyone volunteer?

A. For the reason one does anything—the experience promises

to be congenial to one's temperament. Undoubtedly the slaves who hewed and moved and fit in place the blocks of the first pyramids felt a secret gratification at taking part in the erection of such great monuments. Who can read of the building of Chartres without a smart of envy? By enlisting in the Pyramid Corps, one becomes part of a community devoted to a high and selfless goal, and yet there is no danger, in this case, of unwittingly furthering less worthy aims while pursuing one's own enlightenment. The CIA will have as little patience with pyramids as the church of Rome, but no great animus against them either. Pyramids, being all alike, do not excite the imagination, and so even the least competent of painters, architects, or interior decorators should be able to view their construction with equanimity. What other undertaking could be at once so strenuous and so little self-deluding? This is a purer form even than working for an insurance company of modern, secular monasticism.

Q. Where will they be located?

A. Outside the towns of Fairmont, Pipestone, Moorhead, Bemidji, and Aurora. Anyone who wants to see them should have to make a special effort.

Q. How can I help *now?*

A. Send your name and address to PYRAMIDS, c/o this magazine, indicating whether your interest is in contributing funds or your own labor. When sufficient interest has been demonstrated, a nonprofit Pyramid Foundation will be established, and you will be notified.

When the foregoing proposal appeared in *Harper's* magazine, it evoked a hearteningly large response. A lot of people want to enlist in the Corps, and a few have even proffered funds for such time as a Pyramid Foundation exists. One such volunteer in Austin, Texas, wrote: "Unfortunately, many people are not responding to your article because they think it is, while a worthy idea intrinsically, nevertheless a put-on." Even some of my oldest, closest friends have been given to doubting whether it isn't just a joke. So this is to say, crisscross my heart, that of course it's a joke—but a perfectly *serious* joke. A joke, what's more, that gets better with each ton of stone that's quarried and cut. Therefore, gentle readers, you are all invited to sign on by writing to me, c/o Harper & Row, Publishers. The *Zeitgeist* is on our side and slowly but surely the pyramids *will* go up.

Utopianism may be seen as a recusant (or lazy) form of monasticism. All the first utopias—More's, Campanella's, Bacon's—though written at the gilded dawn of the Baroque, partake of a hodden-gray homeliness that surely has its source in a blurred idealization of monastic life (with complications of pastoral fantasy). This nostalgia for the path not taken persists down to our time and informs even such determinedly secularist works as *Walden Two,* if not in the crucial matter of how we may best lead a devout and holy life, then at least in such domestic protocols as how to arrange a dinner and set table for a family of one hundred.

Though the following tale of monastic life in ancient China speaks very powerfully for itself (and so needs no further introduction), yet I cannot forbear quoting, a little, from Helen Waddell's beautiful book, *The Desert Fathers.* "For the Desert, though it praised austerity, reckoned it among the rudiments of holy living, and not as an end in itself: asceticism had not travelled far from the *ascesis,* the training of the athlete, and the Fathers themselves to their contemporary biographers are the *athletae Dei,* the athletes of God. Human passion, the passion of anger as well as of lust, entangled the life of the spirit: therefore passion must be dug out by the roots. . . . 'Spirit must brand the flesh that it may live,' said George Meredith, who was no Puritan: and Dorotheus the Theban put it more bluntly fifteen hundred years earlier: 'I kill my body, for it kills me.' "

THE ZEN ARCHER

by Jonathan Greenblatt

In a valley in the region of Kweichow in China, not more than a journey of two days by foot from the city of Kweiyang, there was a monastery in which thirteen humble students of the Buddha lived and meditated. The eldest of the monks was named Hsiang K'ung-hsi, and was the most beloved and respected among them. Indeed, there were many who believed him to be a true Bodhisattva, having achieved satori, yet remaining among his brethren for their bettering and guidance.

The youngest of the thirteen, K'uang Chao-yin, was a man of only twenty-two years who had been born of a merchant in Kweichow and had entered the monastery by his own choice at the age of fifteen. He was perhaps, of the monks, the most silent; and yet when he spoke it was with wisdom and the simplicity of the enlightened.

The monks lived at the edge of a forest, a beautiful thick wood that was alive with animals of many sorts and crowded with ginkgo trees, banyans, sago palms and rosewood acacias. They ate the fruit that they could gather, and the nuts of the walnut, the chestnut and the pistachio tree. Also they gathered the medicinal herbs that were to be found—cassia, ginseng and mahuang—and with these bartered for rice and paper with traders from the city.

Their lives were spent in peaceful work and in joyful contemplation of the teachings of the Buddha, especially the Dhammacakka—pavattana-sutta, the Discourse on the Turning of the Wheel of the Law, and the Four Noble Truths. Time seemed to go by quickly, seasons passed like the days of a week; and each man, in his heart, felt that he was drawing always nearer to the moment of revelation.

For K'uang Chao-yin, life was like the fall of a stone into water. The days were indistinguishable, one from the other, and yet in the morning of each new day, when the sun became visible through the trees, he felt closer than he had the evening before to understanding the oneness of the earth, the Universe and himself. The immersion into the All, the unified whole of creation, that was to come as nirvana at the moment of his death, or even before, seemed imminent to him, like the sound of splashing water once a stone has been dropped.

And for him, too, time passed more rapidly than it did for any of the others—even Hsiang K'ung-hsi, who was rushing toward the end of his life. He would meditate on the Four Noble Truths; but it seemed that he began to think of the suffering that was necessary to existence in the world when the first layers of frost and ice appeared on the hard ground, and his mind had not yet had time to turn to the limitation of desires before the thaws and the appearance of the yellow ginkgo fruit.

Yet at moments the earth stopped: time ceased to flow; the sun, the forest, the monastery, all disappeared. It was at moments such as these, as he told Li Shih-min, the monk from Kiangsu, to the distant northeast, that the Four Truths became one, and the One Truth was as the air he breathed. These revelations were his only as he stood with an arrow nocked and drawn in a clearing by an ancient, decayed chestnut tree, deep in the forest.

The bow had been given to him by the closest friend of his father on the day that K'uang Chao-yin first left for the monastery. He had accepted it gravely: a strong, well-polished bow with a cork grip; also a hip quiver that held ten arrows having a fine blue and white fletching. It had seemed to him then, though he respectfully said nothing at the time, that the gift of a hunting bow was an oddly chosen one for the occasion. But years later, when he had grown large enough to handle the weapon, he found it to have an enhancing effect on his meditations.

He would go—often several times during the week, except in the coldest of the winter months—to the clearing, a rectangular patch in the middle of the wood. He carried the bow and strapped the quiver beneath a fold of his black robe, the dress he wore always. Taking his accustomed place about twenty meters from the long-dead chestnut, he would prepare an arrow for firing with the care and observation of form of any other religious ritual. The cock feather was white, the hen feathers blue. He nocked the arrow, gripped it and drew the shaft, against perhaps sixty pounds of pull, until it nubbed his cheek. Then, without ever having looked at his target, a tiny hole in the black bark of the chestnut, he turned his face away, closing his eyes. He began to meditate.

The true meanings of the words of the Buddha came clear to him, with the clarity of a dream. He ceased to think; instead he became a well of understanding. Questions that had troubled his soul disappeared in the blazing white light of revelation. Though he did not know it, often he remained in that position, his arrow drawn and aimed, for an hour or more. He did not feel the pull of the bow wearing at his arm; he was at one with the Universe, at one with the weapon in his hands. The bow had become an extension of his own body, and he did not have to fight it.

And as his understanding fluoresced, he became profoundly conscious of the air around him, and the sounds of insects and birds that it carried. He expanded like the wave caused by the stone fallen in a pool, and he was at one with the living things that surrounded him. He was at one with the earth, and the stones, and suddenly with the ancient chestnut tree: with a snap and fleeting hiss, the arrow leapt from its drawn bowstring and passed cleanly through the fissure in the bark. It lodged in the rotting wood, penetrating to the depth of an inch.

K'uang Chao-yin never fired more than a single arrow. He

would open his eyes after the thwanging vibration of the arrow shaft had ceased, and contemplate for some minutes the truths to which he had awakened. Then he would retrieve the shot, and return quickly to the monastery.

The great wheel of the seasons revolved. In winter the cold was bitter, and the monastery had few visitors. The monks rarely went beyond the stone walls of their dwelling and, for many, winter was the time of a long, meditative fast. In the spring the wood once more blossomed with fruit and herbs, and the monks in their black robes walked the demesne of Nature, among the plicate ginkgo leaves and the sharp green needles of perennial shrubs. Traders returned, bringing news of the cities and of marvelous happenings to the east. The monks thought about right views and right action.

Then two travelers came to the monastery in the evening of a spring day. Hsiang K'ung-hsi offered them a place to stay for the night, and food, if they wished to share in the diet of the monks. The men thanked the elderly teacher, accepting with respectful bows, then came to eat with the others.

The monks sat at a long table in the refectory, a room on the eastern wall with a broad stained-glass window. Hsiang K'ung-hsi showed the travelers to the place of honor.

The larger of the two men spoke for them both. He was uneducated, as they could see, but he was polite and considerate of their hospitality. Hsiang K'ung-hsi inquired about their destination.

"Pichieh," the traveler said, and his fellow nodded. "We're just returning from Tuyün, where we had some business to transact."

"Ah, you have been in the East," Hsiang K'ung-hsi observed.

"Yes," said the traveler. "Already we have been journeying for sixteen days; and perhaps we have six more days ahead of us."

"No," Hsiang K'ung-hsi told him. "Pichieh is not more than

five days' travel from here. If you will allow, we will give you food to last another day of your journey when you set out in the morning."

"You are very kind," said the traveler. "The next time T'ao-chin and I pass through this country we will be very rich and, good monk, we will remember all this kindness you've shown us."

"Ah, we have our own riches here," said Hsiang K'ung-hsi.

"Indeed?"

"Peace," answered the monk. "Serenity."

His guest nodded understanding.

"But how will you become rich?" another monk asked the trader.

He smiled at them with a great, wide grin. The light from the slender, scented candles on the table flashed in his eyes as he looked slowly around at them all. "Birds," he said.

"Birds?" repeated Hsiang K'ung-hsi.

Then the trader laughed, shaking his head; and his long black hair, which had gone untrimmed during the days of his journey, fell across his forehead. He pushed the locks out of his eyes.

"We have seen something marvelous," he told the wondering monks. "In Tuyün there are trained birds, beautiful dark birds with red feathers on their necks. They catch fish. We've seen it, T'ao-chin and I. The fishermen tie ribbon around their necks, or light string, and *whoosh,* let them go. The birds catch fish; they dive into the river and bring them back flapping right to the bank. The fishermen pull them in. Next trip we're going to buy some and bring them to Yangtze. We're sure to be rich."

"Ah," said Hsiang K'ung-hsi.

The monks all looked at each other. Astounding things went on in the East.

"I have heard of such birds in Kiangsu," said Li Shih-min.

"Perhaps," said the trader. "But not in Yangtze. T'ao-chin and I will bring the first ones. We know well what is profitable to trade."

He took a walnut from his plate and chewed it carefully.

"There are strange things all over," he said then. "Even here, in this very forest. Do you know what we saw just this afternoon?" he asked Hsiang K'ung-hsi.

The monk shook his head.

"As we were resting in the forest, deciding which of two paths to take, we saw a man holding a lovely, very powerful bow. It was a fierce-looking weapon. And the oddest thing was this: the man was dressed in a monk's robe, exactly like your own. T'ao-chin and I got as far from him as we could; we didn't make a sound. He must have been a bandit, dressed as a monk for disguise. We got only a brief glimpse of him, and if not for the bow we would almost certainly have been fooled; perhaps robbed. But one does not need to be too clever to realize that a monk does not wield a hunting bow. We waited until he was gone before we moved. If not for this, we might be miles from your company at this moment."

At the far end of the table, K'uang Chao-yin spoke. "I apologize for causing you such difficulties," he said. "I am K'uang Chao-yin, and it was I that you saw today in the wood."

The two travelers looked at him, astonished.

"Remarkable," said the quiet man, T'ao-chin.

K'uang Chao-yin looked down without speaking. The eyes of the other traveler were on him, glowing with equal measures of surprise and curiosity. The monk felt his pulse quicken. If one sees evil where only innocence exists, the thought formed in his mind, then the evil must come from one's own heart. He let these words remain unvoiced.

"Why," said the trader wonderingly, "does a monk of the Buddhist faith, a holy man such as yourself, train with a hunting bow?"

With his eyes still downcast, K'uang Chao-yin answered, "It aids me in my search for enlightenment."

The trader's eyes seemed now to sparkle with a new fire. "Do you shoot well?" he asked.

"It is not important," said the young monk. "My bow is not

a weapon, it is an instrument of learning. My arrows are not meant to harm, only to pierce the darkness of my own ignorance."

The trader brought his fingers impatiently to his lips. "Yes, yes," he said. "But can you actually shoot?"

"Yes," said K'uang Chao-yin.

The trader said nothing for a time, yet all the monks except the youngest looked at him with expectancy. It seemed that he was weighing a thought.

"This is a poor monastery," he said at length.

Hsiang K'ung-hsi answered, "I have told you, friend, we have our own riches here."

"Yet money for books, for paper and food would not be unwelcome." The trader turned to K'uang Chao-yin. "The forest in which you live is rich with animals, with squirrels and monkeys and other small creatures whose pelts are very valuable. If you were to bring these pelts to any nearby town, they would fetch a worthy price; enough to help in this business of running a monastery. There is a great demand for squirrel fur. It is very profitable."

"I must ask you," Hsiang K'ung-hsi said, with embarrassment and discomfort showing in his expression, "to refrain from suggesting any such thing."

K'uang Chao-yin had turned away with revulsion.

"It is a belief of the Zen," the monk continued, "that all living creatures have a right to life, they are all worthy in the eyes of Nature; and that to remove a soul, even of a small beast, from its earthly vessel before time is an act of unholiness and evil."

Now it was the trader who evinced discomfort. "Forgive me," he said. "I was thinking only to repay the kindness you've shown us tonight. I could not, in any case, deal with you, as I will be away soon far to the west. It was only an idea that I thought might profit you."

"We will forget the matter," said Hsiang K'ung-hsi.

"Yes," the trader agreed.

But K'uang Chao-yin did not.

The travelers were sent in the morning from the monastery with food and with the blessing of the monks. The routine of days was resumed.

The image of a red bloodstain on the white shaft of his arrow had infected K'uang Chao-yin's vision. He tried to think of right effort and living, two teachings of the eightfold path; but the swift, straight line of the arrow's travel, the simple inexorable flight from his bow to the quivering target, leapt back into his mind at each opportunity.

He tried to fight it, to empty his mind of such imaginings. But he could not; and neither could he put away his bow and give up the hours of motionless contemplation in the clearing of the forest.

He endured temptation each day of his life as a monk; he endured abstinence from food and from the pleasures of the body, and never had he experienced a moment of weakness. Yet though he had no doubts of the evil of his conception, it bore a fascination whose grip he could not break. He envisioned blood spurting from a tiny heart as his arrow struck and penetrated. And, more than this, he could imagine the feeling of total unity he would experience at the moment of firing—this time with a creature doomed to an immediate death.

He pictured the fatal release, again and again, as he ate, meditated, worked, and even as he slept. He would break off speaking to one of the other monks at times if the idea had recurred to him. The monastery gradually became aware that something was troubling the young monk, but he did not explain to anyone, as he was ashamed.

His preoccupation grew more and more serious. K'uang Chao-yin almost felt that he was becoming ill. Still, he did not confide in the others.

The day was warm and bright. In the sky the thin clouds seemed frozen, and the firmament appeared as a surface of stone, marble or chalcedony. K'uang Chao-yin held an arrow up above his head, and saw that the colors of the fletching were just those of the sky and clouds.

He looked about the clearing and listened carefully. The breeze was fainter than a breath, yet he could hear the light slapping of fronds one against another, and the shivering of leaves in the topmost canopies of trees. He heard low animal noises from deeper in the wood. A few starlings were nesting in a tall banyan or mulberry tree just at the edge of his vision. He sighed, almost imperceptibly, and walked to the familiar spot, across from the decaying chestnut tree.

Then he turned and looked back at the starlings.

He nocked the arrow carefully, white cock feather up. The polished bow glinted in the afternoon sun. He drew back and, turning his face away, brushed his fingertips against his cheek. He closed his eyes.

In his inner eye he kept the image of the forest as he had just seen it. He heard and felt a gentle breeze blow, and he pictured the bending of stalks and the swaying of trees.

Then, just as always before, the illumination of knowledge came to him, breaking like a white sun over the horizon. Understanding filled him as if he were a vessel, then overflowed even beyond the limits of his body. He knew the air, and how it shimmered with warmth, and contained a hundred million tiny insects. He knew each one of the minuscule creatures, seeing them flit to and fro, hearing them buzz their insect messages and intelligence. The bubble of his knowledge expanded, and he knew the trees surrounding him, the sap running through them, the sunlight baking their leaves, the ants crawling on and burrowing into their bark.

His arrow was drawn and motionless.

Then he saw the starling as he was seeing everything else; he knew it and understood it. It lifted its tail and resettled its feathers. The tiny bright eyes were turned to him suddenly. He felt its heart beat as he felt his own. He was at one, completely at one, with his target.

The arrow released itself, and sped the shortest trajectory of all, the line from a thing to itself.

When Hsiang K'ung-hsi discovered that K'uang Chao-yin had not returned to the monastery, he went to the wood in search of the young monk. In the fading light of the evening he noticed a shape lying on the earthen floor of a clearing. He approached, and saw that it was the archer, his hunting bow fallen beside him. An arrow had pierced his heart.

The monk gripped his cloak around himself, shivering.

There was a small black bird, motionless, on the forehead of the dead man. It, too, seemed to the elderly monk to have given up its soul; but then suddenly it twitched, and hopped lightly to the bridge of K'uang Chao-yin's nose. For another moment it remained; then it ruffled its feathers and flew off into the night.

If the Visitor is the basis of most utopian scenarios, the Rebel is just as invariably the focus of dystopian fictions. Obviously, rebels offer larger dramatic possibilities than mere visitors, and dystopias do tend to make for livelier reading. There is a conflict, after all, not just an explanation. (Though there was a time, in about 1960, when every hack s-f novel on the stands was a retread of *1984*, wherein a pair of intrepid freedom-lovers would try to escape from their hateful domed world against hopeless odds, and that got to be as dull as any other hack formula.)

It was my intent from the start to include only real, ameliorative utopias in this book. Consequently there are few certifiable rebels in these pages: Eleanor Arnason's Doubter King, M. John Harrison's Estrades, and the unfortunate conspirators in "I Always Do What Teddy Says." Each of these figures appears in the role of Tempter, and his relation to the protagonist and to the utopia at large is equivocal at best.

Gene Wolfe, however, has found a hero (who really is a hero) who can rebel against a utopia (that really is a utopia). As to the peculiar spelling of the title, Gene insists on *Werwolf*, without the *e*, and the OED allows as how that's possible. As to *why*, I have my own theory: which is, that this is the superfluous *e* in *Wolfe*, and that this story might just as aptly be titled "The Wolf Gene." (Too baroque? Consider that Gene Wolfe followed up "The Island of Dr. Death" with "The Death of Dr. Island," and that the second of these won the Nebula that the first should have got by rights. And that wasn't deliberate?)

Which is not to suggest that what follows is anything but

straightforward. Gene's is the art that conceals art. What's left in plain view is simply one of the most witheringly scary stories this side of Frankenstein and Dracula . . .

THE HERO AS WERWOLF

by Gene Wolfe

> Feet in the jungle that leave no mark!
> Eyes that can see in the dark—the dark!
> Tongue—give tongue to it! Hark! O Hark!
>   Once, twice and again!
>   *Rudyard Kipling*
>   "Hunting Song of the Seeonee Pack"

An owl shrieked, and Paul flinched. Fear, pavement, flesh, death, stone, dark, loneliness and blood made up Paul's world; the blood was all much the same, but the fear took several forms, and he had hardly seen another human being in the four years since his mother's death. At a night meeting in the park he was the red-cheeked young man at the end of the last row, with his knees together and his scrupulously clean hands (Paul was particularly careful about his nails) in his lap.

The speaker was fluent and amusing; he was clearly conversant with his subject—whatever it was—and he pleased his audience. Paul, the listener and watcher, knew many of the words he used; yet he had understood nothing in the past hour and a half, and sat wrapped in his stolen cloak and his own thoughts, seeming to listen, watching the crowd and the park—this, at least, was no ghost-house, no trap; the moon was up, nightblooming flowers scented the park air, and the trees lining the paths glowed with self-generated blue light; in the city, beyond the last hedge, the great buildings new and old were mountains lit from within.

Neither human nor master, a policeman strolled about the fringes of the audience, his eyes bright with stupidity. Paul could have killed him in less than a second, and was enjoying a dream of the policeman's death in some remote corner of his mind even while he concentrated on seeming to be one of *them*. A passenger rocket passed just under the stars, trailing luminous banners.

The meeting was over and he wondered if the rocket had in some way been the signal to end it. The masters did not use time, at least not as he did, as he had been taught by the thin woman who had been his mother in the little home she had made for them in the turret of a house that was once (she said) the Gorous'—now only a house too old to be destroyed. Neither did they use money, of which he like other old-style *Homo sapiens* still retained some racial memory, as of a forgotten god—a magic once potent that had lost all force.

The masters were rising, and there were tears and laughter and that third emotional tone that was neither amusement nor sorrow—the silken sound humans did not possess, but that Paul thought might express content, as the purring of a cat does, or community, like the cooing of doves. The policeman bobbed his hairy head, grinning, basking in the recognition, the approval, of those who had raised him from animality. *See* (said the motions of his hands, the writhings of his body) *the clothing you have given me. How nice! I take good care of my things because they are yours. See my weapon. I perform a useful function—if you did not have me, you would have to do it yourselves.*

If the policeman saw Paul, it would be over. He was too stupid, too silly, to be deceived by appearances as his masters were. He would never dare, thinking him a master, to meet Paul's eye, but he would look into his face seeking approval, and would see not what he was supposed to see but what was there. Paul ducked into the crowd, avoiding a beautiful woman with eyes the color of pearls, preferring to walk in the shadow of her fat escort where the policeman would not see him. The fat man took dust from a box shaped like the moon and rubbed it between his hands, releasing the smell of raspberries. It froze, and he sifted the tiny crystals of crimson ice over his shirt-front, grunting with satisfaction; then offered the box to the woman, who refused at first, only (three steps later) to accept when he pressed it on her.

They were past the policeman now. Paul dropped a few paces behind the couple, wondering if they were the ones tonight—if there would be meat tonight at all. For some, vehicles would be waiting. If the pair he had selected were among these, he would have to find others quickly.

They were not. They had entered the canyons between the buildings; he dropped farther behind, then turned aside.

Three minutes later he was in an alley a hundred meters ahead of them, waiting for them to pass the mouth. (The old trick was to cry like an infant, and he could do it well; but he had a new trick—a better trick, because too many had learned not to come down an alley when an infant cried. The new trick was a silver bell he had found in the house, small and very old. He took it from his pocket and removed the rag he had packed around the clapper. His dark cloak concealed him now, its hood pulled up to hide the pale gleam of his skin. He stood in a narrow doorway only a few meters away from the alley's mouth.)

They came. He heard the man's thick laughter, the woman's silken sound. She was a trifle silly from the dust the man had given her, and would be holding his arm as they walked, rubbing his thigh with hers. The man's blackshod foot and big belly thrust past the stonework of the building—there was a muffled moan.

The fat man turned, looking down the alley. Paul could see fear growing in the woman's face, cutting, too slowly, through the odor of raspberries. Another moan, and the man strode forward, fumbling in his pocket for an illuminator. The woman followed hesitantly (her skirt was of flowering vines the color of love, and white skin flashed in the interstices; a serpent of gold supported her breasts).

Someone was behind him. Pressed back against the metal door, he watched the couple as they passed. The fat man had gotten his illuminator out and held it over his head as he walked, looking into corners and doorways.

They came at them from both sides, a girl and an old, grey-bearded man. The fat man, the master, his genetic heritage revised for intellection and peace, had hardly time to turn before his mouth gushed blood. The woman whirled and ran, the vines of her skirt withering at her thought to give her leg-room, the serpent dropping from her breasts to strike with fangless jaws at the flying-haired girl who pursued her, then winding itself about the girl's ankles. The girl fell; but as the pearl-eyed woman passed, Paul broke her neck. For a moment he was too startled at the sight of other human beings to speak. Then he said, "These are mine."

The old man, still bent over the fat man's body, snapped: "Ours. We've been here an hour and more." His voice was the creaking of steel hinges, and Paul thought of ghost-houses again.

"I followed them from the park." The girl, black-haired, grey-eyed when the light from the alley-mouth struck her face, was taking the serpent from around her legs—it was once more a lifeless thing of soft metal mesh. Paul picked up the woman's corpse and wrapped it in his cloak. "You gave me no warning," he said. "You must have seen me when I passed you."

The girl looked toward the old man. Her eyes said she would back him if he fought, and Paul decided he would throw the woman's body at her.

"Somebody'll come soon," the old man said. "And I'll need Janie's help to carry this one. We each take what we got ourselves—that's fair. Or we whip you. My girl's worth a man in a fight, and you'll find I'm still worth a man myself, old as I be."

"Give me the picking of his body. This one has nothing."

The girl's bright lips drew back from strong white teeth. From somewhere under the tattered shirt she wore, she had produced a long knife, and sudden light from a window high above the alley ran along the edge of the stained blade; the girl might be a dangerous opponent, as the old man claimed, but Paul could sense the femaleness, the woman-rut from where he stood. "No," her father said. "You got good clothes. I need these." He looked up at the window fearfully, fumbling with buttons.

"His cloak will hang on you like a blanket."

"We'll fight. Take the woman and go away, or we'll fight."

He could not carry both, and the fat man's meat would be tainted by the testicles. When Paul was young and there had been no one but his mother to do the killing, they had sometimes eaten old males; he never did so now. He slung the pearl-eyed woman across his shoulders and trotted away.

Outside the alley the streets were well lit, and a few passers-by stared at him and the dark burden he carried. Fewer still, he knew, would suspect him of being what he was—he had learned the trick of dressing as the masters did, even of wearing their expressions. He wondered how the black-haired girl and the old man would fare in their ragged clothes. *They must live very near.*

His own place was that in which his mother had borne him, a place high in a house built when humans were the masters. Every door was nailed tight and boarded up; but on one side a small garden lay between two wings, and in a corner of this garden, behind a bush where the shadows were thick even at noon, the bricks had fallen away. The lower floors were full of rotting furniture and the smell of rats and mold, but high in his wooden turret the walls were still dry and the sun came in by day at eight windows. He carried his burden there and dropped her in a corner. It was important that his clothes be kept as clean as the masters kept theirs, though he lacked their facilities. He pulled his cloak from the body and brushed it vigorously.

"What are you going to do with me?" the dead woman said behind him.

"Eat," he told her. "What did you think I was going to do?"

"I didn't know." And then: "I've read of you creatures, but I didn't think you really existed."

"We were the masters once," he said. He was not sure he still believed it, but it was what his mother had taught him. "This house was built in those days—that's why you won't wreck it: you're afraid." He had finished with the cloak; he hung it up and turned to face her, sitting on the bed. "You're afraid of waking the old times," he said. She lay slumped in the corner, and though her mouth moved, her eyes were only half open, looking at nothing.

"We tore a lot of them down," she said.

"If you're going to talk, you might as well sit up straight." He lifted her by the shoulders and propped her in the corner. A nail protruded from the wall there; he twisted a lock of her hair on it so her head would not loll; her hair was the rose shade of a little girl's dress, and soft but slightly sticky.

"I'm dead, you know."

"No, you're not." They always said this (except, sometimes, for the children) and his mother had always denied it. He felt that he was keeping up a family tradition.

"Dead," the pearl-eyed woman said. "Never, never, never. Another year, and everything would have been all right. I want to cry, but I can't breathe to."

"Your kind lives a long time with a broken neck," he told her. "But you'll die eventually."

"I am dead now."

He was not listening. There were other humans in the city; he had always known that, but only now, with the sight of the old man and the girl, had their existence seemed real to him.

"I thought you were all gone," the pearl-eyed dead woman said thinly. "All gone long ago, like a bad dream."

Happy with his new discovery, he said: "Why do you set traps for us, then? Maybe there are more of us than you think."

"There can't be many of you. How many people do you kill in a year?" Her mind was lifting the sheet from his bed, hoping to smother him with it; but he had seen that trick many times.

"Twenty or thirty." (He was boasting.)

"So many."

"When you don't get much besides meat, you need a lot of it. And then I only eat the best parts—why not? I kill twice a month or more except when it's cold, and I could kill enough for two or three if I had to." (*The girl had had a knife.* Knives were bad, except for cutting up afterward. But knives left blood behind. He would kill for her—she could stay here and take care of his clothes, prepare their food. He thought of himself walking home under a new moon, and seeing her face in the window of the turret.) To the dead woman he said: "You saw that girl? With the black hair? She and the old man killed your husband, and I'm going to bring her here to live." He stood and began to walk up and down the small room, soothing himself with the sound of his own footsteps.

"He wasn't my husband." The sheet dropped limply now that he was no longer on the bed. "Why didn't you change? When the rest changed their genes?"

"I wasn't alive then."

"You must have received some tradition."

"We didn't want to. We are the human beings."

"Everyone wanted to. Your old breed had worn out the planet; even with much better technology we're still starved for energy and raw materials because of what you did."

"There hadn't been enough to eat before," he said, "but when so many changed there was a lot. So why should more change?"

It was a long time before she answered, and he knew the body was stiffening. That was bad, because as long as she lived in it the flesh would stay sweet; when the life was gone, he would have to cut it up quickly before the stuff in her lower intestine tainted the rest.

"Strange evolution," she said at last. "Man become food for men."

"I don't understand the second word. Talk so I know what

you're saying." He kicked her in the chest to emphasize his point, and knocked her over; he heard a rib snap. . . . She did not reply, and he lay down on the bed. His mother had told him there was a meeting place in the city where men gathered on certain special nights—but he had forgotten (if he had ever known) what those nights were.

"That isn't even metalanguage," the dead woman said, "only children's talk."

"Shut up."

After a moment he said: "I'm going out. If you can make your body stand, and get out of here, and get down to the ground floor, and find the way out, then you may be able to tell someone about me and have the police waiting when I come back." He went out and closed the door, then stood patiently outside for five minutes.

When he opened it again, the corpse stood erect with her hands on his table, her tremors upsetting the painted metal circus-figures he had had since he was a child—the girl acrobat, the clown with his hoop and trained pig. One of her legs would not straighten. "Listen," he said, "you're not going to do it. I told you all that because I knew you'd think of it yourself. They always do, and they never make it. The farthest I've ever had anyone get was out the door and to the top of the steps. She fell down them, and I found her at the bottom when I came back. You're dead. Go to sleep."

The blind eyes had turned toward him when he began to speak, but they no longer watched him now. The face, which had been beautiful, was now entirely the face of a corpse. The cramped leg crept toward the floor as he watched, halted, began to creep downward again. Sighing, he lifted the dead woman off her feet, replaced her in the corner, and went down the creaking stairs to find the black-haired girl.

"There has been quite a few to come after her," her father said, "since we come into town. Quite a few." He sat in the back of the bus, on the rearmost seat that went completely across the back like a sofa. "But you're the first ever to find us here. The others, they hear about her, and leave a sign at the meetin'."

Paul wanted to ask where it was such signs were left, but held his peace.

"You know there ain't many folks at *all* anymore," her father went on. "And not many of *them* is women. And *damn few* is young girls like my Janie. I had a fella here that wanted her two weeks back—he said he hadn't had no real woman in two years; well, I didn't like the way he said *real,* so I said what did he do, and he said he fooled around with what he killed, sometimes, before they got cold. You never did like that, did you?"

Paul said he had not.

"How'd you find this dump here?"

"Just looked around." He had searched the area in ever-widening circles, starting at the alley in which he had seen the girl and her father. They had one of the masters' cold boxes to keep their ripe kills in (as he did himself), but there was the stink of clotted blood about the dump nonetheless. It was behind a high fence, closer to the park than he would have thought possible.

"When we come, there was a fella living here. Nice fella, a German. Name was Curtain—something like that. He went sweet on my Janie right off. Well, I wasn't too taken with having a foreigner in the family, but he took us in and let us settle in the big station wagon. Told me he wanted to wed Janie, but I said no, she's too young. Wait a year, I says, and take her with my blessing. She wasn't but fourteen then. Well, one night the German fella went out and I guess they got him, because he never come back. We moved into this here bus then for the extra room."

His daughter was sitting at his feet, and he reached a crooked-fingered hand down and buried it in her midnight hair. She looked up at him and smiled. "Got a pretty face, ain't she?" he said.

Paul nodded.

"She's a mite thin, you was going to say. Well, that's true. I do my best to provide, but I'm feared, and not shamed to admit to it."

"The ghost-houses," Paul said.

"What's that?"

"That's what I've always called them. I don't get to talk to many other people."

"Where the doors shut on you—lock you in."

"Yes."

"That ain't ghosts—now don't you think I'm one of them fools don't believe in them. I know better. But that ain't ghosts. They're always looking, don't you see, for people they think ain't right. That's us. It's electricity does it. You ever been caught like that?"

Paul nodded. He was watching the delicate swelling Janie's breasts made in the fabric of her filthy shirt, and only half listening to her father; but the memory penetrated the young desire that half embarrassed him, bringing back fear. The windows of the bus had been set to black, and the light inside was dim—still it was possible some glimmer showed outside. *There should be no lights in the dump.* He listened, but heard only katydids singing in the rubbish.

"They thought I was a master—I dress like one," he said. "That's something you should do. They were going to test me. I turned the machine over and broke it, and jumped through a window." He had been on the sixth floor, and had been saved by landing in the branches of a tree whose bruised twigs and torn leaves exuded an acrid incense that to him was the very breath of panic still; but it had not been the masters, or the instrument-filled examination room, or the jump from the window that had terrified him, but waiting in the ghost-room while the walls talked to one another in words he could sometimes, for a few seconds, nearly understand.

"It wouldn't work for me—got too many things wrong with me. Lines in my face; even got a wart—they never do."

"Janie could."

The old man cleared his throat; it was a thick sound, like water in a downspout in a hard rain. "I been meaning to talk to you about her; about why those other fellas I told you about never took her—not that I'd of let some of them: Janie's the only family I got left. But I ain't so particular I don't want to see her married at all—not a bit of it. Why, we wouldn't of come here if it weren't for Janie. When her monthly come, I said to myself, she'll be wantin' a man, and what're you goin' to do way out here? Though the country was gettin' bad anyway, I must say. If they'd of had real dogs, I believe they would have got us several times."

He paused, perhaps thinking of those times, the lights in the woods at night and the running, perhaps only trying to order his thoughts. Paul waited, scratching an ankle, and after a few seconds the old man said: "We didn't want to do this, you know, us Pendeltons. That's mine and Janie's name—Pendelton. Janie's Augusta Jane, and I'm Emmitt J."

"Paul Gorou," Paul said.

"Pleased to meet you, Mr. Gorou. When the time come, they took one whole side of the family. They was the Worthmore Pendeltons; that's what we always called them, because most of them lived thereabouts. Cousins of mine they was, and second cousins. We was the Evershaw Pendeltons, and they didn't take none of us. Bad blood, they said—too much wrong to be worth fixing, or too much that mightn't get fixed right, and then show up again. My ma—she's alive then—she always swore it was her sister Lillian's boy that did it to us. The whole side of his head was pushed in. You know what I mean? They used to say a cow'd kicked him when he was small, but it wasn't so—he's just born like that. He could talk some—there's those that set a high value on that—but the slobber'd run out of his mouth. My ma said if it wasn't for him we'd have got in sure. The only other thing was my sister Clara that was born with a bad eye—blind, you know, and something wrong with the lid of it too. But she was just as sensible as anybody. Smart as a whip. So I would say it's likely Ma was right. Same thing with your family, I suppose?"

"I think so. I don't really know."

"A lot of it was die-beetees. They could fix it, but if there was other things too they just kept them out. Of course when it was over there wasn't no medicine for them no more, and they died off pretty quick. When I was young, I used to think that was what it meant: die-beetees—you died away. It's really sweetening of the blood. You heard of it?"

Paul nodded.

"I'd like to taste some sometime, but I never come to think of that while there was still some of them around."

"If they weren't masters—"

"Didn't mean I'd of killed them," the old man said quickly. "Just got one to gash his arm a trifle so I could taste of it. Back then—that would be twenty aught nine, close to fifty years gone it is now—there was several I knowed that was just my age. . . . What I was meaning to say at the beginning was that us Pendeltons never figured on anythin' like this. We'd farmed, and we meant to keep on, grow our own truck and breed our own stock. Well, that did for a time, but it wouldn't keep."

Paul, who had never considered living off the land, or even realized that it was possible to do so, could only stare at him.

"You take chickens, now. Everybody always said there wasn't nothing easier than chickens, but that was when there was medicine you could put in the water to keep off the sickness. Well, the time come when you couldn't get it no more than you could get a can of beans in those stores of theirs that don't use money or cards or anything a man can understand. My dad had two hundred in the flock when the sickness struck, and it took every hen inside of four days. You wasn't supposed to eat them that had died sick, but we did it. Plucked 'em and canned 'em— by that time our old locker that plugged in the wall wouldn't work. When the chickens was all canned, Dad saddled a horse we had then and rode twenty-five miles to a place where the new folks grew chickens to eat themselves. I guess you know what happened to him, though—they wouldn't sell, and they wouldn't trade. Finally he begged them. He was a Pendelton, and used to cry when he told of it. He said the harder he begged them the scareder they got. Well, finally he reached out and grabbed one by the leg—he was on his knees to them—and he hit him along-side the face with a book he was carryin'."

The old man rocked backward and forward in his seat as he spoke, his eyes half closed. "There wasn't no more seed but what was saved from last year then, and the corn went so bad the ears wasn't no longer than a soft dick. No bullets for Dad's old gun, nowhere to buy new traps when what we had was lost. Then one day just afore Christmas these here machines just started tearing up our fields. They had forgot about us, you see. We threw rocks but it didn't do no good, and about midnight one come right through the house. There wasn't no one living then but Ma and Dad and brother Tom and me and Janie. Janie wasn't but just a little bit of a thing. The machine got Tom in the leg with a piece of two-by-four—rammed the splintery end into him, you see. The rot got to the wound and he died a week after; it was winter then, and we was living in a place me and Dad built up on the hill out of branches and saplings."

"About Janie," Paul said. "I can understand how you might not want to let her go—"

"Are you sayin' you don't want her?" The old man shifted in his seat, and Paul saw that his right hand had moved close to the crevice where the horizontal surface joined the vertical. The crevice was a trifle too wide, and he thought he knew what was hidden there. He was not afraid of the old man, and it had crossed his mind more than once that if he killed him there would be nothing to prevent his taking Janie.

"I want her," he said. "I'm not going away without her." He stood up without knowing why.

"There's been others said the same thing. I would go, you

know, to the meetin' in the regular way; come back next month, and the fella'd be waitin'."

The old man was drawing himself to his feet, his jaw out-thrust belligerently. "They'd see her," he said, "and they'd talk a lot, just like you, about how good they'd take care of her, though there wasn't a one brought a lick to eat when he come to call. Me and Janie, sometimes we ain't et for three, four days —they never take account of that. Now here, you look at her."

Bending swiftly, he took his daughter by the arm; she rose gracefully, and he spun her around. "Her ma was a pretty woman," he said, "but not as pretty as what she is, even if she is so thin. And she's got sense too—I don't keer what they say."

Janie looked at Paul with frightened, animal eyes. He gestured, he hoped gently, for her to come to him, but she only pressed herself against her father.

"You can talk to her. She understands."

Paul started to speak, then had to stop to clear his throat. At last he said: "Come here, Janie. You're going to live with me. We'll come back and see your father sometimes."

Her hand slipped into her shirt; came out holding a knife. She looked at the old man, who caught her wrist and took the knife from her and dropped it on the seat behind him, saying, "You're going to have to be a mite careful around her for a bit, but if you don't hurt her none she'll take to you pretty quick. She wants to take to you now—I can see it in the way she looks."

Paul nodded, accepting the girl from him almost as he might have accepted a package, holding her by her narrow waist.

"And when you get a mess of grub she likes to cut them up, sometimes, while they're still movin' around. Mostly I don't al-low it, but if you do—anyway, once in a while—she'll like you better for it."

Paul nodded again. His hand, as if of its own volition, had strayed to the girl's smoothly rounded hip, and he felt such desire as he had never known before.

"Wait," the old man said. His breath was foul in the close

air. "You listen to me now. You're just a young fella and I know how you feel, but you don't know how I do. I want you to understand before you go. I love my girl. You take good care of her or I'll see to you. And if you change your mind about wanting her, don't you just turn her out. I'll take her back, you hear?"

Paul said, "All right."

"Even a bad man can love his child. You remember that, because it's true."

Her husband took Janie by the hand and led her out of the wrecked bus. She was looking over her shoulder, and he knew that she expected her father to drive a knife into his back.

They had seen the boy—a brown-haired, slightly freckled boy of nine or ten with an armload of books—on a corner where a small, columniated building concealed the entrance to the monorail, and the streets were wide and empty. The children of the masters were seldom out so late. Paul waved to him, not daring to speak, but attempting to convey by his posture that he wanted to ask directions; he wore the black cloak and scarlet-slashed shirt, the gold sandals and wide-legged black film trousers proper to an evening of pleasure. On his arm Janie was all in red, her face covered by a veil dotted with tiny synthetic bloodstones. Gem-studded veils were a fashion now nearly extinct among the women of the masters, but one that served to conceal the blankness of eye that betrayed Janie, as Paul had discovered, almost instantly. She gave a soft moan of hunger as she saw the boy, and clasped Paul's arm more tightly. Paul waved again.

The boy halted as though waiting for them, but when they were within five meters he turned and dashed away. Janie was after him before Paul could stop her. The boy dodged between two buildings and raced through to the next street; Paul was just in time to see Janie follow him into a doorway in the center of the block.

He found her clear-soled platform shoes in the vestibule, under a four-dimensional picture of Hugo de Vries. De Vries was in the closing years of his life, and in the few seconds it took Paul to pick up the shoes and conceal them behind an aquarium of phosphorescent cephalopods, had died, rotted to dust, and undergone rebirth as a fissioning cell in his mother's womb with all the labyrinth of genetics still before him.

The lower floors, Paul knew, were apartments. He had entered them sometimes when he could find no prey on the streets. There would be a school at the top.

A confused, frightened-looking woman stood in an otherwise empty corridor, a disheveled library book lying open at her feet. As Paul pushed past her, he could imagine Janie knocking her out of the way, and the woman's horror at the savage, exultant face glimpsed beneath her veil.

There were elevators, a liftshaft, and a downshaft, all clustered in an alcove. *The boy would not have waited for an elevator with Janie close behind him.* . . .

The liftshaft floated Paul as spring-water floats a cork. Thickened by conditioning agents, the air remained a gas; enriched with added oxygen, it stimulated his whole being, though it was as viscous as corn syrup when he drew it into his lungs. Far above, suspended (as it seemed) in crystal and surrounded by the books the boy had thrown down at her, he saw Janie with her red gown billowing around her and her white legs flashing. She was going to the top, apparently to the uppermost floor, and he reasoned that the boy, having led her there, would jump into the downshaft to escape her. He got off at the eighty-fifth floor, opened the hatch to the downshaft, and was rewarded by seeing the boy only a hundred meters above him. It was a simple matter then to wait on the landing and pluck him out of the sighing column of thickened air.

The boy's pointed, narrow face, white with fear under a tan, turned up toward him. "Don't," the boy said. "Please, sir, good master—" but Paul clamped him under his left arm, and with a quick wrench of his right broke his neck.

Janie was swimming head down with the downshaft current, her mouth open and full of eagerness, and her black hair like a cloud about her head. She had lost her veil. Paul showed her the boy and stepped into the shaft with her. The hatch slammed behind him, and the motion of the air ceased.

He looked at Janie. She had stopped swimming and was staring hungrily into the dead boy's face. He said, "Something's wrong," and she seemed to understand, though it was possible that she only caught the fear in his voice. The hatch would not open, and slowly the current in the shaft was reversing, lifting them; he tried to swim against it but the effort was hopeless. When they were at the top, the dead boy began to talk; Janie put her hand over his mouth to muffle the sound. The hatch at the landing opened, and they stepped out onto the hundred-and-first floor. A voice from a loudspeaker in the wall said: *"I am sorry to detain you, but there is reason to think you have undergone a recent deviation from the optimal development pattern. In a few minutes I will arrive in person to provide counseling; while you are waiting it may be useful for us to review what is meant by 'optimal development.' Look at the projection.*

"In infancy the child first feels affection for its mother, the provider of warmth and food. . . ." There was a door at the other end of the room, and Paul swung a heavy chair against it, making a din that almost drowned out the droning speaker.

"Later one's peer-group becomes, for a time, all-important—or nearly so. The boys and girls you see are attending a model school in Armstrong. Notice that no tint is used to mask the black of space above their airtent."

The lock burst from the doorframe, but a remotely actuated hydraulic cylinder snapped it shut each time a blow from the chair drove it open. Paul slammed his shoulder against it, and before it could close again put his knee where the shattered bolt-socket had been. A chrome-plated steel rod as thick as a finger had dropped from the chair when his blows had smashed the wood and plastic holding it; after a moment of incomprehension, Janie dropped the dead boy, wedged the rod between the door and the jamb, and slipped through. He was following her when the rod lifted, and the door swung shut on his foot.

He screamed and screamed again, and then, in the echoing silence that followed, heard the loudspeaker mumbling about education, and Janie's sobbing, indrawn breath. Through the crack between the door and the frame, the two-centimeter space held in existence by what remained of his right foot, he could see the livid face and blind, malevolent eyes of the dead boy, whose will still held the steel rod suspended in air. "Die," Paul shouted at him. "Die! You're dead!" The rod came crashing down.

"This young woman," the loudspeaker said, *"has chosen the profession of medicine. She will be a physician, and she says now that she was born for that. She will spend the remainder of her life in relieving the agonies of disease."*

Several minutes passed before he could make Janie understand what it was she had to do.

"After her five years' training in basic medical techniques, she will specialize in surgery for another three years before—"

It took Janie a long time to bite through his Achilles tendon; when it was over, she began to tear at the ligaments that held the bones of the tarsus to the leg. Over the pain he could feel the hot tears washing the blood from his foot.

Envoi: A Salute to H. G. Wells

In my introduction I spoke of the looming exception of Wells. Again and again, through a career that began in the Victorian Age and continued uninterrupted through World War II, Wells created fictions (and nonfictions) in which the elements of s-f and utopian speculation are indissolubly knit. There has probably never been another writer who has written so many utopias. Inevitably, though he was enormously resourceful in disguising the fact, there came to be a certain sameness to these utopias, just as there is a sameness in a gallery full of Monets.

Wells' utopian proposals are always sane and often inspired, but it is neither his abundance nor his judiciousness nor yet his ingenuity that makes him the supreme Utopian. Rather it is because his utopias have their origin in his certain *knowledge* that there is a better way to live and breathe and be, that utopia begins at home. Or—even closer than home, it begins in your head at the epochal moment that the doors are opened and the windows cleaned. Wells, for all his reputation as a dryasdust progressive materialist, is the great-granddaddy of the counterculture, in witness whereof, and because it is *the* central statement on the subject of utopia in the whole sprawling body of his work, I would like to end this book with an excerpt from Wells' 1906 novel, *In the Days of the Comet.* Never mind the context. It doesn't need one.

THE CHANGE

by H. G. Wells

1

I seemed to awaken out of a refreshing sleep.

I did not awaken with a start, but opened my eyes, and lay very comfortably looking at a line of extraordinarily scarlet poppies that glowed against a glowing sky. It was the sky of a magnificent sunrise, and an archipelago of gold-beached purple islands floated in a sea of golden green. The poppies, too, swan-necked buds, blazing corollas, translucent stout seed-vessels, stoutly upheld, had a luminous quality, seemed wrought only from some more solid kind of light.

I stared wonderingly at these things for a time, and then there rose upon my consciousness, intermingling with these, the bristling golden green heads of growing barley.

A remote faint question, where I might be, drifted and vanished again in my mind. Everything was very still.

Everything was as still as death.

I felt very light, full of the sense of physical well-being. I perceived I was lying on my side in a little trampled space in a weedy, flowering barley-field, that was in some inexplicable way saturated with light and beauty. I sat up and remained for a long time filled with the delight and charm of the delicate little convolvulus that twined among the barley stems, the pimpernel that laced the ground below.

Then that question returned. What was this place? How had I come to be sleeping here?

I could not remember.

It perplexed me that somehow my body felt strange to me. It

was unfamiliar—I could not tell how—and the barley, and the beautiful weeds, and the slowly developing glory of the dawn behind; all those things partook of the same unfamiliarity. I felt as though I was a thing in some very luminous painted window, as though this dawn broke through me. I felt I was part of some exquisite picture painted in light and joy.

A faint breeze bent and rustled the barley-heads and jogged my mind forward.

Who was I? That was a good way of beginning.

I held up my left hand and arm before me, a grubby hand, a frayed cuff; but with a quality of painted unreality, transfigured as a beggar might have been by Botticelli. I looked for a time steadfastly at a beautiful pearl sleeve-link.

I remembered Willie Leadford, who had owned that arm and hand, as though he had been some one else.

Of course! My history—its rough outline rather than the immediate past—began to shape itself in my memory, very small, very bright and inaccessible, like a thing watched through a microscope. Clayton and Swathinglea returned to my mind; the slums and darkness, Düreresque, minute and in their rich dark colours pleasing, and through them I went towards my destiny. I sat hands on knees recalling that queer passionate career that had ended with my futile shot into the growing darkness of the End. The thought of that shot awoke my emotions again.

There was something in it now, something absurd, that made me smile pityingly.

Poor little angry, miserable creature! Poor little angry, miserable world!

I sighed for pity, not only pity for myself, but for all the hot hearts, the tormented brains, the straining, striving things of hope and pain, who had found their peace at last beneath the pouring mist and suffocation of the comet. Because certainly that world was over and done. They were all so weak and unhappy, and I was now so strong and so serene. For I felt sure I was dead; no one living could have this perfect assurance of good, this strong and con-

fident peace. I had made an end of the fever called living. I was
dead, and it was all right, and these—?

I felt an inconsistency.

These, then, must be the barley-fields of God!—the still and
silent barley-fields of God, full of unfading poppy flowers whose
seeds bear peace.

2

It was queer to find barley-fields in heaven, but no doubt there
were many surprises in store for me.

How still everything was! Peace! The peace that passeth understanding. After all it had come to me! But, indeed, everything was
very still! No birds sang. Surely I was alone in the world! No birds
sang. Yes, and all the distant sounds of life had ceased, the lowing
of cattle, the barking of dogs. . . .

Something that was like fear beautified came into my heart. It
was all right, I knew; but to be alone! I stook up and met the
hot summons of the rising sun, hurrying towards me, as it were,
with glad tidings, over the spikes of the barley. . . .

Blinded, I made a step. My foot struck something hard, and I
looked down to discover my revolver, a blue-black thing, like a
dead snake at my feet.

For a moment that puzzled me.

Then I clean forgot about it. The wonder of the quiet took pos-
session of my soul. Dawn, and no birds singing!

How beautiful was the world! How beautiful, but how still! I
walked slowly through the barley towards a line of elder bushes,
wayfaring tree, and bramble that made the hedge of the field. I
noted as I passed along a dead shrew mouse, as it seemed to me,
among the halms; then a still toad. I was surprised that this did
not leap aside from my footfalls, and I stooped and picked it up.
Its body was limp like life, but it made no struggle, the brightness
of its eye was veiled, it did not move in my hand.

It seems to me now that I stood holding that lifeless little creature for some time. Then very softly I stooped down and replaced it. I was trembling—trembling with a nameless emotion. I looked with quickened eyes closely among the barley stems, and behold, now everywhere I saw beetles, flies, and little creatures that did not move, lying as they fell when the vapours overcame them; they seemed no more than painted things. Some were novel creatures to me. I was very unfamiliar with natural things. "My God!" I cried; "but it is only I—?"

And then at my next movement something squealed sharply. I turned about, but I could not see it, only I saw a little stir in a rut and heard the diminishing rustle of the unseen creature's flight. And at that I turned to my toad again, and its eye moved and stirred. And presently, with infirm and hesitating gestures, it stretched its limbs and began to crawl away from me.

But wonder, that gentle sister of fear, had me now. I saw a little way ahead a brown and crimson butterfly perched upon a cornflower. I thought at first it was the breeze that stirred it, and then I saw its wings were quivering. And even as I watched it, it started into life, and spread itself, and fluttered into the air.

I watched it fly, a turn this way, a turn that, until suddenly it seemed to vanish. And now life was returning, to this thing and that on every side of me, with slow stretchings and bendings, with twitterings, with a little start and stir. . . .

I came slowly, stepping very carefully because of these drugged, feebly awakening things, through the barley to the hedge. It was a very glorious hedge, so that it held my eyes. It flowed along and interlaced like splendid music. It was rich with lupin, honeysuckle, campions, and ragged-robin; bed straw, hops, and wild clematis twined and hung among its branches, and all along its ditch border the starry stitchwort lifted its childish faces, and chorused in lines and masses. Never had I seen such a symphony of note-like flowers and tendrils and leaves, and suddenly in its depths, I heard a chirrup and the whirr of startled wings.

Nothing was dead, but everything had changed to beauty! And I stood for a time with clean and happy eyes looking at the intricate delicacy before me and marvelling how richly God has made his worlds. . . .

"Tweedle-tweedle," a lark had shot the stillness with his shining thread of song; one lark, and then presently another, invisibly in the air, making out of that blue quiet a woven cloth of gold. . . .

The earth recreated—only by the reiteration of such phrases may I hope to give the intense freshness of that dawn. For a time I was altogether taken up with the beautiful details of being, as regardless of my old life of jealous passion and impatient sorrow as though I was Adam new made. I could tell you now with infinite particularity of the shut flowers that opened as I looked, of tendrils and grass blades, of a blue-tit I picked up very tenderly—never before had I remarked the great delicacy of feathers—that presently disclosed its bright black eye and judged me, and perched, swaying fearlessly, upon my finger, and spread unhurried wings and flew away, and of a great ebullition of tadpoles in the ditch; like all the things that lived beneath the water, they had passed unaltered through the Change. Amid such incidents, I lived those first great moments, losing for a time in the wonder of each little part the mighty wonder of the whole.

A path ran between hedge and barley, and along this, leisurely and content and glad, looking at this beautiful thing and that, moving a step and stopping, then moving on again, I came presently to a stile; and deep below it, and overgrown, was a lane.

And on the worn oak of the stile was a round label, and on the label these words, "Swindells' G 90 Pills."

I sat myself astraddle on the stile, not fully grasping all the implications of these words. But they perplexed me even more than the revolver and my dirty cuff.

About me now the birds lifted up their little hearts and sang, ever more birds and more.

I read the label over and over again, and joined it to the fact that I still wore my former clothes, and that my revolver had been lying at my feet. One conclusion stared out at me. This was no new planet, no glorious hereafter such as I had supposed. This beautiful wonderland was the world, the same old world of my rage and death! But at least it was like meeting a familiar house-slut, washed and dignified, dressed in a queen's robes, worshipful and fine. . . .

It might be the old world indeed, but something new lay upon all things, a glowing certitude of health and happiness. It might be the old world, but the dust and fury of the old life was certainly done. At least I had no doubt of that.

I recalled the last phases of my former life, that darkling climax of pursuit and anger and universal darkness and the whirling green vapours of extinction. The comet had struck the earth and made an end to all things; of that too I was assured.

But afterwards? . . .

And now?

The imaginations of my boyhood came back as speculative possibilities. In those days I had believed firmly in the necessary advent of a last day, a great coming out of the sky, trumpetings and fear, the Resurrection, and the Judgment. My roving fancy now suggested to me that this Judgment must have come and passed. That it had passed and in some manner missed me. I was left alone here, in a swept and garnished world (except, of course, for this label of Swindells') to begin again perhaps. . . .

No doubt Swindells had got his deserts.

My mind ran for a time on Swindells, on the imbecile pushful-ness of that extinct creature, dealing in rubbish, covering the countryside with lies in order to get—what had he sought?—a silly, ugly, great house, a temper-destroying motor car, a number of disrespectful, abject servants; thwarted intrigues for a party-fund baronetcy as the crest of his life, perhaps. You cannot imag-ine the littleness of those former times; their naïve, queer absurd-ities! And for the first time in my existence I thought of these things without bitterness. In former days I had seen wickedness, I had seen tragedy, but now I saw only the extraordinary foolishness of the old life. The ludicrous side of human wealth and importance turned itself upon me, a shining novelty, poured down upon me like the sunrise, and engulfed me in laughter. Swindells! Swindells, damned! My vision of Judgment became a delightful burlesque. I saw the chuckling Angel sayer with his face veiled, and the corporeal presence of Swindells upheld amidst the laughter of the sphere. "Here's a thing, and a very pretty thing, and what's to be done with this very pretty thing?" I saw a soul being drawn from a rotund, substantial-looking body like a whelk from its shell. . . .

I laughed loudly and long. And behold! even as I laughed the keen point of things accomplished stabbed my mirth, and I was weeping, weeping aloud, convulsed with weeping, and the tears were pouring down my face.